**Publishers **

In this thrilling time travel page-turner, four kids from rural England learn that no less than the fate of the world as we know it will be determined by them. Or, more specifically, by 12-year-old Clara Callenick and how good she is at convincing her grandmother not to sell land that has been in the family for generations. There's only one problem: Gran has already agreed to sell the land to Derek Maunding, a conniving local businessman.

For Clara the trouble all starts when she's overcome by sudden, wrenching headaches that mysteriously occur at specific but inexplicable times. The searing pain occurs at the hours of 1:11 am, 2:22 am, 3:33 am, and so on, every eighth day. At the same time, there are bright, multicolored lights that rocket skyward from the opening of an abandoned tin mine on Gran's property.

Of course Clara is hesitant to talk with anyone about the weird events, but she finally relents, telling school friends Rob Hocking, Hayley Shezell, and Mick Amar. Together they decide to investigate by going down to the mine opening and awaiting the expected light show.

What ensues is a series of hair-raising, edge-of-your-seat events culminating in a delightful story that packs a powerful values punch relevant to both young and not-so-young adults.

THE TIME CRYSTALS

BOOK ONE

TERESA BASSETT

THE TIME CRYSTALS

Winner of The Next Novelist 2013

Shortlisted Amazon Breakthrough Novel Award 2013 (final five in Young Adult)

'a thrilling time travel page-turner ... Hair-raising, edge-of-your-seat events culminating in a delightful story that packs a powerful values punch relevant to both young and not-so-young adults'— Publishers Weekly

Also by Teresa Bassett:

The Mystery of Acorn Academy

CHAPTER 1

CLARA CALLENICK'S day began badly when Jess, her greyhound, was sick all over her history homework. It got worse when she realised she'd left her jam sandwich at home on the caravan table. If schooldays were the best days of your life, as everyone kept telling her, she could only dread what the future held in store.

"It's nothing but excuses from you, Clara," said Miss Grundy as she collected everyone else's essays. "If it happens again, I'll be contacting your parents."

A couple of classmates tittered. Clara sighed quietly, letting her breath out in short bursts. It was now after two o'clock and she was so hungry, even one of her dad's nearly raw boiled eggs would taste delicious.

"Now turn to page ninety-five," continued Miss Grundy. "Today, we'll be discussing the outbreak of the Second World War."

The teacher's monotonous drone came and went as she trotted to and fro. Every so often she paused to nip into the store cupboard where, according to rumour, she kept a bottle of gin.

Clara tried to stop her stomach rumbling and

concentrate on the lesson, but she had far too much on her mind. Her gaze drifted to the window. Five miles beyond the playing fields, in the lush Cornish countryside, lay her family's land. How she wished she were there now, at the top of the tallest fir tree perhaps, the one with the view from the woods up to the Downs. Despite the odd things happening lately, home was still her favourite place to be.

Little wonder, when her school career was proving to be such a disaster. At twelve years old, Clara was in her first year at St Piran's secondary school. She'd hoped to make lots of new friends here, but those horrible Maunding sisters had ruined any hope of that, causing trouble for her every chance they got.

Clara had no idea why they hated her so much. Maybe it was because of the land. Maybe it was because they were rich and she was poor. Whatever, just the thought of them made her queasy.

"Clara! You're day-dreaming again. I asked you a question, girl."

Clara was alarmed to see thirty faces turned in her direction.

"Sorry, Miss."

Miss Grundy leaned in close, drumming nail-bitten fingers on Clara's desk. Clara tried to avoid her eyes, which were pale and bloodshot, like tiny pearls within the folds of a cracked-open oyster.

"Oh, Clara, wake up! I have just asked you what the League of Nations was. Furthermore, I have spent the past quarter of an hour explaining it, so it shouldn't be too taxing, even with your limited attention span."

Clara stroked the lucky St Christopher pendant she always wore, praying for inspiration. The faces watching her all seemed to be smirking, willing her to fail.

Miss Grundy ran a hand through her hair, which was as grey and velvety as a mole's fur. "Come on, girl. We're waiting."

"Um … Is it to do with football, Miss?"

Laughter erupted all around. Miss Grundy sighed and shook her head.

"Clara, you exasperate me. I'd like an essay on the role of the League of Nations between the First and Second World Wars. On my desk tomorrow morning. And no excuses this time."

Clara wondered if her day could possibly get any worse.

It did. Just before her last lesson she made the mistake of dawdling on her way through the cloakroom. The door slammed shut and the dreaded Donna Maunding leapt in front of her.

"Hello, Clara." Donna grinned as she tossed back lustrous, golden curls.

Clara's heart lurched. Muffling a cry, she turned back the way she'd come, but Donna's sister Gail was now barring the way. Together, they hauled Clara over to a bench and dragged her down between them, gripping her arms to hold her in place. Waves of panic surged through her. She didn't mind snakes or spiders. She wasn't afraid of the dark. The one thing she couldn't bear was feeling trapped.

3

"The poor thing's scared stiff," sneered Donna. "She's actually shaking."

Gail grunted. She looked nothing like her sister, being short and thickset, with flat, greasy hair. Sharp, pointy teeth and a sullen expression were the only things they had in common.

"Leave me alone!" Clara tried to pull away, but although she was strong for her slim build, she was no match for the Maundings, both of whom were older, Gail thirteen and Donna fourteen.

Trying a different tack, Clara paused, took a breath and forced a smile. "Ever since I've got to this school you've been picking on me. It's getting boring."

"Is that so?" Donna's lips curved in a smirk, then her face hardened. "Hold her tight, Gail. We need to teach her a lesson."

Clara's mouth went dry. Everyone was in class now, so no one was likely to see them. Her cries wouldn't carry far in this solid old building with its granite walls and hefty oak doors. What could she do?

She remained still for a moment, slowing her breathing, mustering her strength. Then, without warning, she thrust her arms downwards. Startled, the two girls loosened their grip. Clara sprang to her feet and made a run for the door.

Not quick enough. Clara felt a yank on her hair so vicious she thought her neck would snap. Donna laughed while Gail lumbered over and clutched Clara's arm in her meaty paws. Clara couldn't move.

Donna leaned in close and peered at Clara's lucky St Christopher on its silver chain.

"Why d'you always wear that stupid thing?"

Clara glared but said nothing. She would never tell them it had been the final birthday present she had received from her mother before her death, four years earlier.

Donna snatched at the medallion and ripped it from her neck.

"Give that back!" Clara bit her bottom lip to stop it quivering.

Donna slipped the chain into the pocket of her trousers. "Who do you Callenicks think you are, anyway? Our father's going to have that poxy land of yours, though God knows why he wants it. You might as well get used to the idea." She turned to Gail. "Wonder if she'd like one of those burn-thingies Daddy told us about?"

As Gail sniggered, Donna seized Clara's wrist in both hands and twisted the skin in opposite directions. At first Clara felt only mild pain, then her wrist burned as Donna tightened her grip and squeezed harder. Clara gritted her teeth, determined not to let them see how upset she was.

"Get off!" She kicked out with all her strength, cracking Donna's shin.

"Ow!" Donna squealed and hopped on one leg, letting loose a curse.

Gail gave her sister a sly glance. "Why don't we give her a real burn? That'll learn her."

"No, Gail," said Donna with a scowl. "It'll teach her."

"Huh? That's what I said."

"Never mind. Excellent idea."

Clara kicked and struggled, but it was no good. Within seconds the sisters had hurled her back on the bench and pinned her between them.

Gail, who reeked of smoke, produced a lighter from her pocket and flicked it alight. Donna pulled back Clara's sleeve, exposing her forearm.

"There you are, Gail. Your turn first."

Gail brought the lighter slowly forward. Her mean eyes glittered as the flame inched towards Clara's wrist. Dizzy with fear, Clara squirmed and writhed furiously but it was impossible to twist and get a good kick at either of them.

As if in slow motion, she watched the flame bend and lick her skin. Searing pain shot up her arm. The breath caught in Clara's throat as she opened her mouth to scream.

The door burst open.

"Who's in there?" said a voice.

Clara looked up to see a boy with rosy cheeks, his hair fox-red and as bristly as a cactus.

Gail quickly shut the lighter and rammed it into her pocket.

He strolled towards them, swinging his schoolbag casually over his shoulder. "There you are, Clara. You should be in class. What's going on?"

Clara tossed back her mane of chestnut hair. She'd

seen him around, but their paths had never crossed until now. He was clearly trying to help, though, and Clara was quick to grasp the lifeline he offered. Breaking free of Donna's grip, she bounced to her feet.

"I'm on my way," she said, trying her best not to sound mystified. "I just stopped for a chat with these delightful girls."

"Come on, then," he said. "Let's go."

Clara caught the slightest hint of a wink as her new friend led the way towards the classrooms. Clara followed, forcing herself not to bolt. The sisters watched them, Donna with her spiteful eyes narrowed, Gail's eyes blinking in her large, bovine face.

***

"Thank you! Er … I'm sorry, I don't even know your name." Clara studied him as they walked along the corridor, taking in his strong, generous build and the sprinkling of freckles across his nose.

"I'm Rob Hocking. You're Clara Callenick. You live near me, don't you, near Polgrehan?"

"Yes, Polgrehan is just down the road from my place." Clara felt a little embarrassed that he knew so much about her when she knew next to nothing about him.

"What were they doing?" he asked. "Was that a lighter Gail had?"

Clara glanced down at her wrist. The skin felt horribly sore and was turning a nasty shade of purple.

7

All the same, she'd only just met Rob, and she didn't want to burden him with her problems.

"Doesn't matter," she said with a shrug.

Rob's footsteps slowed outside a classroom and Clara peered past him through a glass pane in the door. Inside, thirty Year Eights sat in rows, their full attention on Miss Sitwell, the young Spanish teacher who was so popular with the boys. Today she was wearing a sapphire-blue dress which was perfect for her slim figure.

"Is this your class?" asked Clara.

"Yeah." He looked closely at her. "Are you okay? You look a bit pale."

"I think so." Clara's heart had stopped pounding against her ribs, but she still felt a little shaky.

Rob glanced at his watch. "Look, it's a bit late to go to class now. Fancy going outside for a bit?"

Clara's spirits lifted. "That'd be great."

They sneaked out into the yard. The winter mist had cleared, revealing a mauve sky with mackerel clouds. Clara filled her lungs, glad to be out of the building with its whiff of socks and cabbage. Out here it smelled as though the world had been freshly made this morning.

Edging past the windows, they raced across the playing fields to the area behind a wooden shed, which was hidden from view by a thicket of holly and hazel. It was a popular hiding place for the pupils of St Piran's, a fact confirmed by the swathe of cigarette butts peeping out from the leaf litter.

"How come you weren't in class earlier?" Clara asked.

Rob leaned back against the shed wall. "Dentist's appointment. Just got back. Saw you with those idiots through the window and guessed they were up to no good. I know what they're like."

"Oh! I thought everyone loved them, except me."

"Huh, they're not that popular. They've just got stacks of their father's money to throw around, that's all."

"Well, I owe you a big favour. Did you have to have anything done at the dentist's?"

"Not today," said Rob with a grin. "But I was told I eat too many sweets. Like a mint?"

"Yes, please." Clara's hunger, which had disappeared during her run-in with the Maundings, was back with a vengeance. She was starving.

Rob held out the tube. "So come on, what have the Maundings got against you?"

Clara hesitated. Should she tell him? They'd only just met, but Rob's face was frank and open, and Clara saw only concern in his bright blue eyes. She could trust him, she felt sure. She didn't want to relax too soon, but it looked as though her awful day had just taken an amazing U-turn.

"I think they've got it in for me because their dad wants to buy my family's land," she began cautiously, reluctant to admit how much her family owned. People didn't always believe her, and glancing down at her old school uniform—the pullover threadbare, the skirt faded from maroon to brown—it was easy to understand why. As Clara knew only too well, land

9

wasn't money.

"They call me names," she went on, "because we live in a caravan—well, a mobile home. I like living in a caravan ... but the land belongs to my gran, and old man Maunding wants it for himself."

"Hmmph, I hope he doesn't get it. That lot think they own the place."

"Well they do, almost."

Clara didn't have the heart to mention what Dad had told her and her sister Sally the night before. Granny Callenick had decided to sell. The deal was about to be struck, and Clara would shortly lose her home.

"Our land used to be a mine in the olden days," she told Rob. "A tin mine."

By the time the bell rang, Clara felt as though she'd already known Rob for years.

"Well, thanks again," she told him as they set off across the damp grass towards the yard, where hordes of shrieking students were erupting from the buildings.

"No problem. You're all right, then?"

Clara nodded. Her wrist was throbbing now, and a blister was forming. However, it was the necklace which really upset her. True, it hadn't brought her much luck lately. Yet things could only get worse without it, of that she was sure. She'd have to think of a plan to get it back.

At the school gates, Rob pulled out his phone and began texting. "I'm meeting a couple of mates later in Polgrehan Park. Fancy coming?" He flushed tomato red, including his ears. "One of them's Hayley Shezell.

She's in your year."

"Yes, she is!"

Things were getting better and better. Hayley Shezell attended some of Clara's classes, and Clara had noticed her kind, elfin face. She'd already been looking for a way to get to know her.

Then she remembered. "Oh no, I'm busy tonight. I've got heaps of homework and my Granny wants me to go over and do some stuff for her, too."

For the thousandth time Clara wished her family had a computer … and that Granny wasn't so demanding.

"No worries." Rob looked away, his colour deepening from tomato to beetroot.

Clara chewed her lip, cross with herself for turning Rob down. She'd been longing to make new friends. That was more important than homework, wasn't it? But Granny wanted shopping done, and just getting the list out of her took an age. And after that there'd surely be a hundred other things to do before she could even start on her homework.

An idea struck her. "Would you like to see our place, sometime? It's lovely up on the Downs. Hayley can come too if she'd like."

Clara tried hard to sound casual about it, but she hoped more than anything that Rob would say yes. Before long, the mine would no longer be her home. What's more, this could be the chance she'd been waiting for. The chance to talk to someone about the weird things which had been happening on the family land.

11

Rob stopped walking and beamed. "Cool. I'd like that. At the weekend maybe?"

"D'you know where it is? There are two caravans at the end of the lane. The first one belongs to my Auntie Iris, then you'll get to ours. There's a rusty old motorbike outside."

Rob gave her a thumbs-up. "Okay, got it. 'Bye then." He hurried a few paces along the pavement, then, with a quick wave at Clara, stepped into his father's Audi.

Clara watched the car glide away. What her own father wouldn't give for one of those, she thought as she unclipped her old bone-shaker from the bike rack.

**

That night, Clara lay listening to the owls hooting and the dripping of the rain into the water butt outside her open window. She didn't like the window shut, whatever the weather.

The wind howled through the trees. Normally that would soothe her, but tonight it sounded like people groaning. Even Jess seemed uneasy—Clara could hear her padding about in the lounge, giving an occasional half-bark.

Clara tried to stay awake, reading her book, but the lamp kept flickering and she couldn't concentrate. Despite her best efforts, she drifted off to sleep.

She jolted awake. Her head felt like a metal band was being pulled round it, tight enough to crack her skull. She rubbed her forehead and groaned. The pain was so intense, she thought she might be sick. The rain became fiercer, rattling on the caravan roof like someone desperately trying to get in.

Pulling the duvet over her head, Clara took deep breaths and told herself to stay calm. She tried to think of something else, anything else, but it was no good. Her head now felt like nails were being hammered into it. She tossed the duvet aside.

Her gaze went straight to the little clock radio with its green glowing numbers. She just had to look, even though she knew what it would say. It was eleven minutes past one. 0111. It was happening again.

CHAPTER 2

"WOW!" said Rob. "That's a cool ruin down there. What is it?"

"It's the old engine house," explained Clara. "From the mine that used to be here."

It was Saturday afternoon, cold and fresh, and Rob had brought two friends with him, Hayley Shezell and Mick Amar, who both lived near him in Polgrehan village. Clara had led them to the Downs along a grass track running north beyond her mobile home, and the four of them sat huddled on a granite boulder.

Here they had a stunning view of the surrounding fields and countryside—the best view in Cornwall, as far as Clara was concerned. The sea formed a violet line on the horizon, to the left of which was an enormous clay tip, like a pyramid, part of the clay works where half the people of Polgrehan worked. Best of all, you could see most of the Callenicks' land—the Downs on the hillside with the wood at the bottom, plus the two caravans and the ivy-clad ruin beside them.

Hayley pulled a tissue from her pocket and dabbed at the mud on her shoes. "Tell us about those horrible Maundings, Clara. I hate them. They laugh at me and call me hoighty-toighty and namby-pamby, whatever that's supposed to mean."

"Don't worry about it," said Mick, who was thirteen and in his second year at the school, the same as Rob. "They hate me, too. I don't know why. Do they need a reason?"

Hayley's chin dimpled in a smile. "It's 'cos you're so clever. Mick's so brainy, Clara. He's a genius at maths and science."

"Well, um—" Mick cleared his throat and hunched himself into his big green parka coat.

"Mick's right," Rob said. "You don't want to take any notice of those Maunding girls."

Clara was too surprised to speak. So there were others being bullied by the Maunding sisters, just as she was! For the first time in ages, she no longer felt alone.

Hayley slipped a dainty arm through Clara's. "Is it true the Maunding girls' father wants to buy your family's land? What does he want it for?"

"I don't know. I wish I did. Dad clams up when I try to talk to him about it. Says it's not my business." Tears stung the back of Clara's eyes. She blinked quickly and forced her mind onto something else. "Come with me. I haven't shown you everything."

They followed her down a hillside carpeted with lime-green moss. Clara's sleek black greyhound Jess scampered between clumps of heather, sniffing rabbits, and Rob whooped as he charged after her.

"Isn't she fast!" marvelled Hayley. "You'd think those matchstick legs of hers would snap."

Clara grinned. "She's a rescue dog—a retired racer, though you'd never know it. She's the laziest dog ever."

She led them behind another boulder onto a track flanked with yellow gorse. Hayley brought up the rear, carefully skirting the puddles. Around halfway along the path, at a clearing, Hayley tripped on a root and fell sprawling into the mud.

"Ow!"

In three strides, tall, lanky Mick was by her side, helping his petite friend to her feet. "Rob told you to wear your old stuff, didn't he? Or haven't you got any old stuff?"

"Mum throws it out. It's not my fault." Hayley glared at the serpentine root, as though it had attacked her on purpose.

Fighting their way through a tangle of brambles, they emerged in Clara's wood.

"My gran owns all this," Clara said, waving her hand. "Our ancestors were tin miners. We bought the land over a hundred years ago, after the mining stopped, and we've been here ever since. Granny lives in the Account House on the other side of the wood. That's where they used to pay the miners and stuff like that. People came here to work from miles around. And there's something else."

They followed her between willow, holly and hazel, past copper beech and oaks with trunks as wide as tractor tyres.

Mick stopped suddenly, his face pale beneath black, wavy hair. "What was that noise? Sounded like a Geiger counter."

Clara laughed. "It's only the woodpecker. There's a

16

family of them over by the lake."

She halted in front of a huge wheel by the side of the river. It was around five metres high and overgrown with ivy.

"'Tis the water wheel," said Clara, lapsing into the dialect she reserved for home, to avoid any comments at school.

"Cool." Rob ran across and jumped onto the low wall beside it.

"It doesn't work now," explained Clara. "But it used to take water round. The wheel turned the stamps which broke up the rocks, so they could get the tin out."

"What're stamps?" asked Hayley. "I don't think you mean postage stamps."

Clara smiled. "No, they were like huge iron hammers, pounding the rocks into sand."

Rob grabbed the wheel's edge to see if he could move it, but although he strained and grunted until his face went bright red, the wheel was much too large and overgrown to budge. Clara and Hayley exchanged a glance, stifling giggles.

"Maybe old man Maunding wants the land so he can build a load of tiny houses on it," said Mick. "They cram them in these days. He could make a fortune."

It was as though he'd slapped Clara across the face. Such a horrible thought had never occurred to her.

"What? They'd never let him, would they? It's riddled with mine shafts here. He just couldn't."

"They can do all sorts, these days," said Mick with a shrug.

Clara shuddered. She didn't expect anyone to understand. Maybe to other people it would just mean moving house. But Clara felt passionate about her land. The wood was a living being to her, and she loved it as much as any person. Sometimes more so.

"I was born here," she said. "I keep telling Dad he mustn't let Gran sell up. But Maunding's offering a heap of money. And I know we're lucky to have this land, but, well, we don't have much money." She looked down at her scuffed trainers. She'd had them so long, her big toes were pushing through. "Gran wants us to live in a proper house like she does. But I don't want to live in a house. I like things the way they are."

The four of them went to sit on a tree trunk which had fallen across the river. Clara fell silent, dangling her feet absent-mindedly over the edge.

"What a cool place to live," said Hayley. "I wouldn't want to leave here either. No wonder we haven't seen much of you around Polgrehan." She glanced at Clara. "Clara? What is it? Is there something else?"

Clara's insides were twisting horribly. Could she trust them? She had only just met them, after all. But the urge to tell them was irresistible.

"There is something else. You're right."

"Spit it out, then," said Rob. "Don't keep us in suspense."

Clara felt icy river water seeping into her trainers. "It's—well, it's a bit strange. A bit of a mystery, really."

Hayley clapped her hands. "Please tell us! I love a mystery."

Clara looked at their eager faces, then took a deep breath.

"All right, I will." She gathered her thoughts, wondering where to begin. "One night, a while ago, I couldn't sleep. I had the weirdest feeling, like I should stay awake. I dropped off in the end, but a horrible pain woke me up. It felt like someone was drilling holes in my head. I noticed it was eleven minutes past one. 0111."

Hayley nodded. "You poor thing. My mother gets those evil headaches, too. Have you seen the doctor?"

Clara shook her head. "It was more than that. It was like someone was there. Someone trying to hurt me. Later, the same thing happened again. This time it was twenty-two minutes past two. 0222. Somehow, I managed to get back to sleep." She paused, wondering if her story sounded ridiculous.

"What then?" asked Mick. "Did it happen again?"

"Yeah. The same pain woke me up at thirty-three minutes past three. 0333. The next time it was 0444. By then, I was really scared. I didn't know what was going on."

A blackbird squawked as it flew past, making them all jump.

"That does sound weird," said Hayley. "Scary and weird."

Rob threw a stone into the water, trying to skim it along the surface. "Could be a simple explanation, though. It must have been horrible, but it's not that weird, Clara."

19

"That's not all! At 0555, on the dot, the pain started again, worse than ever. It hurt so much I couldn't move, and I had the same creepy feeling, like someone was in the room. As soon as I could move, I got up. I looked everywhere, even in the wardrobe, I felt so jittery. No one was there. So I went outside for some air." Clara stopped.

"And?" prompted Rob.

"Well, if you look between two tall trees you can see to the top of the Downs—where we were earlier. There's a big mine shaft there. It was pitch black but I looked up that way and I could see lights. A bit like fireworks going off."

There was a pause.

Hayley tucked her neat honey-coloured hair behind her ears. "Maybe it *was* fireworks. Can other kids get in there?"

"Not easily. And it wasn't exactly like fireworks. The lights didn't go up in the sky. I could just see them glowing."

"Did you go and have a look?" asked Hayley.

"I was scared to, on my own," admitted Clara. "They fizzled out after a while and I went back to bed. But just over a week later, the same thing happened again. The horrible headaches woke me up at 0111, 0222, 0333 … and at 0555 I could see the lights."

She was quiet for a moment, not daring to look at them. Had she been right to trust them? It sounded silly now that she'd said it. It was only a few lights after all.

"How many nights has it happened altogether?" asked Mick.

"Three. I marked it in my diary. It's been every eight days. If it happens again it will be next weekend, Saturday morning. Oh, I just know something's wrong."

No one spoke. Clara bit her lip, wondering what on earth they would make of her story.

"Have you told your dad?" Hayley asked at last.

"No." Clara knew her dad had enough to worry about. And Sally, sixteen and in the middle of exams, was hardly ever home.

"Why don't we come along next time?" suggested Rob. "We could check it out together. I'm sure there's a perfectly reasonable explanation."

Clara was stunned. "You'd really come with me? That would be brilliant."

It was much more than she'd expected. She had done the right thing!

But Hayley looked doubtful. "We'd have to get to your place ever so early, wouldn't we?"

"I suppose about half past five," said Clara. "We'd need to be up on the Downs before six."

"Hmm, I'd like to help, but my mum would kill me if she found out. She hates me being out in the dark."

Mick pushed his dark-rimmed glasses up his nose. "Don't let her find out, then. I'll come. It sounds exciting."

Hayley wriggled her feet over the water. "I will, too, then. Mum's just a worrier."

Clara felt a rush of relief, tinged with unease. She

very much hoped the weird things wouldn't happen again. But now she would look daft if they didn't.

***

Two miles away towards St Pirans, in the games room at Pardeaux Hall, the Maunding sisters were busy. Donna sat at a mahogany desk, writing out her Christmas list. Her father had invited her to put whatever she wanted on it, and she was leafing through a pile of catalogues, sucking her little finger. Early in December Daddy always sent one of his minions up to London to get everything.

A TV screen covered half the wall to the back of the room. Beside it lay a pile of unopened educational toys. The Maunding sisters had little interest in growing crystals, building solar-powered radios or making clocks from potatoes. Their bookcases groaned beneath pristine volumes, also unopened. A doll, missing all its clothes and also its head, sprawled on the floor.

Should Donna have an AdZack Z-800i games console with the fantastic graphics, or the Xing-A that came with all the best games including the new Slave Zombies one? She wrote down both.

Over in the window seat, Gail wriggled her tongue in concentration as she attempted to thread a piece of cotton through the broken links of Clara's lucky St Christopher necklace. She cursed as, once again, it fell from her stubby fingers to the floor.

Donna scowled in her direction. "It's only cheap

junk. Why are you bothering?"

Gail grunted as she leaned forward and picked up the necklace. "I want to see her face, like, when she sees me wearing it."

Their mother poked her head around the door holding a tray. "Girls, could you take your father's toast and coffee up to him? And pick up that doll."

Gail tossed the doll into the antique, ivory-inlaid cabinet where they hid their make-up and celebrity magazines.

Together the girls plodded up two flights of stairs to their father's office at the top of the house. It was at the back of the east tower, overlooking lawns as vast and manicured as a cricket pitch.

"Come," said the deep voice as they knocked on the study door.

Derek Maunding always had a slice of toast at half past four, heaped up with the best Beluga caviar. Donna suspected he didn't like caviar, but as he often said, he could afford it, and what good was money if you didn't have the best?

The study was opulent, with elegant furniture and ancient tomes locked away behind glass. The smell of peppermint and aftershave wafted towards them.

Donna deposited the tray on a desk bearing many folders and sheaves of paper, yet only one ornament: a piece of rock on a silver plinth, with a small gold plaque bearing the word Luxulyanite. It was the size of a fist, coal-black with pink crystals and swirls of grey, and as it caught the light it glistened with iridescent sapphire, turquoise and violet, like a peacock's tail. Donna often wondered why he kept it but had never dared to ask.

Smart and imposing in his tailored suit, Maunding looked up from behind the desk and pierced them with his laser beam stare, the one that made Donna feel he could see right through her.

"Now then, girls. Tell me how it went with the Callenick girl. Did you do as I asked?"

Donna tried to ignore the see-sawing sensation in her stomach. Since he'd become obsessed with Clara's land, their father had seemed even more uptight than usual, and his mood could darken at the slightest setback.

Squeezing out a grin, she said, "Of course, Daddy. She's terrified of us, isn't she, Gail?"

Gail nodded, a bead of sweat flying from her forehead.

Derek Maunding bit into his toast, grimaced, then smiled.

"That old witch in the woods is still dithering. Though I suspect ..." Falling silent, he ran a hand through his hair, a slick black mane with a streak of grey which curled into a question mark.

Donna slid her weight from foot to foot, but she knew better than to express her impatience.

"Have you written out your Christmas lists?" he asked, changing the subject. "I need them by tomorrow morning. Half past seven, sharp."

"Yes, Daddy," they both gushed, although Gail was only halfway through hers.

"And I expect you're looking forward to your

24

Christmas party?"

Every year the girls were allowed to throw a big party in the banqueting room, with lavish feasting and expensive presents for everyone. It was their reward for staying at St Piran's school, when he was rich enough to send them to any school in the land.

"Yeah, Daddy, you bet," said Gail, nodding eagerly.

Their father winced, and Donna ground her heel into Gail's foot.

Stifling a small squeak, Gail tried again. "Indeed we are, Daddy."

Waving an imperial hand in their direction, he returned his gaze to the document he was reading. His daughters turned to leave. As they reached the door, he called them back.

"So this girl—Clara, is it? She'll talk to her grandmother, correct? I can expect a capitulation very soon?"

Daddy was always using long words like that. Donna had never heard of a capitulation before, but she assured him that he could expect one. Derek Maunding nodded and waved his hand again, as if swatting flies.

"All right, girls. Good work. I'm sure I don't need to reiterate to you how important this is."

As if we could forget, thought Donna. These days, their father spoke of little else.

They trudged back downstairs to the games room and sat in silence on a peach leather sofa, gazing outside. Through the window, their huge marmalade cat Heidsieck lurked with intent by a hole in the stone wall.

"You told Daddy a lie!" Gail blurted out. "She never said she'd talk to her grandmother at all. That boy came and stuck his oar in and spoiled everything, remember? And what's a capit—cappy thingy, anyway?"

Donna grabbed her arm so tightly Gail squealed. "Shut your stupid face and listen. You heard Daddy. He wants that mine, and we've got to make sure he gets it."

CHAPTER 3

THE village of Polgrehan lay a mile eastwards from Callenick mine, in the opposite direction from the Maundings at Pardeaux Hall. A small village with granite cottages and winding lanes, it boasted one pub, the Flea and Feather, and a shop selling everything from postcards to Cornish pasties.

Rob and Mick lived in Tregurr Close, the cul-de-sac behind the Flea and Feather. Hayley's bungalow was one of a handful squeezed between the Methodist chapel and the chip shop.

The three of them had known one another all their lives, and had whiled away many a lively hour playing in the park, or kicking a football around the cul-de-sac. Tregurr Close was quiet enough for that, even in this day and age.

On Wednesday, Hayley rode the five miles to school with Clara on the new red bike she'd received for her birthday. Hayley's mother had agreed to let her, now that she had someone to ride with.

Clara thought they must look odd together, Hayley on her impressive mountain bike, while she herself rode her prehistoric bone-shaker. She didn't mind, though, not in the least. They had a lot of fun racing each other, and the crisp, cold air whizzing by made a refreshing start to the long school day.

"Any news about your land?" Hayley pulled alongside Clara, her snub nose red from the cold.

"No … no." Clara flinched as a lorry thundered past. Granny wasn't one to talk about her plans. Clara didn't expect to hear anything until the deal was struck and the papers signed. She spent her time in a constant state of anxiety, terrified that at any moment she might be told to pack up, ready to leave.

As they reached the school gates they were passed by the Maunding girls, noses in the air, being driven to school in their father's blue BMW by his chauffeur.

Clara made a face at them. They didn't seem quite so frightening now she had Hayley with her. She had a horrible feeling they were far from finished with her, but with any luck she could stay out of their way.

Since Clara and Hayley were in the year below Rob and Mick, they didn't see them in lessons. On Friday lunchtime they all met up by the shed beyond the playing fields.

Once he'd eaten his final sandwich, Rob fixed Hayley with a solemn stare.

"Right, here's the plan. Mick and I will collect you outside your place tomorrow morning at five fifteen, sharp. Don't be late. We'll cut through the bridleway by Bolton's farm. That'll take us right over to Clara's."

"Are you sure you don't mind?" asked Clara for the fifth time. "I feel bad, putting you to all this trouble."

"No way!" said Hayley. "It'll be an adventure. We'll get to the bottom of it, you'll see. This time next week we'll be laughing about it."

Clara gave a rueful smile. She wished she could believe it. Her stomach twisted with anticipation, her thoughts in turmoil. What if it didn't happen this time? What if it did?

Friday night seemed to go on forever. Clara couldn't stop worrying about what might be in store—and yet if nothing happened, her new friends might think she'd been lying, just to get attention.

She couldn't sleep a wink. Although she noticed it was eleven minutes past one, there was nothing unusual about it this time, and she didn't feel the same agonising headache.

The minutes dragged by. At last it was twenty-two minutes past two. And still nothing! She didn't know whether to be pleased or miserable.

She went to fetch a glass of water. Three thirty-three. Nothing again. Wasn't that just typical?

At five o'clock, still awake, she got up and threw on her jeans and her least frayed fleece. Would the lights be there if the other things hadn't happened? Oh well, it might be a waste of time, but she'd have to go through with it now. Rob, Mick and Hayley would soon be on their way.

She crept about as quietly as she could, but the caravan creaked at every step. Just as she reached the door, her sister appeared behind her.

Sally glared at Clara, arms folded across her pink dressing gown. "What're you doing? You woke me up, sneaking about like that. I've got to get up early enough

29

as it is." Sally worked weekends on the fruit and veg stall at the market.

For a split second, Clara considered confiding in her sister. But she soon changed her mind. There was no point. They might look similar, but inside they were poles apart. Sally would be sure to laugh at her and tell her to stop imagining things.

"I just couldn't sleep, that's all," she muttered instead. "Go back to bed."

Sally narrowed her eyes. "You're so selfish—you'll wake Dad up in a minute."

Clara said nothing. Dad had been testing his new batch of blackberry wine the night before. He was sure to be out of action for a few hours yet.

Grumbling, Sally returned to her room.

A wave of cold air hit Clara as she opened the front door. Jess leapt up from her spot by the wood-burner and tried to slip out with her.

"No, Jess, you can't come," whispered Clara, pushing the greyhound back inside. Jess looked disappointed, her eyes questioning, her tail hanging limp.

Clara sat on a tree stump in the lane. She gazed up at the bright stars overhead, the Milky Way clearly visible, streaking across the sky. She filled her lungs with the night-scented, woodland air.

It was gone twenty-five to six. Her friends were late. Clara shivered, feeling very alone. Should she have brought Jess, after all? No, she couldn't bear the thought of Jess being in danger. It was worse than being in danger herself.

She fiddled with her hair, pulling the chestnut strands out of her eyes and fastening them into a ponytail. Perhaps they weren't coming. Perhaps they couldn't be bothered after all.

An owl hooted, then Clara heard the strangled cry of a fox. How long should she wait? Ten minutes more? After that, she'd go back inside.

She was roused from her thoughts by the glimmer of a torch and soft voices. They had come! She could just make out their silhouettes by the light of the moon. Her heart pounded. As they grew level she smiled mischievously and gave a quick whistle.

Hayley stifled a scream. "Omi—Clara, I nearly jumped out of my skin!"

"Sorry." *Idiot. Why did I do that?* "Thanks for coming. We'd better get a move on."

Hayley rummaged in her tiny backpack. "I've brought some buns. They're saffron."

She offered them round. Clara took one gratefully and munched it as she went along.

"So," said Rob as they ducked into the wood by the side of Clara's caravan. "Did you keep waking up the same as before? Did you get the horrible headaches? Did you see the lights?"

Clara frowned. "Well, no, I didn't. Would you believe it, I was awake all night, and nothing happened." She felt awful now, dragging them all this way. Most likely the lights she'd seen before were caused by kids trespassing and fooling about.

"Oh. That's good, I guess," said Rob, clearly

disappointed. "We might as well check it out, though, now we're here." He shone his torch along the path.

Embarrassed, Clara charged past him, ignoring the beam. They followed at a trot as she headed through the wood towards the Downs.

The wind had got up and rustled and sighed through the leaves. Clara had always felt at home in the woods, but tonight felt different somehow. To raise her flagging spirits she gave the others a running commentary as they picked their way through the trees, trying their best to keep up with her.

"That's where the badger sett is over there. My Auntie Iris puts food out for them and you can hide and watch them … Hear that? That's one of the owls. There are two. During the day they live in the clump of sycamores over by the pond."

"Shhh!" hissed Rob. "Clara, if there is anyone up there, you're doing a grand job of letting them know we're on our way. Do you realise how far voices carry at night?"

"Sorry."

Rob was right. Stop rambling, she told herself. She did that when she was nervous. Sometimes she had to remind herself that to many people, a wood was just a wood. Her friends must be numb with cold and it was practically the middle of the night. She stopped talking, resisting the urge to point out her favourite toadstool, the sulphur-yellow honey fungus which glowed in the dark.

They crossed the river on a rickety bridge made of

three planks and a wobbly handrail. Hayley held onto Mick's parka but still managed to get her foot soaked.

"Oh no," she wailed. "I knew I should have worn thicker shoes."

At the top of the woods, Clara led them through the brambles and along the narrow path lined with gorse. Around halfway along, they came to the clearing where Hayley had stumbled before.

"Stay close behind me here," said Clara. "There's a small track on the left, just there, with a second mine shaft, not far along. You could easily fall in. It goes down miles. You'd never get out alive."

"Shouldn't there be … Is that allowed?" Hayley's voice was small and anxious.

"It's always been like that. There are fences. And signs."

Clara tried her best to sound confident, but her uneasiness was growing by the step. The wood seemed sinister, almost menacing, full of shadows and unseen creatures scurrying near her feet. The darkness was so thick, you could barely tell back from front or up from down.

They emerged from the gorse thicket, stepped around a rocky outcrop and found themselves on the Downs. Clara led them towards the brow of the hill. At least you could see better out in the open. A sliver of moonlight shone down upon the heather, and Clara could make out the sandy mounds of rabbit burrows and misty slabs of granite lurking like ships in a ghostly sea.

Clara quickened her steps. "Hurry! We're going to be late."

They were all panting by the time they reached the top. As they paused and caught their breath, Rob shone his torch beam over a dim shape. "Is that the shaft where you saw the lights? Over there?"

"Yes," said Clara. "That's the entrance. Can you see?"

Nearby, a low wire fence surrounded a hole in the ground, four or five metres in diamcter. To one side was a ramshackle sign bearing the words "Danger, open mine shaft".

Rob peered closely at his watch and grinned. "It's eight minutes to six. What were you so worried about, Clara? We've got plenty of time."

Clara forced a smile, hiding her nervousness. If anything was going to happen, it should start any minute now.

The wind was moaning and the temperature had dropped further still. Despite the cold, Clara felt hot and clammy from the climb and the tension. She began to wish they hadn't come. Whatever the problem up here, nothing was worth the risk of losing her new friends.

Rob paced to and fro. "I can't see anything. There's nothing here."

"Keep away from the shaft," Clara called as he strayed close to the little fence.

Hayley jumped up and down, rubbing her arms to keep warm. "D'you think anything will happen, Clara?" Her voice, high-pitched from excitement, battled against the wind. She delved into her bag and offered them all a second bun.

Everyone said no, except Rob. "I will, thanks. I'm ravenous. I didn't have much time for breakfast. All I could find was a bit of chow mein left over from last night's takeaway."

"Oh, Rob," cried Hayley. "I can't bear leftovers."

Rob's bun disappeared in two bites. "Mmm, not bad, Hayley."

"I made them myself. You can have another one if you like, there's loads … Aaargh!" Hayley shrieked as something rustled nearby. A small dark shape slid behind a granite boulder. The wind dropped suddenly and there was an eerie quiet.

"Are there snakes up here?" whispered Hayley.

Clara shrugged. "A few adders and grass snakes. But don't worry. They're more scared of us than we are of them. Anyway, they'll be asleep."

"Like we should be, probably," muttered Rob under his breath.

Clara felt her cheeks burning and was glad it was too dark for him to see. No doubt he already regretted becoming her friend.

"What if you accidentally stepped on one or something?" said Hayley, sounding unconvinced.

No one was listening. Mick crossed to the fence around the mine shaft and peered into the gloom. "Give us your torch, would you, Rob?"

Just then, there was a rumbling.

Mick jumped back. Hayley grabbed Clara's arm.

"What was that?" said Rob.

Before anyone could answer, there was more rumbling, louder this time.

"It's coming from in there," said Mick, pointing. "Down in the shaft."

They ran across to join him at the fence. It was hard to see much in the feeble moonlight, the hole obscured by stones and tufts of heather around its edge.

Hayley grasped Mick's arm. "Do be careful. We could all fall in."

"Shhh," said Rob.

The sound came again. This time it was as loud as thunder.

"Look!" Within the mine shaft, Clara saw a glow.

"What is it?" Mick was fiddling with his glasses, as though it might help him see better.

A spark of light zoomed out of the hole, like a shooting star.

Hayley screamed.

There was a fizzing noise, then more lights followed—buttercup yellow, scarlet and tangerine. A sharp tang filled the air, like citrus.

"Stand back!" yelled Rob.

They stood motionless on the hillside as the lights grew brighter. A rainbow fountain poured out of the shaft, like an extraordinary firework. The rumbling and fizzing increased until the earth beneath their feet was trembling.

"Run! It's going to explode!" Hayley turned and tried to pull Clara away from the fence. "Come on. The ground feels like it's going to rip apart."

Too late. With a horrible crack, a tube shot out of the shaft.

It was dark red and snake-like, around six metres long and the width of a dinner plate. One end remained in the mine shaft. The top end curved over and circled slowly in the air, as if watching them. Then, with lightning speed, it whooshed towards Clara.

Mick grabbed Hayley and pulled her back, and they fell out of the way just in time. Clara was too slow. The tube's mouth struck her with a thud and moulded itself around her waist like a pair of lips.

There was no time to think about what was happening. Clara pounded the tube with her fists, gasping as it tightened. It felt cold and immensely powerful. She was stuck fast.

Adrenalin coursed through her as the tube lifted her free of the ground. She tried to prise it away, but it was slippery, and she couldn't get her fingers underneath. Moving swiftly, it pulled her through the air, back towards the shaft.

Clara wriggled her feet, too shocked to speak or even scream. She heard Hayley crying, as if from a long way off.

"Do something, quick! Help her!"

Rob appeared below, armed with a stick. Reaching up, he tried to thrash the tube, but Clara was already out of reach. The tube continued to pull back into the mine shaft, clanking and roaring as it went.

It stopped for a moment when Clara was suspended

across the centre of the shaft, and there was a squeak as it rotated and bent, turning her upright. Rob jumped over the little fence and stood on the narrow ledge, before the gaping hole. His face was sweaty as he craned towards her.

"Try to reach me, Clara."

Mick and Hayley appeared beside him. Pale with fright, they too held out their arms.

Clara wriggled and squirmed, but the tube held her firmly in its grasp. However hard she stretched, she couldn't reach their hands. She was jerked violently as the tube moved again.

Peering down she saw that not far below, the shaft had filled with a glowing orange disc. The tube was disappearing inside the disc, taking her with it! She stared at her friends in terror, knowing there was nothing they could do.

As her feet touched the disc, it began to vibrate. The surface felt soft and gooey, like warm butter. She felt a prickling sensation and looked down towards her feet. They were no longer there. Whatever the disc was, Clara was sinking through it.

"I can't reach you." Rob teetered on the edge, his arms slicing the air.

Clara's eyes met his. She was still too stunned to speak, already knee-deep in the disc.

She heard an ear-splitting yell as Rob jumped in after her.

"Rob, come back!" Hayley's shrill voice was almost lost in the roar. "Rob, you idiot."

Rob landed feet first on the disc. His arms flailed as he tried to find his balance. Then he gave a cry as he, too, began to sink through.

The gloopy substance had now reached Clara's shoulders. She felt it seeping into her clothes, stinging where it touched. In moments, she would be suffocated.

Mick and Hayley stood motionless by the shaft, their arms still outstretched.

The disc closed around Clara's neck. It smelled corrosive, like burnt almonds. She clamped her jaws together and shut her eyes, then grabbed a last breath of air as it smothered her nose.

She was certain of only one thing: that she and Rob were about to die. And she had no idea what they were dying for.

With a sickening slurp, the disc closed over her.

CHAPTER 4

CLARA and Rob screamed as they plopped through the bottom of the disc and landed on a hard surface just below. Clara coughed and spluttered, struggling to catch her breath. Above them, the disc vanished, like an eye shutting. They were left in total darkness.

Fighting hysteria, Clara stretched out her fingers and recoiled as she felt something slimy. "This is crazy! What's going on? It feels like we're moving."

"Keep calm." Rob's voice sounded firm, but higher than usual. "There must be a logical explanation."

"That stuff ... I thought we were going to suffocate."

"It must be a—a layer of some kind."

Remnants of the orange buttery disc still clung to Clara's hair, eyes and nose, stinging where they touched. She wiped at her face, trying to rid herself of them.

"Oh, Rob, why did you jump in? We might never get out again!" Clara's voice echoed in her ears. *This can't be happening. I'll wake up at any moment.*

"Don't panic. It won't help. Would you rather you were here on your own?"

"Of course not." The thought of facing this alone— whatever it was—was unbearable.

The rhythmic clanking, coming from somewhere

below, was growing louder. Clara reached for the tube at her waist, which still held her fast in its fish-like mouth. She fingered along its length as far as she could stretch, grimacing at the wrinkled, sticky feel of it. She couldn't tell for sure in the dark, but it seemed to be joined to the floor near her feet.

"I think we're being dragged down the shaft," said Rob. "Ow!"

"What?"

"My hand bashed against something. The walls are moving. It's like we're in some kind of lift, with no sides or roof. Just a floor."

"How big a floor? Don't move too far. You could fall off."

"Tell me something I don't know, Clara."

"Try putting your foot out. Hold on to me."

"All right …"

Clara made a grab for where she judged Rob to be, but her hand sliced through empty air. After a few more attempts, Rob's hand found her wrist and gripped it tightly.

"Be careful," she told him.

Seconds passed. In between the clanking and whooshing, Clara heard Rob muttering.

"We're definitely being pulled down. That's the side of the mine shaft slipping past. We're on a small platform." Rob let go of Clara's arm.

Clara gritted her teeth. She'd hated cramped spaces since the age of six, when the door to the caravan bathroom had jammed shut, and she'd been trapped inside for what seemed like hours. As the floor continued to descend, she tried to forget how hemmed in they were, but could think of nothing else. Her lungs felt tight and crushed as a familiar blackness flowed over her, like a curtain being pulled down.

"I can't breathe … I'm claustro—claustro—"

"Claustrophobic?"

"I just said I was, didn't I?"

"Okay, okay … Um, try to think of something nice."

"I'm being sucked down a mine by a horrible eel-thing! How can I think of anything nice?"

"Only trying to help. Wait there. Let me see if I can free you."

"How can I go anywhere?" Clara shouted. She knew she was being unfair, but she couldn't help herself. Panic was getting the better of her.

With a great shudder, the movement stopped. There was a loud reverberation underfoot.

"The walls have stopped," said Rob. "Maybe we're at the bottom."

Clara gulped air like a fish out of water. Down here the citrus scent had vanished, replaced by a ghastly musty smell, like the one which had whooshed out of a cupboard once when a mouse had died in Dad's boot.

There was silence all around. Clara tried to slow her breathing. To think that, just days ago, she had been anxious about school. What she wouldn't give right now to be dozing her way through Miss Grundy's history lesson.

"Thank God Mick and Hayley stayed clear," she whispered.

"They'll get help. They'll call the fire brigade. Maybe this is some sort of machinery left from mining times."

"The fire brigade? How on earth—"

Clara stopped herself. Rob could be right. Mick and Hayley knew exactly where they had disappeared. Maybe the fire brigade would be able to reach them somehow.

"I've lived here all my life," she continued. "No one's ever been able to get into the tunnels. They're all blocked or fenced off."

"Shhh," hissed Rob. "Something's happening."

A vertical sliver of green had appeared in front of them, like a glowing snake. A door was opening, sliding slowly aside. Dim light filtered through, reflecting off the slimy walls of the mine shaft around them. At Clara's side, Rob's face gleamed like a pale moon. He put up clenched fists, jaws clamped together.

Together, they looked towards the gap. Bit by bit, the door receded into the rock.

A man was revealed.

Stooped over a wooden cane, he wore a grubby cloak made of rags stitched together. His face appeared sickly in the green light, the skin stretched and sallow as though barely able to cover his features. He peered in at them, his eyes like bright black beetles.

Rob jumped in front of Clara, shielding her. "Who the hell are you? What's going on?"

The old man gazed past him towards Clara.

"Are you Clara Callenick? Of Polgrehan?" His voice

quivered, and his sharp eyes were wide with something like amazement—or fear.

"I … I …" Clara gave a small nod. *He seems to know me! How can that be?*

"It *is* you!" He thumped his cane onto the ground, disturbing a thick layer of ashy dust. "And who the Granite have you brought with you?"

Clara stared as a hundred questions clamoured at her brain. What was he doing inside the mine tunnels? How did he get in and out? Why had she never seen him before?

"Come with me. Quickly!" The old man turned and set off along the dimly lit tunnel.

Rob called after him. "How is Clara supposed to move with that horrible tube-thing stuck to her?"

The man glanced over his shoulder. Mumbling, he strode back, his pace surprisingly brisk. With a skeletal finger, he pressed a button in a panel to the side of the shaft. The suction relaxed, and, with a squelch, the wrinkled tube released Clara. She watched in disgust as it shrank back into the round platform beneath them. Its mouth, the last bit to go, was ringed with folds, like toothless gums.

She cast her eyes down over herself anxiously, half expecting to see a gaping hole in her stomach where the vile thing had been. Luckily, she appeared to be still in one piece.

She brushed herself down and tried to rub the last gobbets of slime from her face. The stuff smelled rank and vinegary now, making her queasy. Rob had some, too: a splodge on his cheekbone.

As the old man vanished into the tunnel, Clara and Rob raced to catch up with him.

Rob tapped him on the shoulder and glared, arms crossed. "I want an explanation. Why have you brought us here? When are you taking us home?" Under his breath he said to Clara, "Did you bring your phone?"

"No. I can never get a signal at the mine, anyway."

The man gave a harsh laugh. "Mobile phones. Ha, I wish."

"There's no reception?" asked Rob. "We're too far down, is that it?"

The man kept walking. "Hurry up. There isn't much time."

Clara gazed around, trying to make sense of her surroundings. The ground beneath her feet was sandy and uneven. She couldn't tell for sure, but they seemed to be climbing gradually upwards.

Pictures lined the walls: paintings, drawings, scraps of paper from magazines. She noticed one of a rose, one of a weird fish with a lantern growing out of its head. Another showed a field of some crop or other, potatoes possibly.

"Odd décor." Rob raised his brows at Clara and smiled.

Clara tried to smile back, but only managed a grimace.

"You've got gloop on your face," she said, pointing to the blob of slime.

Rob rubbed at it, cursing.

"He must have found some way to get into the disused mine workings," Clara whispered. "I don't understand it. What's he doing here? Did he build that lift thing?"

Rob shrugged. "Guess we'll find out."

The tunnel ended at a stone door. Propping his cane against the wall, the old man turned to a panel of buttons and tapped in a complicated sequence. Clara saw that the cane's handle was finely worked in silver, shaped like a horse's head.

The door slid slowly back. They now found themselves on a narrow ledge, with stone staircases running down to left and right. Clara gawped in amazement. In the dim light, a cavern was revealed.

***

The cavern stretched as far as Clara could see. It reminded her of an aircraft hangar she had seen on TV, with a high roof and a lot of echoing space. In the centre was a metallic cylinder, perhaps two metres across, which rose vertically from the floor and disappeared into the stone ceiling ten metres or so above. Other tubes led from its centre, like the spokes of a wheel, open at one end and big enough to walk into. The whole contraption looked like a metallic spider's web.

The rest of the cavern housed ramshackle buildings, some barely standing, others ultra-modern in appearance, all looking as though they had grown organically out of the floor.

Between the buildings, Clara saw people.

She grabbed Rob's arm. "Look! Who are they?"

It was impossible for Clara to take in. Their strange companion wasn't the only one to infiltrate the family mine—there were others, too. Dressed in ragged clothes similar to the old man's, they scurried to and fro, as if on urgent business. Not one of them glanced in their direction.

Rob was peering to the right, at a long, low building, blood-red in colour, near which another tunnel cut into the rock.

"There are tunnels along the walls," he said, keeping his voice low. "Maybe one of them is a way out."

Clara nodded, although she didn't feel too hopeful. She dreaded to think how far they must be below the surface of the earth.

In the distance, beyond the buildings, Clara could just make out the far wall of the cavern. It appeared to be one huge window comprising several smaller ones, all hexagonal, like honeycomb. Beyond this window, there was only darkness.

They descended the rough-hewn staircase and stepped into the cavern. Clara felt relieved to be out of the tunnel. However, the cavern was stiflingly hot, and the air smelled even mouldier.

"I don't believe this," she said, shaking her head. "It can't be real. We're dreaming, right?"

"We must both be having the same dream then. It seems real enough to me."

Rob had never looked so pale. Even his hair appeared drained of its normal bright colour.

"But he knows me," said Clara. "How can he? What's going on?"

"I don't know any more than you." Rob flashed her a shaky smile. "What have you got me into, Clara Callenick?"

Clara hung her head. Rob must wish he'd never set eyes on her. She'd brought him nothing but trouble.

The stranger crossed to a bench carved into the cavern wall, and sat down heavily. With alarm, Clara saw that his bony shoulders were heaving, his eyes glistening.

"Rob, I think he's crying." Clara had never seen an adult cry before. Not even her father, when her mother died.

Shuddering even more, the man tapped his stick on the ground. A compartment below the silver horse's head sprang open, and he grabbed a small lozenge from inside. He tossed it into his mouth and chewed.

Gradually the colour returned to his face. He looked at his two captives and coughed.

"I'm, ahem, sorry about this."

Clara quailed. Did he mean he was sorry for bringing them here? Or was he planning to do something horrible to them?

"Who's in charge?" demanded Rob.

The man ignored him. His mouth worked strangely, the thin lips violet, moist with spittle. He looked sad and pathetic, and Clara was finding it difficult to stay angry with him. With a sigh, she flopped down beside him on the bench.

"Was all this planned? Did you deliberately set out to capture us and bring us here?" Images of home crowded Clara's mind. Her sister Sally lounging on the sofa, Jess the greyhound snoring by the embers of the wood-burner.

The stranger stared into his lap, saying nothing.

"I want to go home," she pleaded. "Take us back, now!"

Rob sat down on his other side. "Why pick on Clara, anyway?" he asked. "Or would anyone have done?"

The old man recovered enough to turn to Rob. "That I can't say."

"Oh great," said Rob. "You can't say? That's really helpful. Why not? You'd better say something or—"

"All right." He gave a loud sigh. "The truth is, Clara is sensitive. Many children are, and Clara especially so. If she weren't, we'd never have been able to contact her."

With so much going on, Clara had forgotten about the weird headaches and the lights which had started all this. Things began to fall into place.

"You mean, it was you who gave me those horrible headaches? That's how you were trying to contact me?"

"There's no time for questions. Clara, listen to me. Try to understand. My name is Zeno. You must trust me. What you do next is of the utmost importance. More important than you could ever know."

Clara appealed to Rob, wondering if he were as mystified as she was. Their captor—Zeno—had clearly lost his mind.

Rob gave a puzzled frown. "This is mad," he told Zeno. "You're not making any sense."

As Zeno fell silent, Rob stood up and paced to and fro, rubbing at his throat and wiping his forehead. "Do you have anything to drink? I'm parched. It's boiling hot in here."

Zeno got to his feet and shuffled a few paces, almost tripping over the hem of his patchwork robe. The garment might once have been colourful, but grime had darkened all the pieces to shades of brown.

Rob leaned across and whispered in Clara's ear. "He's off his head. We've got to get out of here."

"Great plan, but how? We don't even know where we are."

They watched as Zeno tapped a panel in the stone wall of the cavern. A little door slid back and he reached inside and withdrew a plastic pot, like a yogurt container. He handed it to Rob, then sat down again.

Rob peered inside, sniffing suspiciously. "Very generous, I'm sure."

Clara grimaced at the drop of brackish liquid in the cup. "Don't drink it, Rob. It could be poisoned."

"I don't think he'd go to all this trouble to get us here just to poison us, do you? I'm so thirsty I could drink a puddle." Ignoring Clara's protests, Rob took a sip—then spluttered and spurted droplets all over his jeans.

"Ugh! Tastes like something scooped out of a swimming pool. It would make a puddle taste like champagne."

"I did warn you," said Clara, trying not to sound smug.

Rob put the cup down on the ashy ground. For a while, no one spoke. Clara decided to try a different tack. "Mr Zeno, could you tell us a bit more, please?"

Zeno was so quiet and still, he seemed to have gone into a trance. He looked really awful now, beaded with perspiration, his face as yellow as an egg yolk.

"I don't feel so good," he murmured.

"Should I fetch someone?" asked Clara, worried despite herself. "Do you need help? Where's the chief?"

Zeno shook his head as he batted her away. He breathed heavily for a moment, then got up stiffly and walked to the left, alongside the rock wall.

"Follow me."

Having little choice, they set off after him. Rob grinned at Clara, his teeth green in the light. "Chief? You've been watching too much TV."

"What would you have said? Take me to your leader?"

Zeno picked his way along the wall, tracing the edge of the cavern clockwise, prodding the ground before him with his cane. Clara and Rob followed behind, gazing left and right for clues.

Clara felt as confused as ever. It was hard to believe that they were really beneath her hillside. Could they have ended up somewhere else, somehow? And who were all these people? There must be a good hundred of them, mostly middle-aged or older, who all ignored Clara and Rob completely.

Within ten minutes, the three of them arrived at the hexagonal windows. Close up, they were huge, each one big enough to contain a van. They fitted together to form one gently curving slope against the side of the cavern.

Clara peered through the glass. All she could see were shadowy shapes in the darkness, at the back of which was a glowing line, like a hot copper needle.

"Where are we?" asked Clara. "Have we reached the outside? It doesn't make sense. If this is the side of the hill, I should be able to see my wood through here."

"That is indeed outside," said Zeno. "Just there you can see the sea."

Clara's stomach churned. "What, that orange line is the sea? But the sea is three miles away from Callenick mine. We can't have come all that way. Where's my wood? Where are the Downs? I can't stand it. Tell me where we are!"

"Not where," said Zeno. "But when."

CHAPTER 5

CLARA stared, speechless, through the giant windows, then stepped close to Rob. "What does he mean, when? It sounds like he's saying we've travelled in time or something stupid like that."

"At last you get it!" announced Zeno. "Full marks."

Rob glared at him. "You're actually trying to tell us that—"

"Correct. It will be getting light soon. Then you will understand more. Follow me." He walked alongside the windows, towards the other side of the cavern.

Clara glanced at Rob, chewing her lip to stop it trembling. She hoped to find him laughing it off. He wasn't.

Could Zeno be telling the truth? No way! It was impossible. And yet … surely what had happened to them up until now was impossible. What Clara could see with her own eyes was impossible.

Lagging behind, she tapped slyly on the giant window. "It feels very strong," she whispered to Rob. "I don't think we could break it."

"Well done, Shylock."

"I think you mean Sherlock," said Clara.

Although Zeno was a good few metres ahead, his hearing seemed remarkably good. "The windows are made from osmothene," he called. "It lets all our … waste gases out. It also protects us from the outside elements. Every entrance and exit is sealed with it."

Clara shuddered. Zeno spoke as though he never went outside. She couldn't begin to think how awful that would be, never to smell fresh air or feel rain splashing her face, never to look up and see the stars.

Fighting back a growing sense of dread, she forced herself to look around, to concentrate. Beyond the windows, the line of sea grew brighter. Above it, a tangerine streak glimmered as dawn approached. But all she could see on the ground was a strip of glittering blue-violet ash.

After they had passed the windows, Clara spotted another tunnel leading from the cavern. She tapped Rob's arm and pointed, lowering her voice. "Distract him for a bit, Rob. I'll take a quick look."

Nodding, Rob caught up with Zeno while Clara slipped inside to investigate.

A few paces in, beside the path, the tunnel was skewered by a mine shaft, a vertical stone chute leading all the way to the surface. It was obviously not the shaft they had come down in, and Clara wondered if it might be the second shaft—the one just off the gorse path between her wood and the Downs. She felt a surge of excitement, wondering whether they might escape that way.

Then she realised how impossible it would be. The inside surface of the shaft was smooth and damp, with no handholds or footholds. It was too wide to crawl up by straddling, and the mouth of it looked a long, long way up. Far above she could see the first glow of dawn, a small, dim circle. She longed to reach out and touch it.

She retraced her steps back into the cavern. Zeno and Rob were waiting just ahead. Rob gave Clara a sheepish grin. His attempts to distract Zeno had clearly failed.

"I see you've found the Skeleton Shaft," Zeno said, his beetle eyes glinting. "We use it to collect rainwater. The water runs down through a purification membrane."

"Why's it called the Skeleton Shaft?" asked Clara.

An uneasy look crept across Zeno's face. "Best not to tell you that."

They arrived at the low, blood-red building they'd seen from the ledge. It appeared to have neither doors nor windows, but Zeno tapped out a sequence in another panel and a door slid back.

The light in this room was much brighter than in the cavern, and revealed a handful of shabby computers on wooden desks. Between them were scattered microscopes, test-tubes and a haphazard collection of other scientific equipment. Messy heaps of papers spilled from benches and shelves. A stained tarpaulin was spread across the floor.

Four people worked quietly at the computers, two men and two women, none of whom appeared to notice Clara and Rob. Near the door, however, a man with wild butter-yellow hair gazed at them with widened eyes, his hands clasped together across a patched boiler suit.

"Isn't it stupendous?" he cried, bobbing up and down in yellow wellington boots which matched his hair. "Here they are, by Corundum! They've come! Ha ha ha, I can't take it in."

Rob glowered at him. "We were kidnapped, actually. We're hardly emmets on a day trip."

"Emmets, you say?"

"He means tourists," explained Clara, grateful that at last someone apart from Zeno was taking notice of them.

Zeno waved the younger man away. "Get on with your work, Jed. Time is Rock after all."

Jed looked about to object, then shrugged. "Okay, you're the boss."

Clara made a face at Rob. Zeno was in charge?

Jed moved off, but kept glancing over. Zeno gestured for them to sit at a table, then sank onto a stool nearby.

Looking round, Clara saw a large screen on the far wall. Beside it were shelves heaped with jars and bottles in shades of orange, yellow and red, the colours of the lights which had poured from the mine shaft.

Zeno waved an arm. "This is the laboratory. These people are our scientists."

The scientists had not looked at them once. They had moved quietly to the end of the room and were busy measuring liquids into containers.

"I've been working on this project for years," said Zeno. "Finally we have this breakthrough." He banged his cane on the floor, stirring up dust from the tarpaulin.

"Ha! We should be sipping champagne. Celebrating!" His gaze travelled across the room to where yellow-haired Jed was bent over a computer screen.

"Right," said Rob firmly. "Let's hear it. You owe us an explanation and we want it now. What is this place?"

Zeno was out of breath again. He took another lozenge from the small compartment in his cane, tossed it into his mouth and gulped. Ignoring Rob, he turned to Clara and sighed.

"You're not really supposed to be here. It might be quite the wrong thing to do. But we're desperate. We have no other choice. We need help, Clara. I don't admire melodrama, but facts are facts. You are our only hope."

"If that's not melodrama, I don't know what is," Rob muttered.

Clara said nothing. There was something about the way Zeno spoke. Something that chilled her to the core.

At that moment, a shout came from the other end of the room. Jed scooted up to Zeno and they murmured together conspiratorially. Clara heard a few words: "Project Gigi ... tempoplas ... can't maintain the field."

"Start without me." Zeno sent Jed back to his work.

Slowly, Clara said, "You're saying we've travelled in time?"

Zeno nodded.

"Okay. So what year is it, then, according to you?"

"I can't exactly say," replied Zeno. "Really, the less you know the better ... I can tell you that you are from my past. That much will become clear. You have to

57

trust me. It's vital for everyone that you listen to my instructions and carry them out."

Clara looked at Rob, then back to Zeno. "Why should we believe you? You can't expect us to help you without knowing what's going on."

"Yeah," added Rob. "You might be trying to take over the world or something, making up all this future stuff to scare us. Can you prove—aargh!" He jumped at the sound of scuttling on a nearby shelf. "What was that?"

The noise had come from a wire cage filled with tubes and boxes.

"I can't see any—" began Clara, leaning forward. She shrank back in fright as a huge purple insect, shiny and oval, with long black antennae, scurried along a tube and dropped onto the base of the cage.

Zeno smiled for the first time since they'd met him. "Those are Felix and Fido," he said softly, his eyes glistening. "Our cockroaches. Aren't they wonderful? That's Felix. Fido is a mottled grey."

Clara now saw the second cockroach, peeping out from behind a piece of cardboard.

Rob made a face. "They're disgusting. For experiments, are they?"

Zeno ground his cane onto the floor. "Have you any idea how resilient and clever a cockroach is? A cockroach is the ultimate survivor. It can hold its breath for up to forty minutes. It can withstand vastly more radiation than a human being can, perhaps fifteen times as much. And it can survive for a whole week—without

58

its head! Could you?"

"Okay, calm down," said Rob.

Zeno warmed to his theme. "It can go for days without food."

"Rob couldn't go for one hour without food," said Clara with a grin in Rob's direction.

Rob met her gaze and laughed. "Thanks for that, Clara. But you're not wrong."

Zeno pulled a weather-beaten watch out of his pocket and heaved himself to his feet. "Wait here a moment."

He walked to the end of the lab and began talking to the scientists. While he was gone, Rob slipped across to a shelf near the door, where something was glimmering.

"What is it?" Clara whispered, coming up behind him. "Anything useful?"

The shelf held a tray of eight spheres, the size and colour of apricots, made from clear film filled with liquid. Each had a round disc on top, giving it the appearance of a large orange eyeball. Rob touched one and stepped back as it squelched.

"Don't touch those!" boomed Zeno from the far end of the room.

Rob raised his brows. "Wow, he's got eyes in the back of his head."

Zeno made his way towards them. "They're lightballs. We use them in the Siri shaft—that's what we call the time portal. They're essential to the time-travelling process, but the light they produce is truly blinding. Come on; I want to show you something."

Clara and Rob followed Zeno out of the lab. The cavern was now flooded with a watery gleam from outside, which made the ash on the ground sparkle. There were fewer people around, but those remaining strode purposefully about their business. Zeno led Clara and Rob towards the wall of windows. They stopped by the nearest hexagon.

Clara gasped. The sun had risen in the tangerine sky, illuminating scattered rocks of various sizes. But beyond that there was nothing. No people, no animals, not even an insect, no trees, not a blade of grass. It looked like a vast, monotonous beach sloping down to the sea, but instead of sand there was only ash.

Zeno's voice was quiet, but they could hear the bitterness in his words. "How do you like the future?"

Clara gazed through the window, transfixed and silent.

"It can't be," she said at last. "There's nothing there."

A siren rang out, ear-piercingly loud. Clara covered her ears as the cavern people began to race to and fro, joined by others from the tunnels. They darted up stone staircases to the left and right of the hexagonal windows.

"Warning. Warning. Yellow Alert," whined a nasal voice amid the wailing of the siren. "Osmothene breach section G6. Warning. Warning. Proceed with caution."

Zeno seized Clara's shoulder. "Quickly."

He steered Clara and Rob away, back across the cavern. Clara glanced behind, struggling to make sense

60

of what was happening.

"Rob!" she cried, pointing to the windows. "There are people out there!"

Rob wheeled round.

Zeno tried to push them onwards. "Hurry. Ignore them."

Clara held back, frozen with horror. The people outside were dressed even more raggedly than those in the cavern. But unlike the cavern people, they had weapons. They were hurling themselves at the windows, attacking the osmothene with hammers, axes, poles, some just with their bare hands. She couldn't hear their cries. It was enough to see their bulging eyes and livid, furious faces.

The worst thing was their skin. Any part exposed to the air was covered with purple boils, some as large as eggs, oozing pus.

"Don't look!" Zeno tore Clara away from the windows and the nightmare outside.

The last thing Clara glimpsed was a girl, not much older than herself. She was dressed more smartly than the others, in brown overalls. Her boot sliding against the frame, she was attempting to climb the outer face of one of the hexagons.

The girl couldn't possibly see Clara from this distance. All the same, her eyes seemed to stab Clara's like needles, and they were full of contempt.

Zeno groaned in pain as he ushered them back the way they'd come, what seemed an age ago. The door at the top of the stone steps stood open. Zeno pulled them after him into the dimly lit tunnel.

He spoke breathlessly as they ran. "You can see …
The planet … Our only hope … try to change …" He
leaned against the wall, convulsed by a coughing fit.

"Who are those people?" demanded Clara, holding
his cane for him while he caught his breath.

"Grammets," he spluttered. "The ones who were left
behind. They don't live long, the air's too poisonous.
They try to get in. One day soon they will succeed."

He staggered off again. Clara and Rob chased after
him. At last they reached the end of the tunnel.

Zeno shoved them inside the mine shaft. They stood
on the circular floor of the lift.

"Here's what you must do," Zeno said as his fingers
danced across the keypad. "There's a man in your time
called Derek Maunding. Have you met him yet, Clara?
He's the father of Donna Maunding, whom you will
know. Under no account must he buy your family's
mine!" He glanced at Rob. "You must help her.
Whatever it takes, don't let him get it."

The lift door slid across. When it was nearly closed,
Zeno grasped the side and poked his head through the
gap. "Come back to the shaft in eight days' time. If I
can, I will contact you."

He let go the door and it snapped shut. There was a
trembling which shook the earth, followed by clanking
and whooshing.

The lift began to rise.

***

At first, Hayley and Mick had been unable to do more than stare in disbelief at the shaft where Clara and Rob had disappeared.

"That can't have happened," cried Hayley. "What're we going to do? They've gone!"

"But—but—" Mick took his glasses off and rubbed his eyes.

The shaft now looked perfectly normal in the first light of dawn. A ghostly mist hung above its mouth, like breath exhaled in the cold.

Hayley grabbed Mick's sleeve and pulled him after her. "We'll have to get help. Come on!"

They scrambled down the hill and through the wood. As they stumbled out by the two caravans, they saw a light shining in the window of one of them.

"That's where Clara's Aunt Iris lives, isn't it?" asked Mick.

"I think so. We'll have to tell her." Hayley was shivering so much she could barely get out the words.

"Don't be daft. She'll think we're mad. We haven't even met her before."

"We've got to!" Hayley cried, her voice shrill. "Anything could've happened. We've got to rescue them. Oh, we're going to be in such trouble. I knew I shouldn't have come."

"Too late now."

"I know. You're not helping, Mick." Hayley bolted up the caravan steps.

In the gathering light, a figure inside the caravan had

already seen them.

The door opened to reveal a striking woman in an olive silk dressing gown, her auburn hair coiled above her ears. Tall and willowy, she was graceful as a fern.

She peered at them through inquiring jade green eyes, similar to Clara's. "A bit early for visitors, isn't it? Is something wrong?"

***

"Here, try this." Aunt Iris handed Hayley a glass of herbal tea. "You're not making much sense, my dear."

Hayley grimaced as she sipped the odd-smelling liquid. "I know. But they just disappeared." She was shaking violently. Two big tears rolled down her face and dripped into her glass. "You don't believe me. I knew you wouldn't. But it's true. It's true."

Mick sipped his tea quietly, saying nothing.

Iris frowned. "Clara's always running about in the woods and playing up on the Downs. I'm sure she's fine. She'll be hiding somewhere. She's played a trick on you, that's all. 'Tis very naughty of her. I'll give her a good talking-to when she gets home. What were you all doing up there so early?"

A dog barked. Through the window, Clara's dad Tom came striding up the path, closely followed by Jess.

"What the hell's the matter with you today?" he shouted to Jess. "Be quiet."

Jess ignored him and carried on barking.

"Iris! Eye!" Tom rattled the doorknocker.

Iris crossed the lounge and opened the door. Tom stepped inside, filling the doorway with his robust frame, his head almost touching the ceiling.

His words came out in a rush. "Iris, have you got a spare tea bag or two? I didn't get to the shops yesterday. Jess, come back here. Grab her, Eye, she's lagged in mud. Jess! Come here." Only then did he spot Mick and Hayley. "Oh! What are you two doing here?"

Jess bounded up to them and pranced about as they patted her.

"They're friends of Clara's," explained Iris. "I think Clara's been having a bit 'o fun with them. Bit early for shenanigans, if you ask me."

Mick and Hayley had met Clara's dad briefly the week before, but he had been snoozing in front of a snooker match with the pages of The Bugle strewn across him. They weren't sure if he'd noticed them.

"That girl," Tom said crossly. "She's no use to me lately."

Hayley began to sob. "Got to get them. It isn't a joke. In the mine! Clara and Rob." She pulled out a tissue and blew her nose.

Jess leapt to the door and began to scratch at it.

Tom scowled. "What are they talking about, Eye? 'Tis like a foreign language."

Iris looked at her brother with a puzzled, worried expression, as if she didn't quite know whether to take the story seriously or not.

"Clara needs help, Mr Callenick," said Mick.

Tom huffed, then shook his head. "Dammit, can't I

65

ever spend a Saturday in peace? All right then. We'll go and take a look."

***

They set off towards the Downs, following the grass track which skirted the wood. Jess raced ahead at full pelt. Rooks cawed and flapped into the air.

At the end of the track they turned onto the Downs. Jess had disappeared, but they could hear her barking in the distance.

"'Tis a waste of time," muttered Tom. "I know Clara. She'll be off up a tree somewhere, reading a book. She's a dreamer, that girl."

Mick raised his eyebrows at Hayley. Iris strode quietly through the muddy puddles, her lips set in a thin line.

They trudged up the hill. Approaching from this side, the mine shaft and the fence around it were obscured by a stone hedge covered in heather and rabbit burrows.

Suddenly there was more frenzied barking and the sound of voices. As they stepped through a gap in the hedge, Clara and Rob came running towards them.

CHAPTER 6

CLARA bolted out of her history lesson and waited for Hayley in the corridor. Through the open door Miss Grundy could be seen banging chairs about, her whiskery nose bristling with indignation as she re-arranged the classroom. A curse escaped her lips as she reached for a sweet wrapper on the floor.

Hayley's eyes had a glazed look as she pulled the classroom door shut behind her. "How can anyone make the rise of Hitler sound so boring? The Grundy must have repeated herself five times. It's like her mind's not on the job. She seems kind of angry all the time … Don't you think so, Clara?"

Clara wasn't listening. Since her ordeal at the weekend she'd found it impossible to think about anything except the terrible things she'd seen. This was the first proper chance she'd had to discuss what had happened with her friends.

"I told Rob and Mick we'd meet them outside the gym," Hayley said. "We can walk up to the shed together. It's a bit more private up there." Glancing sideways past Clara, she cringed and recoiled. "Uh-oh."

Clara's gaze followed Hayley's and her heart jarred. The Maunding sisters were standing right next to them.

"Oh look, Gail, it's Crazy Callenick," said Donna.

Sneering down her nose at Hayley she added, "She's got herself a little doll."

Hayley's mouth dropped open. Clara clenched her jaws as she turned to face them, determined to stick up for herself and her friend.

Gail stepped into Clara's path and folded her arms. "We want a word with you," she said darkly, her spiteful eyes boring into Clara's. Flicking her gaze towards Hayley she added, "Your little doll can crawl back under her stone."

At Clara's side, Hayley appeared frozen to the spot, her face pinched and anxious. Clara's mind raced and she prayed for inspiration, but no words came.

"Let's go somewhere quiet, shall we?" Donna planted herself firmly beside her sister.

Clara balled her hands into fists. Then, beyond Donna's shoulder, she spotted Jean-Pierre Vaucluse rounding the corner. A tall, blond demigod, tanned from year-round surfing, he was said to be the best-looking boy in the school. Hadn't Clara heard somewhere that the sisters had a crush on him?

"Hi Jean-Pierre," she called loudly, nodding in his direction.

Both girls whipped their heads round. Jean-Pierre looked startled—Clara had never spoken to him before—but to Clara's satisfaction and relief, the sight of him seemed to mesmerise Donna and Gail. With a brief scowl back at Clara, they turned as one, shrieking and beckoning him to their side.

"Come on," whispered Clara. "Let's get out of here."

As they moved off, Clara looked over her shoulder to see that Jean-Pierre had joined the sisters. Donna simpered, leaning against the wall, and Gail giggled inanely as she fiddled with the collar of her shirt.

"Beastly girls," said Hayley with a shudder.

"They don't bother me," Clara said, surprising herself. She had much more important things to worry about—although it did disturb her that Zeno seemed to know the Maundings. What possible link could he have with them?

"They'll be going on about that Christmas party of theirs, no doubt," said Hayley. "Inviting Jean-Pierre, I expect."

Clara glanced at her friend. "Hayley! Why have you gone red? Is it Jean-Pierre? Do you like him?"

"Oh no!" Hayley shook her head a little too emphatically. "Not really. Besides, he'd never look at me."

"Why d'you say that?" Clara couldn't imagine anyone not liking her friend.

Hayley reddened even more. "I'm too quiet for his sort. I reckon he likes Donna."

"Well, more fool him."

Mick and Rob's karate lesson had over-run, so Clara and Hayley waited by the gym door. A group of students in white, belted robes stood watching Mick and the instructor, robotic Mr Fender. Mr Fender kicked out and sent Mick crashing to the ground. Mick groaned as he got to his feet, rubbing his arm.

Mr Fender gave a grim smile. "Okay, kids, that's

enough for today. Next week I'll show you what Mick should have done."

"I'm always the guinea pig," Mick complained as they made their way across the playing fields to the school shed. It was really cold today, and his wavy black hair was thrown sideways by a vicious wind.

"It's 'cos you're so tall, Mick. It makes old Fender look stronger when he knocks you down." Hayley patted his sore arm.

"Ow!"

Clara felt desperate to hear what her friends had to say. On Saturday, her father had been so furious that he'd sent them all home with no chance to explain. Clara had tried to talk to Aunt Iris, but even she remained convinced that it was all an elaborate joke, despite Clara's protestations of innocence. Clara was incensed by the unfairness of it all. She would never dream of trying to frighten anyone like that.

They sought out a spot on the wall running beside the shed, as far away as possible from the other students who congregated nearby. For the next fifteen minutes or so they went over and over Clara and Rob's story. As they talked, Mick handed round bhajis, samosas and naan bread from his massive lunchbox, courtesy of his step-father, who ran the Taj Mahal restaurant in St Piran's.

"Do you really think you were in the future?" he asked.

Clara, who had unearthed only two stale biscuits for breakfast, savoured her bhaji. "We can't think of any other explanation."

"But you can't have been," Hayley said. "It's impossible."

"Well, maybe, maybe not." The winter sun glinted off Mick's glasses as he pondered. "Just because we haven't discovered time travel yet, doesn't mean it won't be discovered in the future. Mind you, it could cause a rift in the Space-Time continuum—"

Rob held up his hand. "I'll stop you right there, Mick. That's science fiction. Not real."

"Yes, but I've often noticed on old sci-fi programmes that they show things that didn't exist in reality back when the programmes were made. Now they do exist. Take mobile phones. They weren't even around when my mum was a girl! Time travel could be the same. What I'm saying is, everything gets invented sooner or later."

Mick's theories were met with silence.

"Maybe Clara had a hallucination," suggested Hayley.

Hayley's words upset Clara more than she cared to admit. Hayley clearly didn't believe what had happened. It would be too unbearable for words if her friend decided Clara was attention-seeking. It was bad enough that her dad and Aunt Iris thought that.

Rob came to the rescue. "But Clara and I were both there! And you and Mick saw things too. You saw the tube-thing, the lights."

"Wow, just think if it is true," said Mick. "I wish I'd gone. I'd love to see the future. So cool. It can't be true, can it? And yet …"

71

Hayley scrunched up her eyes and shuddered. "It sounds like a nightmare. I certainly wouldn't want to see it. Not at all."

"It wasn't nice." Clara rubbed her arms, chilly in the December air. "Look, I can see you don't believe us, Hayley. Maybe I wouldn't myself, if I hadn't been there. But I've made a decision. I'm going to do what Zeno asked. I'm going to do everything I can to stop Maunding getting hold of my land. It's what I want, too. It's all wrong. I just hope it isn't already too late."

Hayley put down her samosa and gave a nervous smile, as though she wanted to believe Clara and Rob, but couldn't quite manage it. "But Clara, what could Maunding be planning to do? How could the sale of your little mine lead to, well, all the things you saw?"

"I don't know. I've wondered the same thing myself."

"Maybe it isn't just the sale of your land," said Mick. "I've read about stuff like this. I do a small thing now— say, swat a wasp. Well, that wasp might have gone on to sting someone and kill him. And that person might have become a horrible dictator, Hitler or someone, and murdered thousands of people."

Everyone chewed for a moment.

"A wasp sting wouldn't kill you, Mick," said Hayley.

"You know what I mean. Anyway, it might do, if you were allergic."

They waited while an excitable group of students hurtled past them towards the tennis court.

"You say it's all sealed down there?" asked Mick.

"That's what Zeno told us," said Clara.

"What do they do for air, then?"

"We didn't get a chance to ask." Clara looked at Rob, who was scratching his arm, a pained expression on his face.

Mick drummed his fingers on his thighs. "What about food? What do they eat?"

"Dunno," Rob said.

Mick frowned. "You didn't find out much, did you?"

Rob stopped scratching and scowled. "Well, Mick, as it was, we were a tiny bit busy escaping from a violent, pus-covered mob. Speaking of which—Clara, have you had any trouble with your skin?"

"I have!" Clara rolled back her sleeve. Her wrist still bore the mark of her run-in with Gail Maunding's lighter flame. But now, next to that, was a patch of raised spots.

"I'm itching all over," she added uneasily, remembering the disgusting boils on the people beyond the hexagonal windows, the people Zeno called the Grammets.

Hayley leapt up to inspect Clara and Rob. "You've got tiny spots on your faces too. You'd better get them checked out." Glancing aside, she added, "Ooh, watch out, here comes Mr Parsnip."

Their head teacher, Mr Pasternak, was marching across the fields, rounding up the students.

"Why do you call him that?" Clara asked with a grin.

"It's what his name means—parsnip! In Russian or something. Cool, isn't it?"

73

Rob pushed himself to his feet. "Never mind that. We're agreed on the plan, right?" He turned to Clara. "You and I will skive off school tomorrow and visit your gran."

"Skive?" Hayley's eyes were round. "Clara, are you sure? We've got a maths test, remember. My mum would be hopping mad if I skived."

Rob snorted. "Hayley, I think this is a little bit more important than a maths test. But you can carry on as normal until next Sunday morning. That'll be the eighth day, so we'll go to the shaft and see if Zeno contacts us." He picked up his bag and strode off. "Five fifteen, same as last time, okay? Clara will wait for us in her lane."

"Okay," Hayley agreed, though she sounded far from enthusiastic.

"Mick?" asked Clara. "You'll come too?"

Mick's face was lit by a fire Clara had never seen before, and his dark eyes glittered like gemstones. He almost quivered as he threw his lunchbox into his bag.

"Just try and stop me … I've never looked forward to anything more. You're sure you didn't pick up any clues about what date you went to, or what had gone wrong? Was it in our lifetime, do you think? Or was it far, far into the future? Don't you have any idea?"

"I'm sorry," said Clara. "Zeno wouldn't say. He said it was for our own good."

Hayley paled. "Imagine if it is in our lifetime. That means, whatever it is, it will happen to us."

Clara said nothing. She had already realised that. It

was hard to think about anything else.

Hayley tugged her sleeve. "Hurry up. We're late already."

"You go on. I just want to sit here for a minute."

Clara heaved a sigh as the other three disappeared across the fields. It was all too much. The thought of losing her home had been painful enough. Now there was this terrible future to worry about.

She had already believed the mine mustn't be sold. The very idea filled her with dread. Maybe it had always been more than wanting to stay in her beloved wood.

Zeno had called her sensitive. Did he mean she possessed a sort of sixth sense? Somehow, it rang true. There was the time Sally had fallen off her bike and broken her wrist. Clara knew something was wrong before anyone told her. Another time she dreamt about Dad's car breaking down. The next day, he had a puncture. And once when Jess went missing, Clara knew exactly where to look. Now that she thought about it, there were lots of things.

She would do what she could for Zeno. But dying planet or no dying planet, she knew from bitter experience that nothing would stop Granny Callenick once her mind was made up.

The sound of movement snapped her from her reverie. Oh no!

The Maunding sisters emerged from some nearby shrubs, grinning as they brushed the cobwebs from their pullovers.

Clara leapt up. "You've been spying on us!"

75

Donna laughed. "As if we'd be interested in anything you losers have to say. Can't a girl have a quiet fag in peace?"

Clara looked left and right. There was no one within hollering distance.

"You're lying," she cried, in as firm a voice as she could manage. Donna and Gail must have overheard Hayley mentioning their plan to come to the shed, and sneaked up here ahead of them while they waited for Mick and Rob to finish karate. How much had they heard?

"Aah, she's upset," sneered Donna. "Diddums."

Clara took a step away from them, poised for flight. She didn't want to run, but it was best to keep her options open. They were bigger and stronger than she was—her only advantage was that she was swift on her feet. What was that funny thing Dad sometimes said? Discretion is the better part of valour.

Donna tossed back her golden curls. "Don't worry. We don't want to hurt you. We just want to talk."

Well, this was new. Clara swallowed. "What about? As if I didn't know."

"Just think about it," said Donna. "Don't be an idiot. Face facts: your family could do with the money, and what good is an old mine with a poxy load of trees? You could buy a proper uniform for a start. I don't know how you've got the nerve to show your face in those tatty rags." Her lip curled as she eyed Clara's skirt.

"I've still got something you want, though, haven't I?" Clara said slyly. On the plus side, it seemed Granny hadn't told Maunding yet of her intention to sell. All the same, within days, Donna and Gail might be gloating at her like cats over a bowl of mice.

Donna smiled, her eyes glinting. "You're playing a dangerous game … Gail, do you remember that old duffer who wouldn't sell Daddy that pub he wanted?"

Gail sniggered, stroking her shirt collar in an exaggerated way. "Oh yeah. The one who fell in front of a truck. Sad, that. Wouldn't it be awful if something like that happened to her weak old grandma?"

Clara felt her skin prickling. Were they just bluffing, or could their father really be as ruthless as that? As she glared back at them, she realised what Gail was fiddling with. It wasn't her shirt collar at all.

"My St Christopher! You give that back."

Trembling with fury, Clara ran full-throttle at Gail and pushed her to the ground, falling on top of her. Gail squealed like a rat caught in a buzzard's beak. Donna thundered across and grabbed Clara from behind.

"Gerrov!" rasped Gail. "Get her off me. She's killing me."

There was a loud yell. "Girls! Girls! Stop that."

Clara turned her head to find Mr Pasternak striding across the grass. He stopped in front of them, nostrils flaring, and peered down the long bridge of his nose. "Stop that right now. What the blazes is going on here?"

Clara released Gail, who burst into noisy and unconvincing sobs. "She—she attacked me, didn't she, Don?" She dabbed at her neck, coughing theatrically.

Gideon Pasternak turned to Clara. "Is this true? It's

77

Miss Callenick, isn't it?"

Clara clenched her fists, too angry to speak. Her school career had been pretty disastrous up until now, but she'd never come face-to-face with the headmaster before.

Pasternak drew himself up to his full height. "Get along now, all of you. You're nothing but hooligans. Don't let me catch you fighting again."

"But she's got my necklace," protested Clara. "They stole it!"

"Do I have to repeat myself, Miss Callenick? Move."

Gail was smirking through her sobs. Clara knew she hadn't really hurt her. But their teacher had never looked so furious—and he obviously blamed Clara.

She gazed towards the horizon, in the direction of home. Bands of sunlight and shadow rolled down the hills as the sun forced its way through the clouds. An exposed tree flailed miserably, bent double by the wind. Clara knew exactly how it felt.

She stepped away from Gail, from all three of them. "Oh, what's the use!"

Blinking back tears, she bolted across the fields.

CHAPTER 7

EARLY the next morning, Clara crept out of her caravan and set off down the lane to meet Rob. Together they would go over to Granny Callenick's and try to talk her out of selling the mine.

Clara's stomach writhed. What if Granny wouldn't listen? Clara had no idea what else she could do.

Clara's dad and her sister Sally had already gone out. Dad had a day's decorating work lined up with his friend Gover, and Sally was at school. But Auntie Iris was a herbalist, and worked from home, so there was still a need for caution if Clara wasn't to be spotted and hauled over the coals for skiving.

It was raining heavily. Aunt Iris's hens looked sorry for themselves, huddled in one corner of their coop. Xavier, the Rhode Island Red cockerel, strode up and down beside them, looking for a gap in the fence.

Clara didn't have long to wait before Rob came hurtling along on his bike. He skidded to a halt in front of her, throwing up a spray of mud.

"Thanks, Rob!" Clara wiped the mud from her face with the back of her hand.

Rob gave a sheepish grin as he climbed off his bike and leaned it against the hedge, ready to collect on the way back. "Sorry."

Clara grinned back. "That's okay."

Walking along the lane in silence, Clara reflected that their trip down the mine shaft already seemed unreal. A day of school and the humdrum familiarity of home life had made that terrible future seem impossible. Yet it was no delusion. Clara knew, deep in her heart, that it was real. That future would happen—unless she could stop it.

As they tiptoed past Iris's caravan, Clara was relieved to note that her aunt must have gone out after all. Her vintage white Mini Clubman was still there, but the caravan had an empty look about it, and she could see no one inside.

A movement nearby startled her. "Quick, Rob, run! Xavier's escaped."

Her aunt's cockerel was bearing down on them with a psychotic glint in his eye. They pelted along the path and ducked into the woods. Xavier flapped after them for a few metres, then gave up and headed back to the hens.

"Auntie Iris got him from Farmer Bolton," Clara told Rob. "He's a lunatic. Attacks everything that moves—Xavier, that is, not Farmer Bolton!"

"Glad to hear that," said Rob, laughing.

Farmer Bolton owned the fields between Callenick mine and Polgrehan village, which were grazed by his herd of black-and-white dairy cows.

"Why does your aunt keep him?" asked Rob as they wove between the sodden trees. "My dad would've had him in a casserole by now."

Clara smiled. "She reckons he's better than a burglar alarm. And she loves the big scarlet comb that flops over his eye like a beret."

Clara led Rob along a muddy path behind the water wheel. Jess joined them, sprinting ahead, bootlace tail flapping.

"So, what are you going to say to your gran?" asked Rob. "Have you got a plan?"

"Not sure. Granny can be a bit … difficult. She's eighty-two, you know."

"So what? My dad's uncle Ken is eighty-three and he's as nice as pie."

"Granny likes to be in control," explained Clara. "She's strong-willed. You'll see for yourself in a minute. You'll meet Coles too. He's a bit … unusual."

"What does that mean, Clara? Who's Coles?"

"Len Coles. He's Gran's unofficial lodger and helps to look after her, though to be honest I don't think he's much younger than she is."

At the end of the path they arrived at the Account House Clara had spoken of before. It was from this cottage, in times gone by, that the tin miners had been paid.

It was a solid granite cottage with a pitched slate roof. A stone trough lay to one side, planted up with purple and yellow winter pansies. From the chimney, a curl of smoke battled against the rain.

As they approached, Clara heard raised voices coming from inside. She stopped and signalled to Rob to be quiet. They inched towards Granny's window and crouched beneath the sill. Clara felt rain seeping through the knees of her jeans.

A strangled cry sounded from within. "How could you?"

It was Aunt Iris! But Clara had never known her sound so upset.

"'Tis my land, Iris," came the voice of her grandmother. Clara felt an icy trickle of fear. Were they already too late? She pushed the thought from her mind. They mustn't be.

Her aunt was shouting now. "I've warned you about him. If it was up to me he'd be flying down the path with a bullet in his backside. You're impossible, Mother. Why don't you ever listen to me?"

There was the sound of a chair scraping. The door flew open and Iris shot out. Clara and Rob scrambled guiltily to their feet.

"Oh!" Iris stopped. Her cheeks were pale, her eyes red-rimmed.

Clara opened her mouth to speak, but Iris pushed right past her and was swallowed up by the wood.

"Huh!" said Clara, stunned.

"Should we go after her?" asked Rob.

"No, not now. Let's get this over with."

She glanced through the window and tapped on the glass. Granny Callenick sat eating her porridge at a Formica table. She smiled at Clara beatifically, as if she hadn't a care in the world.

"You'll have to wait here, Jess," said Clara as the greyhound tried to nose through the door. "She'll kill

Gran's cat if she sees him," she explained to Rob. "That'd be all we need."

They stepped in, leaving a forlorn Jess outside.

"Hello, Gran."

Granny Callenick looked up from her porridge and blinked sharp, bluebell-coloured eyes. A neat woman with feathery white hair, her face was still unlined, despite her years. At her elbow stood Leonard Coles, pouring tea. Gran's cat, Pickles, lay draped about his shoulders like a fur stole.

"Hello, my bird." Maud Callenick's face lit up with another beaming smile. "And who's this then?"

"This is my friend, Rob. Gran, what was that all about? What's the matter with Aunt Iris? She rushed past me without a word."

Clara had already guessed what the matter was, but had to broach the subject somehow.

"What day is it? Why aren't you in school?" Granny continued to eat her porridge, which was sprinkled with brandy-soaked raisins. She ate slowly and methodically, like a determined tortoise.

"Gran, tell me what's going on."

"Nothing for you to worry about, child."

Clara looked from her to Len Coles. A gaunt man with sorrowful fish eyes, Coles took a seat and began to fill in a crossword. He was almost trembling with delight, Clara noticed. Coles was never happier than when the family fell out, or so it seemed to her.

"How's school?" Granny asked between mouthfuls. "Still causing mischief?"

It was quite a while since Clara had caused any mischief. She tried again.

"Were you and Aunt Iris talking about selling the land? Is that why she was so upset? You haven't signed anything yet, have you? You mustn't! I want to stay."

Coles got up and went into the tiny adjoining kitchen. Clara felt certain he wanted to listen without appearing to eavesdrop.

Gran huffed. "My gore, Iris has just been bending my ear. I need the money, Clara. This place needs a new roof, for a start, not to mention decent heating. I just can't manage, and things can only get worse. Your dad wants to go. He agrees with me, it'll be better for you girls to live in a proper house. With the money Mr Maunding's offering I can buy a lovely big place in town for you lot, with a nice little annexe in the garden for me—and Len too, if he wants."

"But … you haven't told Maunding yet, have you?" Clara held her breath.

Coles shuffled in with a tray bearing two glasses of lemonade.

"Get the liqueur chocolates out of the cupboard, Len," said Gran.

Coles set the tray down carefully on the table, crossed to a cupboard and rummaged about in it noisily.

Clara pressed on. "I can't bear the thought of leaving. That Maunding man, you can't trust him. He's—" But what was he? She'd never actually met him. And she still didn't know why he wanted the land.

"These ones?" cut in Coles. With Pickles still draped

around his shoulders, he held up a box of chocolates. Clara recognised them as the box she had given Gran last Christmas, nearly a year ago.

"Yes, open 'em up," said Gran with relish.

Coles sighed elaborately as he battled with the cellophane and cardboard.

"And what about Auntie Iris?" protested Clara. "What's she supposed to do?"

Coles meandered across the room and held the chocolates in front of Rob. Rob reached for one, picked it up, then wrinkled his nose. Following his gaze, Clara spotted the sheen of powdery mould on it. At any other time, she would have laughed.

"Never mind about Iris," said Gran. "She'll be all right, always had a wilful streak in her. Besides, she's got that boyfriend to look after her."

Auntie Iris had recently begun to date Archie Rowlands, who taught science at Clara's school.

Clara gritted her teeth and tried to remind herself, as she often had to, that Granny Callenick was born into a very different world, nearly a century ago. She'd worked hard all her life, and it was the practical things which were most important to her.

Clara tried a different tack. "It's really important, Gran. It's so special here. You can't just sell up. You never wanted to before."

Granny scraped the last morsel of porridge from her bowl, then looked up and rested her bluebell gaze on Clara.

"Things change, Clara. 'Tis decided. 'Tis my land, I

85

can do whatever I want with it. I can give it to the cats' home if I want. Can't I, Len?"

Coles was engrossed in his crossword again, or pretending to be. "Hmmm, whassat, Granny C?" His words dissolved into a coughing fit which threw the cat from his shoulders. Pickles shot off with an angry miaow. Coles got to his feet, still coughing, leaning against the wall for support. He disappeared into the bathroom, from where unpleasant phlegm noises could be heard.

Gran leaned forward conspiratorially. "He's bought this ole tobacco from one of his cronies down the Flea and Feather. Prison tobacco. Dusty stuff. I tell him to go outdoors, but he takes no notice. I don't think he believes in this massive smoking."

Rob clapped a hand over his mouth, stifling a grin. Clara forced herself not to meet his eye. "I think you mean passive, Gran."

There were more hacking noises, then Coles returned, very red in the face.

"I'm sorry, my bird," said Granny. "You'll understand one day. But it isn't really your business."

Clara felt despair welling up. She looked from Granny to Coles, then at Rob, silently imploring him to say something brilliant. But Rob merely shook his head and stood up.

"Come on, Clara. Let's go." He thumped his glass down on the table. "Thanks for the lemonade, Mrs Callenick. And the chocolate."

"Nice to meet you, Rod," said Granny.

As Rob dragged Clara to the door, she made one last desperate attempt.

"Gran, what if I could give you the same amount of money Maunding is offering? Would you sell the land to me instead of him?"

Granny burst out laughing, barking like a seal. Coles smirked.

"Well, that's a new one," Gran said. "What are you going to do, win the lottery? We can all dream, chield."

"Yes, but would you?" demanded Clara. "Say if we gave you twice as much as he is? I'm serious."

Granny was still chuckling. "You are a one, Clara. Give me the same as he is and you can have it, of course you can. 'Tis as broad as 'tis long. You'll have to be quick, though. My mind is made up."

"How quick?" Clara went cold.

"That's for me to know and for you to wonder."

"Tell me, Gran. Please."

"Sooner the better, no point dragging it out." Granny Callenick turned her head stubbornly aside.

Her cackling followed them as they trooped out of the door.

"Buy it instead, I ask you!" came her querulous voice. "The ideas these kids get."

Reunited with Jess, Clara and Rob headed back through the wood.

CHAPTER 8

"WELL, that went well," muttered Rob as they trudged through the mud and dripping trees.

"Much as I expected, really," said Clara with a shrug. She was used to Granny's ways, though it didn't stop disappointment seeping through her like icy water.

Rob gave a slow shake of the head. "I honestly thought we'd have it in the bag by now."

"Nice thought." Their failure came as no surprise to Clara, who had strongly suspected the visit would be a waste of time and effort. "Rob, you didn't say much."

"Huh? What could I have said? Not my business, is it? I was there for moral support."

The hurt look in Rob's eyes filled Clara with regret. "Sorry, Rob. It just all feels so hopeless."

The rain was easing, but they were already soaked.

"You say you've talked to your dad?" asked Rob.

"Till I'm blue in the face. I'm not even going to bother any more. There's no point."

Back at Clara's caravan, they knelt by the wood-burner, which was kept ticking over round the clock. Jess squeezed herself between them, vying for the warmest spot.

"She's not easy to talk to, is she, your gran," said Rob.

Clara sighed. "She's a character all right."

"Hmmph, not the word I'd use. Ignoring you like that. Talking in riddles. As for that man …"

Clara went pink. She didn't mind criticising her relatives herself, but she didn't much like it when other people did, even if they were right.

Rob began to whistle, stroking Jess's velvety ears. "Clara! Jess has got writing in her ear."

"Yeah, it's her identification tattoo. She came with a number, one in each ear. It means she comes from Ireland."

"Poor Jess. That must've hurt."

Lapping up his attention, Jess wriggled sideways, shunting Clara out of the way with her powerful long legs and gazing up adoringly into Rob's eyes.

"So what d'you think, Clara?" Rob asked. "Any ideas? D'you think Granny's signed anything yet?"

Clara shook her head. "Doesn't sound like it. But her mind is made up, that's for sure, and when Granny's mind is made up …"

"Why wouldn't she answer your questions?" asked Rob. "Why make such a mystery of everything? After all, it does affect you, too."

"I know. But that's not Granny's way. What's hers is hers, that's how she sees it. And I'll tell you something else. She won't tell anyone when she's going to sign the deal, not even Dad. She'll just go ahead and do it, and tell us when it's done."

Clara lapsed into silence. Then an idea struck her with the force of a hurricane. She scrambled to her feet.

"What's up?" asked Rob.

"Granny said I could buy the mine if I paid her the same as Maunding. You heard her. Rob, what if I could get the money? What if I could win the lottery?"

Rob laughed. "Nice idea. But she was only pulling your leg, Clara. She thinks you've got as much chance of that as flying to the moon."

"But if I did? She'd have to let me buy it. I'm family, after all. You wouldn't sell to a stranger rather than to your own family, would you?" The ways of her elders were often a mystery to Clara, but Granny wouldn't be that unfair, surely.

"But Clara, you know what the odds of winning the lottery are. Millions to one. We're not even old enough to buy a ticket."

Clara was grinning. "Ah yes, but we do have a curious advantage."

Rob raised an eyebrow—then beamed. "Oh, I see! You think someone from the future might be able to give us a little bit of help?"

"More than a little."

Suddenly hungry, Clara loped into the kitchen and began opening cupboards.

"It's worth a try, isn't it? Zeno's from the future. He might be able to find the lottery numbers for us if we give him a date. Oh, who's that?"

Through the kitchen window she had spied a large car squelching down the lane towards the caravans. She ducked down. "Psst. Come here, Rob. Don't let them see you. We're supposed to be in school, remember?"

Rob crept along the floor and they crouched down in front of the sink, below the window.

"That's some cool motor," said Rob, taking a peep. "Top of the range BMW, that is."

"I've seen it before," murmured Clara, struggling to recall where. Dad had been trying to teach her all about cars, but she still didn't know her Rover from her Renault.

The BMW's privacy glass prevented anyone seeing who was inside. They watched in silence as it pulled up by Iris's caravan. Two men got out. The driver was a fat man with a bulbous forehead and a lopsided grin.

The other was tall and smartly dressed. As the wind ruffled a springy streak of grey in his black hair, Clara gasped.

"That's Derek Maunding! I'm sure it is. I haven't met him but I saw him once leaving Gran's. That man he's with drives the girls to school."

Maunding scowled at a spray of mud above one wheel arch. "Trundle! Get that cleaned off. Now!"

The chubby man grabbed a cloth from inside the car and began wiping mud off the glossy blue paintwork.

Derek Maunding disappeared along the path to Iris's door, which was on the far side from Clara and Rob, out of their view. Shortly afterward, getting no answer, he reappeared and strode towards Clara's caravan.

"He's coming this way," cried Clara. "What shall we do? Should I talk to him? Maybe I can persuade him to leave us alone."

"Dream on," scoffed Rob. "Like he's going to listen

to you."

"Shhh, he'll hear."

Maunding had reached the door, next to the kitchen window. He rapped firmly.

Clara swallowed, her mouth dry. Jess sauntered over to the door and snuffled through the letter box. Reluctant to give up, Maunding gazed through the window. He had the oddest eyes, Clara noticed, like pond water. The cold expression in them chilled her to the marrow.

She bobbed further down, hoping the reflective glare would prevent him from seeing them. She had the eerie feeling he knew they were there. However, after what seemed an age, he turned and set off down the path.

His driver, Trundle, waited inside the car, reading a newspaper. Maunding took a notebook from his pocket and began to walk about, making notes as he went.

"Perfect, perfect," Clara heard him say.

"What a cheek!" she huffed, more loudly than she'd intended. "He thinks he owns the place already."

Maunding whipped his head round. Clara held her breath. A few seconds passed, then Maunding gave a small shrug, as though he hadn't heard anything after all, or if he had, he didn't care. He continued on his rounds, up to the edge of the woods and back. Finally, he headed towards the car.

Out of nowhere, Xavier the cockerel came storming down on him. Maunding shrieked as Xavier thudded into his legs.

Maunding tried to hop out of the way, but Xavier

attacked again, stabbing with claws, spurs and beak. Maunding kicked back fiercely. Undaunted, Xavier squawked and pecked at the flailing legs. Smears of blood appeared on Maunding's expensive-looking trousers.

Maunding screamed to the man inside the car. "Don't just sit there, you oaf. Run it over."

None too quick to lower the newspaper, Trundle gave his employer a quizzical glance.

Clara and Rob peered over the kitchen sink. Rob was snorting with glee. Clara covered her mouth with her hand.

Finally, Trundle started the car. Churning the mud, the vehicle charged towards the cockerel.

"Oh no!" Clara shut her eyes, then peeped through two fingers.

The car skidded to a halt, a centimetre from Xavier. Maunding dashed to the passenger side and leapt inside. Trundle reversed and tried again. Just in time, Xavier shot back to the coop, cleared the fence and fell in among the hens.

Rob was helpless with laughter. "I'm so glad that bird didn't go in the pot."

***

Clara found a couple of bags of crisps which had fallen behind the cracker barrel, and she and Rob sat munching them by the fire as they discussed the days ahead.

"I suppose we might as well go back to school for the rest of the week," said Clara.

"Yeah … I'm glad Mick and Hayley are coming with us on Sunday. I'm still not convinced they believe us."

"Me neither," said Clara with a frown. "They'll have to, though, when Zeno contacts us. Maybe this time he'll come up the shaft himself."

"Hmm, dunno. Maybe he can't. He would've done that before, wouldn't he, if he could? Why bother to bring you down to them, if he can come back here?"

Clara shuddered. "I hated it there. The way they live in the cavern. Not to mention those horrible people outside, those Grammets."

Worn down by the gimlet stare, Rob threw Jess his last crisp. She set to it daintily, balancing it between her paws.

"You're being a bit unfair. The Grammets must be desperate. Wouldn't you be? Living in poisoned air, while others are safe inside their own little bubble?" Rob scrunched up his crisp bag and tossed it into the wastepaper basket.

"I suppose so." Clara hesitated. "Rob, did you see that girl, as we left the cavern? The one with the Grammets, who was trying to climb the hexagons?"

"Just a glimpse. Why?"

"Well, I only got a glimpse too, so I couldn't be sure. But the more I think about it, the more convinced I am."

"About what?"

"The girl. She looked like Donna Maunding."

CHAPTER 9

DURING the weekend there was extensive flooding and hail. As Clara waited in her lane at half past five on Sunday morning, a rumble of thunder sounded as a bolt of lightning lit the sky.

Clara cursed under her breath, worried that the storms might put her friends off coming. But no, here they were, just on time. Clara felt guilty for doubting them—let alone dragging them out of their warm beds in such atrocious weather.

The four of them set off with barely a word. Rob had a new wind-up torch, and the beam tried its best to penetrate the darkness and the driving rain. The lane was water-logged, awash with muddy puddles. It was also freezing, and they hurried along to keep warm.

"So, did you get the headaches in the night?" whispered Hayley.

"No, I didn't." Clara felt almost disappointed. Had they stopped now that Zeno had made contact, or did it mean something had gone wrong?

They slipped quietly past the caravans, then plunged into the wood. It was even darker there, the wet trees blocking out the sky. Owls hooted and an animal cried out as if in pain.

Clara ignored the torchlight and strode confidently ahead.

"How come you can see so well?" asked Rob, struggling to keep up.

"I'm used to being out here in the dark."

"Well, can you slow down a bit?"

"Sorry." Clara waited for a moment, then set off again, Rob at her side.

"Do you think I should mention something to Zeno," she whispered, "about Donna Maunding?"

"No point," Rob whispered back. "The girl you saw can't have been her. As you said yourself, you didn't really get a good look. Must have been a resemblance."

"Yeah. I suppose."

"What's that about Donna Maunding?" asked Mick, who was following with Hayley just behind.

"Nothing," Rob said quickly.

"Tell us! You shouldn't keep secrets from us."

Rob sighed. "Well, Clara saw a girl who looked like her, in the future, that's all."

"Like Donna? That's interesting." After a short while he added, "Hayley, are you all right? You haven't said a word."

"Fine. It's just … Isn't anyone else scared?"

Mick chuckled. "I'm not. It's so exciting! Just imagine. We might be about to see someone from the future. I've always dreamed of something like this. I never believed it would really happen. You don't have to come, though. I'll take you back if you want."

"No way! I don't want to be left out. My mum treats

me like a five-year-old."

Rob came to a sudden halt. Mick and Hayley bumped into him. Everyone cried out.

"Shh!" said Rob. "I think I heard voices."

They were still for a moment, but it was impossible to hear much above the howling wind and the rustling of thousands of leaves. Rob wound his torch up, making a grating ratchety noise which put Clara's teeth on edge.

As they came to the clearing halfway along the gorse path, Clara told them about the second shaft she'd seen inside the cavern, the one Zeno had called the Skeleton Shaft.

"I think it could be the one along the track here. It's smaller than the one at the top. I'll have to show it to you sometime."

"That's okay!" Hayley muttered. "I don't mind not seeing it. All these horrible great holes everywhere. I've seen quite enough of them, thank you very much."

Thwack! Hayley fell to the ground, her foot caught once more on the snake-shaped root.

"Oh, Hayley," chorused the others. Rob shone his torch back for her as she struggled to her feet.

"Here we go again," said Hayley. "Ever since I've known you, Clara, I seem to be plastered in mud all the time."

They popped out onto the Downs and continued up the hill. Shadows cloaked the main shaft at the top, with its post and wire fence and the hand-painted "Danger" sign.

It was exactly six o'clock when they got there. The bad weather had slowed them down. The wind died away suddenly, and the rain turned to drizzle.

Clara was breathing in gulps. She had raced up the hill, worried about missing Zeno, but as yet there was no sign of anything happening. The hole gaped before them, sinister in the dark.

Rob paced up and down and peered at his watch, shielding it from the rain with his hand. "Zeno's late. Do you think something's happened?"

Clara stared towards the shaft, feeling more guilty than ever about bringing her friends up here. How long should they wait? Half an hour? They would freeze.

Minutes ticked by.

"Something's not—" began Clara.

"Shhh!" hissed Rob. "Did you hear it? There it was again."

"What? I can't hear anything."

"It's gone now. Like voices, whispering. D'you think someone could've followed us?"

Clara scanned the ghostly hillside. "There's no one here, Rob." A memory was tugging at the depths of her mind, but it refused to come to the surface.

"Why would anyone be here?" asked Mick.

There was a sudden rumbling as the sky lit up.

"Was that thunder?" said Hayley, her voice shaky.

The rumbling sounded again. This time there was no mistaking it. It came from deep within the earth.

Although Clara had been expecting something to happen, it still felt like a shock. She stood and watched the light show, adrenalin surging through her as spears of orange, scarlet and yellow poured from the mine shaft like fireworks, illuminating the ferns and nearby trees.

A clanking, whooshing sound came from within the mine shaft. Then, just below the top edge, the orange disc appeared, wobbly and faint at first, then becoming clearer and more solid.

Clara looked at it more closely this time. It was perfectly round and shimmered like the sea, rippled by a breeze. One moment it looked hard and buttery. A second later, it appeared fluid. As she watched, the wrinkled tube poked out, like an eel breaking the surface of a pond.

Hayley trembled between Clara and Rob, clinging to their arms. Mick craned forward, clearly unafraid.

The tube swivelled slowly, as if searching for them. When it was directly facing Clara, it came to a halt. Clara quailed, wondering if it would attack her again, remembering the sensation of being stuck to its fish-like mouth.

The tube hissed and crackled. Then there was a boom, so loud that Clara covered her ears.

"I told you to come alone." The words were faint, barely audible through the distortion and hissing. All the same, Clara recognised Zeno's voice.

She glanced at Rob, who shrugged.

"You didn't say that at all," she said in a clear voice, addressing the tube.

There was a pause. "Well, I should have done."

The orange disc began to vibrate. Clara could see swirling shapes in it, like spirals of marmalade in custard.

"Tell me if you have succeeded," Zeno continued. "Have you done as I asked?"

Clara took a deep breath. "I haven't had much luck, yet."

"What? Speak up girl. Has the deal been stopped? Is that man going to get your land?"

"I can't get my Granny to change her mind," shouted Clara. "She's determined to go ahead. I don't know what to do." She felt useless. It was all very well for Zeno. He didn't know Granny Callenick.

There was more hissing and crackling, then Zeno spoke again: "I can't … you."

Clara groaned and tried again, but it was no good. She couldn't get him to understand.

"You'll have to … down," Zeno said, his voice fading. "Get onto the tempoplas … plasma. Hurry!"

"No!" It was the last thing Clara wanted. "Just listen."

The hissing stopped dead. The link with Zeno was broken.

"Now what?" Clara looked at the pale faces of her friends. "What should I do?"

No one spoke. Clara stared at the tube, willing Zeno's voice to come out of it. It remained obstinately silent.

"What can you do?" asked Hayley. "He's gone."

Clara shut her eyes briefly, screwing up her courage.

She looked at the orange disc, which still glowed, illuminating the dark sky.

"I'm going down."

Hayley stepped backwards and tried to pull Clara with her. "Clara, you can't. It's not safe."

Clara shook herself free of Hayley's grasp. "I have to … You three stay here. I'll be back before you know."

She wished she felt as confident as she sounded, but no way did she want any of them to get into danger again on her behalf. They had done enough already. Dreading the feel of it on her skin, she hopped over the little fence and jumped onto the disc.

As the buttery substance swirled over her feet, Clara wobbled and almost fell. A sharp smell of citrus filled the air. She began to sink, shuddering as the stuff oozed through her clothes, stinging like a hundred nettles.

"Wait for me," yelled Rob.

Before she could object, Rob leapt in after her. He fell forward as the gloop sucked at his trainers.

"Rob, go back! You too," Clara said to Mick and Hayley, who were gazing at them in alarm. Before she could stop him, Mick too had jumped over the fence and onto the disc.

"Mick!" cried Hayley. "Don't leave me here. What d'you think you're doing?"

Clara's legs had already disappeared, and Rob had sunk in up to his knees.

With a high-pitched shriek, Hayley cleared the fence and bounded in after them.

The four friends vanished. The eye of the disc closed.

***

The eerie glow faded. There was silence once more upon the Downs. Then, not far away, two figures emerged from behind an enormous tree. At first, Donna and Gail could do nothing more than cling to one another, quivering with fear. Then, blubbering and shrieking, they fled into the darkness.

***

Fighting back nausea, Clara squeezed her mouth and eyes shut and held her breath as she sank through the disc and began to emerge from the lower side. Her skin crawled as though hundreds of creatures were scuttling over her, and her lungs felt like they would burst. Finally, the disc released her with a plop. She freewheeled for a second before crashing onto the hard floor of the circular platform below.

Her three friends plummeted down beside her, and they clutched at one another as they tried to stand up. Above them, the lights and the disc faded away. They were left in complete darkness.

"Ugh, that was ghastly!" shrieked Hayley, coughing and spitting. "What is that horrible stuff? It stings!"

"Try not to move," said Rob. "It's like—like a lift. There aren't any sides, though, and there are gaps around the edge. Take any chances and you'll slip off."

"Will it take the weight of all of us?" croaked Hayley.

"We should have thought of that before," said Mick.

The tube seemed to have retreated into the floor. At least, this time, Clara didn't have to put up with its repulsive mouth clamped around her waist. She still had marks on her skin, where it had bruised her the last time.

She put out her hand and felt the cold, clammy sides of the shaft moving past. Gingerly, she extended a foot, then pulled it back quickly as it bashed into a stone.

"Ow!"

"What did I say?" said Rob. "Just keep still."

The whirring and clanking continued as the lift descended.

"How long does this bit take?" Mick's voice crackled with impatience.

"Ages," said Clara. "The cavern is a long way down."

***

Gail ran so fast her belly wobbled and a stitch gnawed at her side. She tripped on a root, fell flat and scraped her knee on something sharp. Ignoring the pain, she got up and ran again.

Her mind filled with the images she'd seen. Clara jumping into the mine, the other three leaping in after her. The fizzing bright lights, like fireworks coming out of the shaft. What could it all mean?

Stumbling blindly, she realised she'd left the Downs

and had been swallowed up by the wood. Cold drizzle whipped her cheeks and trickled inside her collar. A branch stabbed her in the ribs, winding her, and she stopped and felt in her pocket for the torch. Damn, Donna had it.

"Donna," she called in a quavering voice. "Where are you?" She was answered by the sorrowful hoot of an owl. "Donna, don't play games, it isn't funny. Answer me!"

There was only silence.

"I hate you, Donna," she muttered through clenched teeth. "I hate, hate, hate you."

She remained still for a moment, trying to accustom her eyes to the dark. An unseen animal scurried over her foot. She squealed and kicked out, expecting a snake to clamp its jaws around her leg.

"Donna!" Wet foliage clawed and scratched at her as she pounded on, and every path was strewn with gnarled roots. It was as if Clara had booby-trapped the place on purpose.

Bellowing now, she no longer cared who heard. Her face was sticky with tears. Even if one of Clara's awful family found her, anything would be better than this. She raced on, plunging further into the wood.

Then, a glimmer of hope. She could still barely see, but the trees seemed to have opened out around her. She stretched a foot in front. The ground felt smooth and there was no undergrowth. It must be a path.

A feeling of sweet relief rippled through her, like chocolate melting in her veins. She stepped forward eagerly. The path would lead her out of this godforsaken place. This must be the way she'd entered the wood.

After a few steps, however, she wasn't so sure. Everything looked dark and threatening. The shadowy lumps of the trees looked alive, as if waiting to pounce. Their rustling leaves sounded like reedy voices: "Shh. Get Gail... Shh. Shame on her... Shh. We want you, Gail."

The rain pelted down, soaking her through to the bone. In despair, she spun about wildly. Nothing made any sense at all.

Clara's St Christopher necklace seemed to burn into her, so much so that she had to rub the nape of her neck. The silver of the chain felt fiery hot. She could almost smell singeing where the metal touched her skin.

She felt an odd sinking sensation. If she had the words to describe it, she might call it a sense of dread, even of doom ...

What was happening to her? It was all that ghastly Clara's fault. If it wasn't for her she'd be at home in bed, asleep. But Daddy's obsession with Callenick mine grew more desperate by the day, and he needed their help more than ever. Last night he'd given them a stomach-churning ultimatum: if they made no progress by the end of term—just a week away—he'd have no choice but to cancel their Christmas party. He might even cancel Christmas altogether.

"Donna!" She paused, ears alert, but heard only pattering raindrops and the wind sighing in the trees.

Had they gone through the woods, then along the

105

path up the hill to the Downs? Or was the path before the wood? Where were the caravans? Gail felt completely disorientated.

Then she thought she made out a fence. At last! Perhaps she'd reached Clara's gran's house. Daddy had told her the old witch had a cottage on the other side of the woods.

The fence was low and felt like it was made of wire. Nearby, she spotted a pale oblong, like a signpost, level with her knees. Something appeared to be written on it, but she couldn't see what it said. The name of the house, maybe?

She felt along the wire for a gate, but, finding none, stepped carefully over the top. Peering into the gloom, she tried to recognise anything ordinary. All around her was the earthy scent of dead leaves and wet foliage. Was that the cottage just there?

Gail almost giggled. She'd made it! In the cottage there would be light and people and comforting everyday things, even if she was in trouble.

She took a step. Then another.

The ground gave way beneath her. With a scream, she fell, hurtling through space.

CHAPTER 10

THE lift door slid back to reveal Zeno peering in. His eyes widened and his mouth tightened into a thin line.

"What the Granite! Now there are four of you. By Corundum, Clara, this is most grievous. We can't afford to disrupt the temporal equilibrium any further."

"See, I told you," cried Mick. "He's talking about the space-time continuum! It's not science fiction at all. It's science fact." He gazed in wonder at Zeno and squinted past him into the tunnel. "We're Clara's friends, sir." He grabbed Zeno's hand, then yelped and let go. "Ow! Tingles a bit. Like an electric shock I got from a tap once." He seemed more fascinated than alarmed.

Zeno, by contrast, seemed older and wearier than ever. The lines were etched more deeply into his face, and his beetle eyes looked dull and forlorn. He twisted his cane with its silver horse-head handle and knocked it distractedly into the ground.

"Well?" he asked Clara, fixing her with an angry, disappointed stare. "Why did you bring them?"

Clara had been terrified that Zeno wouldn't be there, that they'd be trapped forever in the shaft. Now, her relief at seeing him evaporated. By letting her friends come, it seemed she might have made everything worse.

"I'm sorry, Zeno." Embarrassed and upset, Clara

gazed down at the ashy ground, cringing from his gaze. "I didn't mean to bring anyone. It just happened."

"It just happened," he repeated sourly.

Hayley peeped out from behind Mick. "We've brought buns! I put cranberries in them."

She pulled out a package which had been squashed into her tiny backpack.

Ignoring her, Zeno glared at each of them in turn.

"All right then," he said at last, as though reaching a difficult decision. "You might as well come. If we don't get this sorted, nothing much will matter anyway."

He turned and set off along the tunnel.

"Doesn't he even want to know our names?" asked Hayley.

They picked their way along the ash-strewn tunnel in the green light. Mick dashed to and fro, examining the pictures and drawings on the walls.

"Mick doesn't want to waste his time here, does he?" remarked Clara.

"Oh no, he'll want to take it all in." Rob smiled.

Up ahead, Mick turned and darted back. "I can't believe you were right about this."

"Well, we did tell you," said Clara. It was good, at least, to be able to prove that she and Rob hadn't made it all up.

"Although," went on Mick, "we still have no proof that we are in the future."

"Just wait and see." Clara peered at Mick's face. "Oh, you've come out in those little red spots Rob and I have got." She looked behind at Hayley. "You have, too."

108

Hayley clasped her hands over her nose, a look of horror in her eyes. "No! It must be something to do with coming through that horrible slime. Oh, please don't let it be anything serious."

The tunnel led them upwards on a gentle incline. This time Clara looked more closely at other tunnels branching off the main one. They smelled like drains, and looked gloomy and uninviting. Clara squinted, trying her best to see what was there, but they had no wall lights. She could see nothing.

"What was that? A scuttling noise." Hayley grabbed Clara's arm. "Could it be a—a rat?"

Zeno rounded on them. "If you only knew. Do you have any idea how amazing it would be to see a rat? You just didn't get it, in your time, did you? You thought things would last forever." He stalked on, shaking his head and muttering to himself.

Hayley's shoulders slumped. Clara shot her a sympathetic glance, though she couldn't help feeling triumphant. Hayley, too, could now see for herself that what Clara had said was true.

They reached the end of the tunnel. Zeno keyed a sequence into the panel and the door slid slowly back.

"I can't wait," Mick said in a choked voice. Clara had never seen him so animated.

Zeno led them through the gap. They found themselves on the ledge, overlooking the cavern.

Rob grinned at Clara, then waggled his eyebrows at Mick and Hayley. "Now do you think we imagined it?"

Mick appeared rigid with shock, his eyes wide in his

white face. "Wow," he breathed.

Hayley's mouth dropped open as she stared ahead and blinked, clearly too amazed to speak.

Clara gazed in silence at the vast, green-glowing space, wondering if anything might have changed. But it looked just the same. There was the huge metal column in the centre, with its radial tunnel-spokes. Ranged around it were the shacks and buildings, and in between them scurried people, rushing to and fro as though they hadn't a moment to lose. In the distance she saw the network of hexagonal windows. Beyond that, darkness.

Zeno stepped aside onto the stone staircase to the left. "Come with me."

They followed as he snaked between the buildings, across the cavern. The air was stifling, smelling of sweat and chemicals, and their feet stirred up particles of blue ash, making them cough.

Rounding a corner, Zeno led them towards the blood-red laboratory Clara and Rob had been in before. A woman wrapped in a tattered patchwork robe was striding in their direction, but when she spotted them, her steps faltered. With a curt nod at Zeno, she went to pass by, but Mick stepped into her path and thrust out his hand.

"Hi, I'm Mick Amar," he said. "Pleased to meet you."

The woman shrank back as though he were a slavering wolf. Her lip quivering, she turned in appeal to Zeno.

"On you go, now," Zeno told her in a steely tone.

"Haven't you got work to do?"

Saying nothing, the woman scuttled off.

Mick squinted after her. "Why's she afraid?" he asked Zeno.

"No, no, she's not afraid."

"What then?"

"You ask too many questions, young man." Turning swiftly, Zeno set off again.

Mick raced after him. "Can't you tell us? Please?"

Zeno stopped, appraising Mick for a moment, then sighed. "All right, it might be best that you know. Fact is, our people are under strict instructions to ignore you—we're aiming for the bare minimum interaction. Too much could do irreparable damage to the temporal equilibrium. It's bad enough you're here at all."

Mick nodded twice in a knowing way. "Aha, I see. I did wonder about that."

The two of them set off together, waving their hands, deep in conversation. Clara followed, crestfallen. It had irritated her from the start, the way the cavern-dwellers ignored them. Why hadn't she thought to ask about it herself?

Outside the laboratory, Zeno entered the code into the panel. The door slid back and they stepped inside.

This time, only two scientists were there. One was Jed, the younger man Clara and Rob had met previously. The other was a woman of perhaps forty, who peered through a fringe of curly dark hair at a computer terminal, paying them no attention.

Jed, however, rushed to meet them, shaking Clara's

hand as if she were an old friend. A bolt of electricity shot up Clara's arm, and both of them yelped as they pulled apart.

Jed shook his head and grinned. "Amazing. That's the first time I've actually experienced the Farrula Effect."

"You mean that tingling feeling when we touch you?" asked Mick.

Jed gaped at him, eyebrows raised. "Well done, young man. Named after Giacomo Farrula, a pioneer in the field. I can touch your clothes. But if we make actual contact, it's as though time resists."

Here was something else Clara hadn't noticed. No one had shaken hands with her the last time.

"You're a friend of Clara's too?" Jed gave Mick a warm smile.

Mick nodded.

"And I am," piped up Hayley, peering out from behind him.

"You're all welcome. It's wonderful to see you, simply dobzha." Jed's butter-yellow hair was wilder than ever and waved to and fro as he spoke.

Turning to Zeno he said, "Are they going to help us, Dad?"

Clara and Rob stared at one another. "You're Zeno's son?" asked Clara.

Jed seemed to swell with pride. "Zeno's my dad, yes. Didn't you know?"

Clara felt even more cross with herself. Now that she thought about it, it was obvious. Zeno and Jed had the same features. But Jed had a more hopeful gleam in his eye. He had not yet been beaten down by life.

Zeno seated them around a table near the big screen on the far wall.

Rob scratched his chin. "What are these itchy spots we've got? When are they going to go away?"

Jed looked uncertainly at his father. "They're nothing to worry about, are they, Dad? They're a side effect of the tempoplas—the temporal plasma in the Siri shaft. Yes, I'm sure they are."

"Why don't I feel reassured?" hissed Rob to Clara.

Zeno fixed Hayley with a beady stare. "You said you've brought buns, girl?"

Hayley nodded eagerly, retrieving the package from her backpack. "You can take the cranberries out if you don't like them."

Zeno tore the package open, took out a bun and began to devour it. Clara shared a glance with Hayley, astonished by the excited snuffling sounds he made.

"Real food!" He grabbed another bun and tossed it to Jed. "Here, try this. You won't have tasted anything like it."

Jed caught the bun and held it up to the light, turning it this way and that, examining it carefully. He held it to his nose and sniffed, then brushed it with the tip of his tongue. Slowly, he bit off a small piece and chewed. His eyes widened and his lips curved into an angelic smile. In five seconds flat, he munched his way through the rest. At the final bite he hesitated, as if torn between the pleasure of eating and regret at seeing the bun disappear forever. Then he tossed the morsel into his mouth.

He rubbed his stomach as though he had tasted the finest steak. "By Corundum. That was amazing. What did you say it was? A bum?"

Hayley giggled.

Jed looked at her and gave a sad little shake of the head. "All I've ever eaten is habas."

"Enough of the pleasantries," boomed Zeno. "Now then, Clara, tell us what progress you have made. Our communication devices need more work. There was too much interference from the temporal plasma. What were you trying to tell me?"

Clara chewed her lip, bracing herself for his anger. "I've tried to stop the sale of the mine, I really have. But Maunding has won my grandmother round. I've talked to her, but she's determined to let him buy it."

Jed turned away, disappointment clear in his eyes.

"Is this all you have to say?" said Zeno.

Clara shook her head. "Well no ... I do have a plan!"

Jed's face lit up. Hayley and Mick exchanged a puzzled glance. Clara realised she hadn't yet told them about her plan.

She took a deep breath. "I need money."

"Money!" thundered Zeno. "I expected better of you. Money! The first thing that interests people when it comes to knowing the future. After all we've been through to get you here!"

Clara felt her cheeks burning.

"What's money, Dad?" asked Jed.

"Quiet," Zeno barked.

Rob jabbed a finger in his direction. "You might listen to the rest of Clara's plan. She doesn't want money out of greed."

Zeno glared at him, lips pursed. "Really? Fine, well if that's the case, I am sorry. Go on, Clara."

Clara shut her eyes for a moment, trying to compose herself. It unnerved her that they were hanging on her every word. It was worse than being asked a question in Miss Grundy's history lesson.

"I made my gran promise to sell me the mine instead of Maunding—if I can get the money. She doesn't believe I can, of course. But this is where you come in."

Zeno snorted. "That's ridiculous. You think we have money to give you? Look around."

"Please just listen." Clara blinked back tears. Her plan seemed daft now. But she had no other ideas to offer.

Jed touched her hand briefly, making her skin tingle. "Father's just upset. We know you're trying to help. Go on."

"Well … All right then." Her words tumbled out in a rush. "In our time, we have a thing called the lottery. You might remember it. I don't know, because you won't tell us how far in the future we are. Anyway, the point about the lottery is that it pays out a lot of money. And it's easy to win because all you've got to do is predict six numbers. Easy if you know someone from the future, that is."

Clara looked at Zeno, hopeful and anxious.

Hayley patted her shoulder. "That's brilliant, Clara."

Zeno remained silent. Eventually he said, "We can't get these numbers for you. I'm sorry. You don't understand our situation. You'll have to think again. We have no records, no paperwork from your times. Nothing."

He got up wearily, catching Jed's eye. They both left the lab. There was a shuffling noise as, hugging the walls, the curly-haired scientist slipped past like a shadow and scurried after them.

Clara sat stony-faced and miserable.

"Well that went well," said Rob, flashing her a smile.

He was trying to be kind, which only made things worse. Clara looked away, her eyes blurring with tears.

Hayley squeezed her arm. "Where d'you think they've gone?"

"They're discussing how useless I am, I expect."

"Oh Clara! You tried your best." Hayley stood up and wandered about the untidy lab, stopping in front of the cage where the cockroaches lived.

"Yikes!" she clasped her hands together as the mottled grey one hurtled along a transparent tube.

"They're Felix and Fido," Rob told her, rolling his eyes. "Pet substitutes."

Hayley crept back to her chair, her face pale.

The door slid back and Zeno and Jed strode through, their faces solemn. Zeno sat down next to Clara and spread his hands. "I'm afraid, Clara, that if that's all you've come up with, there's no hope for us."

Rob leapt to his feet, fists clenched. "You're so unfair! Why don't you tell us more? You haven't

116

explained anything. If you tell us what happened here, we might be able to think of a better way to help."

Jed hissed in Zeno's ear. "Dad, the boy's right. What difference can it make?"

Zeno shook his head. "You're forgetting the temporal equilibrium, Jed."

"As if I could! Look, Dad, you've said it yourself. If we don't sort this out, nothing will matter anyway."

"Hmmph." Zeno was silent for several moments. Then he slumped in his chair, a defeated look in his eye. "All right, Jed. You win. As you say, things could hardly be any worse."

Jed jumped up and dashed towards the door. "Come on then, everyone. Follow me."

CHAPTER 11

"ARE you going to explain what went wrong?" Mick asked breathlessly as they strode across the cavern.

"I think I'll have to," said Jed. "But first, let me show you how we live, down here." He pointed to the large wheel apparatus at the centre. "That's our Energy Hub. We get all our power from there."

"Where does the energy come from?" Mick asked.

Jed stared at him as if he were mad. "Why rock, thunderhead! Oh, apologies, I keep forgetting. In your time, the power of rocks was only just beginning to be discovered. Of course, it's obvious when you think about it, because rocks are made up of an accumulation of everything—animal, vegetable, mineral—over millions and millions of years. They absorb everything around them: events, emotions, atmosphere, et cetera, et cetera. Which is why they are so important in the science of Temporal Dynamics."

"What's he on about?" Rob whispered in Clara's ear, making her grin.

"Apologies, time travel," explained Jed, waving his bony arms in excitement.

They had been circling the hub. Inside one of its spokes, a side chute leading to the centre, Clara spotted a woman pushing a cart containing what looked like gravel.

"What's she doing?"

"She's feeding the system." Jed pointed to a nearby building. "That's the processing room, where we prepare the fuel."

This building had none of the hi-tech secrecy of the lab. It was just a large, ramshackle shed attached to the inner wall of the cavern.

"Can we go in?" asked Mick.

Jed pressed his lips together. "All right, but don't talk to anyone. Stand just inside the door. We have to fetch the raw material, the stone, from the rock face at the back there. Then we process it."

Clara watched the twenty or so men and women in the room. Some of them stood around a large vat, adding various liquids and stirring the contents with long poles. Others were strapped to a tall wooden framework, three on each side, turning handles. Inside the framework, vertical steel rods pounded rocks into rubble.

"Oh! It's like the water wheel in my wood," Clara said. "It used to move hammers like that—stamps—to break up tin ore. Except you haven't got a wheel. Those poor people have to do it instead."

Jed nodded. "I expect you're right. I know little of your times."

"It was before our time," Clara said, fascinated. It was hard to comprehend that her ancestors, the tin miners, had once worked in this very place.

The workers in the processing room wore very few clothes, yet sweat poured from their bodies. One

119

woman sat in a corner looking completely exhausted, her tangled, dirty hair hanging down over her face. At the far end, a handful of burly men coated the rock face with steaming dark liquid from jugs. The rock fizzed and hissed as clumps of stone fell, blackened, to the ground. The men collected them carefully, put them into a barrow and wheeled them over to the press.

"Don't you have any machines that could do this?" asked Rob.

Jed gave a rueful smile. "We save our resources for the lab. We produce only what we need to survive, and keep our energy use to the bare minimum. It's tough work, but we try to be fair. Everyone helps with the hardest jobs. Everyone except Zeno, that is. We won't let him. He's the oldest and also a genius, our best hope for finding a way out of this mess."

They left the processing room and walked on. "Your dad seems a bit, well, fierce," Hayley said.

"He's under a lot of strain. It's been very hard for him, and losing my mum of course …"

"What happened to your mum?" asked Clara.

Jed looked away, then turned to face her, a look of inconsolable sadness filling his eyes. "My mother died when I was six. The Grammets managed to get in and they … they desiccated her. My father never got over it."

Clara wondered what desiccated meant, but didn't dare ask.

"I wish you knew Dad as he used to be," continued Jed. "Why, once when I was little he stayed up all night

120

sanding and carving some rejected stones. He made a little game for me and the other children."

Suddenly it hit Clara. "You were born here, weren't you?"

Jed nodded as he set off again. Clara thought of her wood, the Downs, all the places she loved. She couldn't bear to imagine a life without fresh air, plants and animals all around her. Jed had spent his whole life cooped up here below ground, in this stale, stuffy atmosphere.

Rob asked, "Have they managed to get in, the Grammets, since the time when you were young?"

"No. But we fear they will, soon. They have hardly any food. Yet, right from the time of the Disaster, they managed to find, or make, weapons. Much better weapons than ours. And there are so many more of them than there are of us. Things would be different if they were reasonable. We would be glad to share what we have. But, oh, they're plain evil. During that last attack, we lost many of our people besides Mum. Others, they took away."

Tears glistened in Hayley's eyes. "Why? What did they do to them?"

"We never did find out. They put them to work, I suppose … or even … after all, there isn't much else to eat. But let's not … Anyway, I was lucky. I was the youngest person here, and everyone tried to protect me. Dad managed to hide me in one of the tunnels. Unfortunately, since that time, no children have been born to us. We think perhaps the Grammets brought

121

some sort of virus with them—perhaps intentionally, since it doesn't seem to affect them."

Clara had noticed the absence of children here, of course. But as Jed spoke, the reality of his words sank in. There was no one younger than Jed in the cavern. He was the last one.

"You need to protect yourselves," said Rob gruffly. "Get organised. Form an army. Build better weapons."

Jed nodded. "You're probably right, young man, but, as I said, all our efforts go into our survival. And our research, of course."

"They've got their priorities all wrong," Rob whispered to Clara. "Can't they see they have to fight fire with fire?"

Clara spotted the tunnel with the second shaft skewering it, the one Zeno had called the Skeleton Shaft. Mick stepped inside, just as Clara had done on her previous visit, and stood peering upwards into the shaft, towards the hole far above.

"What's that shaft in there?" he asked as he came back out.

Clara opened her mouth to tell him. At last, a question she could answer!

Jed beat her to it. "Aha! Good question. That's part of our water system. We've managed to adapt the osmothene at the top, so it lets in rainwater and air. It must be decontaminated, of course. We call it the Skeleton Shaft."

He marched off, stirring up clouds of blue ash. Clara raced after him.

"Why do you call it that?"

Maybe Jed would tell her what Zeno hadn't.

Jed looked wary. "I probably shouldn't say, but, well, when we were first working on it, we found a human skeleton at the bottom."

Clara shuddered. "How awful."

"What a dreadful way to die," murmured Hayley.

By now, Clara was convinced that this second shaft was the one just off the gorse path between the Downs and her wood. It made sense when she compared the distances between them.

As Jed strode off, he caressed a chain worn beneath his patchwork boiler suit. "We found a pendant around the poor skeleton's neck. I wear it as a talisman. I don't know why."

Clara felt a trickle of fear. She ran after Jed, craning to look, but only a sliver of chain was visible at Jed's collar bone.

"Can I see?" Her voice was hoarse. Was there any chance it could be her St Christopher necklace?

Jed eyed her suspiciously, drumming his fingers on his chest. "No. I never show it to anyone. It would be unlucky."

"But—" began Clara, then stopped. It was just a necklace, after all. She shuddered and walked on.

They arrived at the hexagonal windows and stood still, gazing out. The sun had risen, a tangerine globe. Not far off they could see a glowing line of copper-coloured ocean.

Mick gave a low whistle. "Wow, I never thought I'd

see anything like this. What's happened to the sea? Why is it that strange colour?"

Jed stared down at his feet in their ragged yellow wellingtons. "Poisoned. All poisoned. Dad said it used to be different shades of blue." He looked up, his eyes taking on a moist, dreamy look. "Is that right? That must have been breath-taking."

No one answered. Jed was quiet for a while, then gave an odd little laugh. He ran his hands through his hair, dragging it out into points. "It's not completely useless, funnily enough! I think you'll be impressed. We have a pipe running from here to the sea, and we siphon seawater off into purification tanks. You can see some of them over there." He pointed to four square tanks lined up against the cavern wall.

"Takes a mind-boggling amount of work, mind you," he added.

"The air is bad too," explained Rob to Mick and Hayley as they moved on. "They can't go outside. The Grammets live out there, but they're ill, they're always trying to get in. There's not much to eat and the rivers are poisoned."

"Not much to drink either, then," said Mick.

"If we have a surplus of habas or water, we put it out for them," said Jed. "But that isn't often. We need all we can produce. And they never appreciate it."

Jed sighed and rubbed his eyes. He looks so tired, thought Clara, tired and sad.

"What poisoned everything?" Mick asked. "Is it really as bad as that? There must be something

124

somebody can do. Is it only this area that's affected?"

Clara tapped him on the shoulder and leaned in close. "Mick, you're wearing him out. Can't you see how exhausted he is?"

Jed smiled. "It's all right, I don't mind. You'll understand shortly. First, I want to show you the lower level."

This was an area Clara and Rob had not yet seen. They followed Jed along a tunnel to the left of the hexagonal windows. It sloped downhill for some distance and was so dimly lit they could barely see their way ahead.

Clara tried not to think about how narrow the tunnel was, how far from the outside, how much solid rock lay between this tunnel and the surface. Whenever those thoughts entered her head, the familiar panic threatened to flood her mind and snatch the breath from her lungs.

As the light grew stronger, she and Hayley stopped to admire images etched into the rock—life-sized portraits of human beings.

"Who are these people?" asked Clara as she studied a carving of a severe, weary-looking man.

Jed doubled back to look. "Oh, that's old Sloggett. Died just over a month ago. We don't have much time for art, but we do like to honour our dead with a drawing or a carving somewhere."

"It's so lifelike," marvelled Hayley. Parts had even been coloured in with blood-red paint.

"What do you do with people, when they die?" asked Rob.

125

Hayley's hand flew to her mouth. "Rob! You can't ask him that."

"I just wondered. I mean, it's not as though there's a way out."

They all looked at Jed, who turned crimson. Eventually he said, "We do have a chute near the top of the Skeleton Shaft which we can open. But we think it's more respectful to … ahem … Old Sloggett, especially, would have hated the thought of going to waste." He chuckled. "Sloggett was quite a stickler like that."

Jed strode on. Rob caught up with him. "What do you mean, going to waste?"

Jed cleared his throat. "Er, well, yes. I mean the things that went on in your time. Nothing goes to waste down here. Our old friends live on with us. In our tools, our fuel, our furnishings. I won't go into details. Glue … Paint …"

Hayley fanned her face with her hand. "I think I'm going to pass out."

They came to a flight of stone steps. At the bottom was a large wall, flanked by a narrow walkway. Jed tapped a panel and a blue light flickered on.

"This is where we sleep."

Looking up, Clara saw that the wall was honeycombed with around fifty rough-hewn hollows, each big enough to take a person. Peering inside the nearest one, she noticed a few scraps for a mattress— cotton rags, cardboard, even scrunched-up paper—and a pillow, which looked suspiciously like a bundle of human hair.

Going up the face of the cells, there were handholds made of metal.

"Which one do you sleep in?" asked Clara. Her cosy caravan with its little bunk seemed the height of luxury by comparison.

Jed chortled. "There's a thought. It's not as easy as that, I'm afraid. We have to work around the clock to get the stone processed and the water purified and the habas made. We just crawl in where there's a space. The younger and fitter of us climb as high as we can to leave room for weaker ones below."

He led them back up the steps and along the tunnel. Just before they reached the cavern, Clara noticed a tiny room to one side, scarcely larger than a cupboard. It was triangular, the rock ceiling sloping to ground level at the back. The thick metal door was open, but nothing was inside.

"What's that place for?" asked Clara.

Jed pressed a finger to his chin. "You don't need to know everything."

"You might as well tell us." Something about the place made Clara shudder. It looked horribly small in there.

"It's just … sometimes it's all a bit too much. People go mad. We have to shut them away."

They continued in silence. Clara saw from her friends' dazed faces that they found it just as hard as she did to take in the tragedy of the cavern people's existence.

Back in the cavern, she tried to think of something

cheering to say. "What are these habas you keep mentioning?"

Jed shrugged. "Oh! You know, habas. What we eat."

"You mean those little things Zeno gets out of his stick?"

"That's it. Habas."

"What are they made of?" asked Mick.

"Rock, of course! It's the only food we have. Although it does require a lot of processing, by Corundum. Come and see."

They followed Jed into a shack. Here people flitted between rows of desks, pouring jugs of materials, like different grades of sand, into bowls of various sizes.

"This is the food lab, where we make the habas." Jed nodded to a potbellied man who was walking up and down, testing the contents of the bowls and pausing occasionally to reprimand a worker. The man returned Jed's nod, looking right through the rest of them. Clara stifled a gasp as a bead of sweat slid down his nose and splashed into one of the bowls.

Hayley had seen it too. They caught one another's eye, aghast.

"Can I try one?" Rob asked Jed.

"What? Try a haba? Why the Granite would you want to do that, when you have such dobzha food in your own time?"

"Go on, I'd really like to."

Jed walked over to the fat man and murmured something in his ear. The man wrinkled his brow as he took a few lozenges from a bowl and handed them to

Jed. Eyeing Jed secretively, he made a note in a little book he carried.

Jed came back and gave them one each. The habas were of all shades of grey, from dirty cream to jet black. Clara and Hayley exchanged another glance, but Clara was starving by now, and curious to know what they tasted like.

They threw them into their mouths, even Hayley.

Like chewing the lead from a pencil, thought Clara.

"Interesting," said Mick.

Rob screwed up his face. "A bit hard. Not much taste."

"Yuk!" Hayley spat hers daintily into a tissue.

Jed saw her and tutted.

"Should I give it back to him?" she whispered to Clara.

"We tried to develop flavours," Jed said. "But you must understand how little time and energy we have to spare. They keep us alive, that's the main thing. Oh, that reminds me. There's been a stupendous development in the food lab. Come and see."

He took them to the far side of the shack. Sealed within a padlocked wire cage was a plastic container half-filled with clear liquid. Suspended in the liquid was a plant.

Its long tap root stretched vertically downwards, with lots of other little hairy roots branching off. Four-toothed leaves poked out of the liquid—one withered— and a big yellow sun-face drooped to one side.

Jed's face shone with childlike wonder. "Look.

They've actually managed to get this flower to grow. Dad calls it a dandy lion, though I've no idea what it's got to do with a lion. They were big yellow animals with fur on them, weren't they? Maybe it's the colour. Anyhow, some seeds were discovered jammed in a water purifier. We didn't know there was anything like that left! It's caused a sensation. If we can keep it alive we might be able to get it to reproduce." Jed clapped his hands. "Just imagine, real food! Leaves. Dad told me what it's like to eat leaves. He said people even used to make a drink from the roots or the flowers. Boar, I think he said." He gazed into the distance.

Clara felt puzzled, then smiled. "I think you mean beer, Jed. My dad makes it."

"Ha ha, yes, beer, that's it. Father told me that in the old days before the Disaster, the Pre-D days we call them, people drank things like that to make them laugh and feel happy. Do you drink it in your time?"

"Yes. Not us, though. We're too young." Clara crossed her fingers behind her back. Dad always let her have a glass of elderflower champagne with Christmas lunch.

"I see," said Jed, although clearly he didn't.

Rob's face was shiny from the heat. "Let us get things for you, Jed. We could bring you all kinds of seeds. Tools too."

"We could bring you food and clothes," added Clara. "Whatever you want."

Jed smiled. "Maybe. It's a kind thought. But I'm not sure there's any point."

Clara saw a chilling look of defeat in his eyes.

"There is one thing you can do, though," he added, brightening. "That dandy lion is the only leaf, the only flower, I've ever seen. In the flesh, that is. I have seen a picture. If you come again, could you bring me another flower? I would so love to see a rose."

Clara nodded. The longing in his voice, in his eyes, was unbearable. She didn't have the heart to tell him that roses didn't bloom in December.

CHAPTER 12

OUTSIDE the lab, Hayley stopped to peer suspiciously at the blood-red paintwork. Clara, Rob and Mick charged inside. The curly-haired scientist was once again working quietly at her console. Zeno sat on a bench, draped against the wall as though his backbone had melted.

"Your cavern is amazing," said Mick.

Zeno gave him an uneasy glance. "You enjoyed your tour? Do you understand better the life we have here? The half-life? For Jed, this is the only life he has ever known. I, at least, knew what it was before."

"I'm going to show them the film, Dad," said Jed. "They need to understand what went wrong."

He seated them in front of the large screen mounted on the wall, then fiddled with a panel to one side.

Mick frowned. "Excuse me, Jed."

"What is it?" Impatience clouded Jed's normally sunny features.

"I was wondering … Couldn't you just send us back in time, to when it happened? So we could see it first-hand, like?"

Jed and Zeno laughed.

"By Corundum," said Zeno. "That's a good one. Young man, you have no idea how much effort has

132

gone into creating just the one link, between your time and ours. And each of those collisions uses up so much raw material."

"Oh." Mick's face fell.

Jed went to press a button, then stopped and turned to them.

"Before I show you this, I need to explain something. Hmm, where to start … You may have heard of MORE?"

"More what?" asked Rob.

"I mean MORE. M.O.R.E. No? Well, MORE is—was—the Maunding Original Research Establishment. Headed by Derek Maunding."

"Oh, that horrible man," said Hayley. "I wondered where he fitted into it all."

"Yes, quite. Well, at the beginning, Maunding ran MORE from an office in your town of St Pirans. Derek Maunding wasn't a clever scientist himself—a fact he could never accept—but he was very persuasive. He managed to bring together some of the best scientific brains in the land. He dreamed of making a brilliant discovery, something which would make him the greatest man in history. What interested him most was the secret of time itself!

"As I explained earlier, in your time, the power of rocks was only just beginning to be understood. But, at the same time, new research into neutrinos turned everything on its head. Everything changed—all the assumptions about the universe up till then. Even $E=MC^2$, Einstein's principle, which was thought to be

133

embedded in the fabric of the universe."

Clara glanced at Rob and Hayley to see if they understood this any better than she did. Their faces were utterly blank.

Mick, however, was nodding eagerly. "Cool! I've read about that."

Jed smiled fondly at Mick, then went on with his explanation. "Einstein understood the speed of light to be the maximum speed at which anything could travel. But the neutrino research convinced many of our scientists that particles could be in two places at once, or could arrive at their destination before they had set out on their journey! They realised that time travel might be possible, after all."

"What did Maunding do?" asked Clara. A feeling of dread was creeping into her bones.

"His team was making progress every day. But they needed more of a special rock named Luxulyanite. It's a rare type of granite containing tourmaline crystals. Luxulyanite was named after Luxulyan, the village near you where it was first discovered."

"I was there last week," exclaimed Hayley. "My cousin lives there."

Jed ignored her. "In Clara's mine, Maunding found what he was looking for. You see, Clara's mine was a treasure trove of Luxulyanite. What's more, Maunding realised he could build himself a spectacular laboratory here, underground, where he could carry out his temporal experiments in secret, away from prying eyes. He wanted to keep all the new discoveries and inventions for himself."

Mick put up a hand. "Jed, sir, can we see some of this Luxulyanite? Please?"

Jed whistled through his teeth for a moment. Then he crossed the room and fetched a small bowl from a shelf.

He held it out for them to see. "Take a good look. Those, my friends, are Time Crystals."

The bowl was half-filled with tiny, shimmering crystals—salmon pink, milky-white, slate-grey or black and shiny like crushed coal.

"Wow!" Mick ran his hand through them, letting them cascade through his fingers. As they caught the light they cast peacock hues around the room: sapphire, violet and turquoise.

Jed's eyes were ablaze. "Amazing to think that this rock was in the ground for thousands, millions of years, and no one knew it harboured the secret of time travel … But sadly, this is all that remains. Enough for one final experiment. Two, at the most. When it's gone, there will be no further time travel."

Clara scooped up a few of the crystals. She didn't feel any tingling the way she had when Jed had shaken her hand. That "Farrula Effect" Jed had mentioned must apply only to people, not to things.

Jed returned the bowl to its shelf. "Now, where was I? Oh yes. As soon as he got control of the mine, Maunding set to work building his underground lab. He took away part of the hillside and created this cavern. He moved MORE here. Lied to the authorities. Told them he was working on a new method for stabilising old mines, so that people could build on them."

Jed stopped talking and stroked his cheek.

"What happened?" prompted Mick.

"All went well for a time. Several years, wasn't it, Dad?"

Zeno nodded. He had a faraway look in his eyes, as though he was watching his past unfold in front of him. Clara sensed some of the horror he must have endured, the regret and loss.

Jed smiled. "By this time my father had been recruited. And, although I say so myself, Dad was the cleverest scientist MORE had ever had. Without going into details, he was the first person to successfully react Luxulyanite with Mintaxalic acid to produce temporal plasma."

"That was not going into details?" whispered Rob.

Clara and Hayley giggled.

"So," went on Jed, "Maunding was able to carry on with his experiments with little interference from the authorities. He ignored safety checks and regulations. This was where the trouble began."

A yell came from the back of the room. The curly-haired scientist ran up to Jed and thrust an object into his hand.

"It's finished!" she cried, jumping up and down in excitement. With her patched green tunic, round face and shining, rosy cheeks, she reminded Clara of an apple.

"Thank you so much, Gina." Jed's thanks were so

effusive, she blushed even redder. "Look, Father. The trilloscope! It's ready to test."

A rare smile transformed Zeno's face as he rose stiffly and shuffled across to join them.

The object had the look of a white pebble, but was perfectly spherical, the size of a tennis ball. As Jed held it up to the light, Clara saw tiny perforations in it.

Jed smiled round at them. "The trilloscope," he repeated, but explained no further.

He handed it to Zeno, who took a seat nearby, gazing at it, beetle eyes gleaming. Jed nodded to the scientist named Gina. Her gaze lingered on him for a long time, even after he turned away. Finally she retreated to the far end of the laboratory, where she busied herself with some papers.

As Jed resumed his story, Clara saw her glance back. But this time, it wasn't Jed she was watching. This time, the woman's heavy-lidded eyes rested on her. She must be curious about us, thought Clara. Could it really matter how much interaction they had? Zeno seemed to think so—but he and Jed had already revealed so much. Just thinking about it made Clara's skin prickle.

"My father was worried," said Jed. "He could see Maunding wanted everything done too quickly. Dad explained to him that the experiments weren't safe. Maunding's answer was to sack him!

"Unfortunately, Dad wasn't the only one who knew how to make the plasma. On the very day he was clearing his desk, his partner, Arnold Snell, carried out the biggest experiment yet. Snell reacted all the

Mintaxalic acid they had with the main seam of Luxulyanite inside the mine. Snell and Maunding believed this would lead to a fantastic harvest of plasma. Enough to make the first time tunnel."

Jed touched a button. The screen flickered to life. "We saved all the footage we could from the Disaster," he said quietly. "Even so, most of it is lost."

The screen was blank for a while. Then, terrible images appeared. Skyscrapers juddered and collapsed into rubble. Gaps yawned in the earth and sucked streams of cars from buckled motorways. Waves swept away houses and tossed cars into trees. In every scene, people ran, their faces contorted with fear and disbelief.

Hurricanes uprooted pylons and smashed buildings to the ground. Planes fell from the sky. Crowds fled walls of water as high as cliffs.

There were some clips of newspaper headlines. "Biblical deluge submerges most of Europe," said one. "New York Quake Horror," screamed another. The next sequence showed a TV presenter leaping up halfway through a bulletin as the studio crumbled around him.

Clara looked at her friends. Hayley's hands were pressed against her mouth. Rob and Mick stared at the screen, their faces pale and shocked.

Clara felt sick. She had suspected it for some time, but now the proof was inescapable. The future they were seeing was not some fantastical event which would threaten the world hundreds, perhaps thousands, of years away, long after she and her friends were dead and

138

gone. From Jed's words, from the images she saw, it was clear these events were horrifically close. They would happen in Maunding's lifetime. They would happen in hers.

"I don't understand," she murmured. "How could one experiment do all that?"

Jed's voice was sombre. "Something went terribly wrong. The reaction was too powerful. It went deep into the core of the earth, destroyed the equilibrium of the whole planet. It was … Dad says it was like something called an allergy, where a tiny bit of something might make you ill. Might even kill you."

"Like a peanut allergy?" suggested Hayley. "My mum's got that."

"Maybe. That was how it was for our planet. Although the poison was a small thing in itself, it quickly spread to affect the entire earth. There were earthquakes, tsunamis, floods. Everything went wrong all at once."

Rob's temple twitched. "So—so all this happened because of Maunding's greed."

Zeno looked over at them. "Well, you could say that Maunding's experiment just speeded things up. Oil had almost run out. Climate change was causing chaos, with all the governments babbling about it but doing too little, too late. A new class of pesticides had wiped out most of our insects, which had devastating consequences for crops …"

"But yes," continued Jed. "Maunding's experiment made everything a hundred times worse. The

139

earthquakes destroyed the nuclear power stations. Caused them to spill their radioactive poisons into the sea, into the air."

Hayley wiped the tears from her wet cheeks. "What did people do? How did they cope?"

"Overnight, the life people had known was swept away. Not just in places where such things happen all the time, but here in England, too."

Zeno stood up and began pacing up and down, leaning on his cane. "Within days, there was no food on the supermarket shelves. No traffic on the roads. Buildings lay in rubble, and what wasn't destroyed was washed away. Communication lines were down, the towers destroyed. The internet collapsed. Technology was lost."

"It was known as the Disaster." Jed sat silently for a moment, then threw a haba into his mouth and chewed. The effort of explaining had clearly taxed him.

"What happened here?" asked Clara. "What happened to my wood?"

Even as she asked the question, she knew the answer. Her wood could not have survived.

"I'm sorry, Clara." Jed's voice was gentle. "The sea level rose. Most of Cornwall now lies beneath water."

Clara looked down at her hands, struggling to control her emotions, fighting back a veil of darkness.

"However, we're quite high up here," Jed continued. "Amazingly, parts of the mine, of the laboratory, were still intact. Dad and his colleagues were able to create this refuge, before the poison, violence and disease had made life impossible on the surface."

Mick wrinkled his nose. "How? Hadn't he just been fired?"

"Yes, I had," said Zeno with a glare, "but you can't imagine the chaos, the despair. Snell fled when he saw what he'd done, and I was able to take over."

Jed smiled at his father. "I'm so proud of Dad. He brought my mother Siri here, together with as many other people as he could. I've heard the stories many times—how, working round the clock, they managed to seal off the outside before it was too late. Together, they built some sort of a life. My father persevered with his experiments and succeeded in creating the time portal. The Siri shaft, he called it, in honour of my mother. He had one aim: to discover a way to go back in time and prevent the Disaster from taking place."

On the screen, images of the Disaster continued to play. Plague victims, dead and alive. Gangs fighting each other and destroying what was still standing.

"What happened to Maunding?" asked Clara.

Jed opened his mouth to speak, but Zeno cut him off. "We can't tell you that. On the day of the Disaster he, his wife and daughter disappeared."

He means daughters, thought Clara, but let it pass.

"It seemed an impossible goal," said Zeno, his tone breathless. "Then, a few weeks ago, we had a breakthrough. We found a way to bring people forward from the past, from your time. We were able to lock onto Clara! We succeeded in getting her to the Siri shaft. We weren't expecting you others, of course."

141

He eyed Hayley beadily.

Mick frowned. "Why couldn't you just go back yourselves and sort it out?"

"A good question. Of course we've tried. But so far we've only managed to bring people forward. You can get back—I suppose because you don't belong here. We can talk to you there, but that's all. We can't go back. It won't take."

Clara went cold. It all sounded so uncertain. Had Zeno even known, that first time, whether she and Rob would be able to get back safely to their own time?

"We're working on it," Jed told them.

"If you four can't stop Maunding soon, we will run out of time," said Zeno. "You are our last, and only, hope."

There was another shout from the end of the room. The apple-like scientist was calling Jed, her voice loud and excited. Jed scooted off to join her, and they talked in animated whispers.

Mick stared at Zeno. "I don't understand why there's no time. Surely that's the one thing you do have. You've achieved time travel, after all. Let's say we don't succeed in stopping Maunding this time. Well, you could contact Clara further back, give her a nice long time to sort it all out."

"Mick's right," said Rob. "Or ... you could go further back again, stop Maunding being born."

Zeno put his head in his hands. "No, no, no. It doesn't work like that. Hmm ... How to explain?" He sat down near them and drummed his fingers on the

142

table. "You see, when we established the link with Clara, it was like we had set two twin stopwatches going. It's an ongoing link. That is, the amount of time which passes in each place will be the same. We don't have the raw materials to keep the link going for much longer. As for us ... Well, you can see. The planet is dying. If the Grammets get in, they will destroy my laboratory, no doubt. So we really don't have much time."

Jed raced back to Zeno. "Project Gigi—there's been a development."

Zeno's eyes gleamed. "Well, that's something. A good day all round." He stood up. "Right, time is Rock. Let's go. We must return you four to your proper time."

"But—" objected Mick.

Zeno was already hurrying them through the door. Numbed by all she had seen and heard, Clara followed her friends through the cavern and along the tunnel towards the Siri shaft.

"Do you understand, now?" Zeno asked, dropping back, his voice unusually soft.

Clara nodded. "I'll keep trying. You're sure you can't get the lottery numbers?"

"Quite certain. We saved as much information as we could. But it's scientific stuff, useful stuff, from the time of the Disaster. You're talking about one particular date, a long time ago. Long ago to us. You'll have to think of something else."

"But Zeno—"

"Quick now. Get into the Siri shaft. I'm needed for the Gigi Project."

They bumped into Hayley, who was gazing at a picture on the wall, next to the lift. It showed the head and shoulders of a serene-looking woman.

"Who's that in the picture, Mr Zeno?" she asked.

Zeno's eyes misted. "That's Siri. A little drawing I made of her using ground ash."

"It's beautiful." Hayley's voice was a whisper.

Clara agreed. The picture really was striking. Using just ash, Zeno had captured the liveliness in Siri's eyes and the humour in her smile.

"What is the Gigi Project?" asked Mick, bobbing with impatience.

Rob tugged his arm. "Come on, that's enough questions for one day."

A siren shrieked. Zeno raised his eyes heavenward. "Oh, not again!"

"Red alert. Red alert," boomed a female voice. "Please take your stations immediately. Proceed with utmost caution. Red alert."

"Quick." Zeno pushed them into the Siri shaft and punched a code into the panel.

As the door began to close, he thrust his arm through the gap and pressed something into Clara's hand.

"Take the trilloscope. It's the new device we've been working on. You might be able to speak to us with it. Early stages, I'm afraid. A mere prototype. But take it, Clara. It's eighty-one per cent pure Luxulyanite, you know."

Clara closed her hand around the chalky white ball.

144

Mick shouted to make himself heard above the wailing siren. "Didn't you say you couldn't send things back to the past?"

"People, no. Things, yes. Hopefully."

"How does it work?" yelled Clara above the din.

"You'll need to use ethanoic acid. Make sure it's sitting on granite. A base of at least a metre." Zeno let go of the door.

None of this made any sense to Clara. She stuck her foot in the gap. "What if it doesn't work? Will you contact us?"

A shadow crossed Zeno's face. "The link won't be stable for much longer. We may not speak again."

"But Zeno—what happens to you, if we succeed, if we change things? Will you disappear? Will you cease to be?"

Zeno dismissed her with a wave. "Try, Clara, all of you. Try. Don't worry about us, it doesn't matter. You hear? It doesn't matter."

The door shut with a clang. The floor began to vibrate.

CHAPTER 13

GAIL MAUNDING stirred from a sleep filled with weird dreams, shivering from the cold.

"Donna, don't," she murmured sleepily. Donna must have come into her bedroom and pulled off her duvet. She often did that. She said it was to help Gail get down for breakfast on time. Daddy got angry if they were late.

She tried to open her eyes, but the lids wouldn't budge. What had she done yesterday? She must have worn herself out. Her eyes seemed stuck together, puffy, as though she had been in a too-deep sleep. She tried to raise a hand.

Her left hand wouldn't move. She managed to get one eye open a crack. Blurry shapes swam into view, dark shadows, not the view of her bedroom she was expecting. She wasn't just cold, she was freezing. She couldn't feel her feet ... or her arms.

Of course ... she'd got up early that morning. She and Donna had ridden their bikes to Clara's place ... and then ... No! Frightening images flooded her mind. Hiding behind the fat tree. The glowing mine shaft. Clara jumping in.

She remembered running away, getting lost in the Callenicks' creepy wood. Finding the cottage—or so she thought. There was delicious relief. And then ... nothing.

Her eyes opened wide, her heart see-sawing violently in her ribcage.

Where was she?

It was dark all around, but she could see a circle of dim light high above. Fear pulsed through her as she tried to move. She was wedged fast. But in what? Wriggling a fraction, she felt pinpricks all over her body. She moved her right hand slowly forward. Something pierced her finger, making her yelp and draw back. Tears seeped from her eyes.

The air felt like ice in her lungs, and smelled of damp and decay. She gave a bellow of fury, then lay still.

After a while, she stretched out her right hand in another direction. It brushed the tip of something sharp, then bashed into something slimy, wet and hard.

As her eyes became used to the gloom, the cogs of her brain began to turn. It was a long time before the reality of her situation sank in. Finally, she had to face it.

She wasn't at home in bed at all. She was trapped in a hole. A very deep hole.

The circle of light looked frighteningly distant, a faint glow, high above. How far had she fallen? A freezing draught came from below. She wasn't sure, but the hole seemed to fall away beneath her for a good many metres still.

She was spread-eagled across a bush, her legs entangled in its thickest branches, her arms sprawled across its prickly green foliage. Somehow, the bush had managed to root itself in the stone wall and grow out horizontally across the hole.

The foliage lurked, shadowy and menacing, ready to stab her at the slightest movement. There was a faint whiff of coconut.

Gail didn't know the names of many plants, but she recognised this one as gorse. Its horrid prickles explained the puffiness of her eyes and the burning sensation all over her skin. She felt as though she had been hurled onto a bed of needles.

Her left arm, flailing in front of her, must have helped to break her fall. But when she tried again to lift it, she was winded by excruciating pain. She tried to work her fingers. Nothing happened.

She let loose a string of curses. Against Clara, against Donna, against the tree itself for stabbing her.

Numb and growing ever colder, she tried to move her legs. The bush strained, and she heard the chilling sound of something breaking loose. She held her breath. One second, two seconds, three seconds. There was a muffled clatter as a stone landed far below.

Were there any handholds or footholds? Stretching her right hand out behind, she could find nothing to grip. Panic throbbed in her veins. Every tiny movement seemed to further loosen the roots of the bush. It could fall at any moment, taking her with it.

Where was Donna? She was sure to be back soon with help. But would she be able to find her? Gail had been running for ages before she fell. This godforsaken hole could be anywhere.

The minutes dragged by. She heard the tchack-tchack of jackdaws, high in the sky. The only other sound was an eerie scraping, echoing through the shaft as the bush was wrenched slowly from the stones.

***

The journey through the wood had scared Donna almost more than the incredible goings-on around that mine shaft. In the dark, she had tripped on a root and fallen flat on her face. She had lain for what seemed hours in the mud, snivelling, unable to move. She was exhausted by the time she managed to hoist herself to her feet and limp back to the road.

Once she thought someone called her name, but at the same time birds in a nearby tree flapped into the air. It must have been their cawing, that was all. She didn't plan to hang around to find out.

Donna was convinced that Gail had gone home without her. When, at last, she arrived at the clump of trees where they had hidden their bikes, she frowned in puzzlement. Both bikes were still there. What game was her stupid sister playing? Just wait until she saw her!

It was already gone seven a.m. Leaving the bikes to their fate, she limped down the road until she could get a signal on her phone.

She called the taxi firm her father sometimes used. A car came within minutes and dropped her off by the driveway to Pardeaux Hall. She charged the fare to her father's account, despite having forty-two pounds in her pocket.

Donna was horrified, yet oddly satisfied, to see that

her ankle had swollen to the size of a grapefruit. As she sneaked up to her room, she glanced through Gail's open doorway, expecting to find her sister already there. But the room was empty. Gail's phone lay abandoned on the carpet. A faint sense of disquiet clutched at Donna's heart.

She sat at her dressing table and brushed her golden curls, admiring the way they fell in neat waves about her shoulders, the perfect frame for her china blue eyes. Where on earth was Gail? She'd better hurry, or she'd miss breakfast, and Daddy would not be pleased.

There was a rap at the door.

"Donna?" It was her father. "Carpe diem, Donna my dear, carpe diem."

Donna had no idea what this carpe diem was, but her father was always carping on about it. She got painfully to her feet. "Just coming, Daddy."

Trying to ignore the taut feeling in her chest, she hobbled downstairs after him.

In the kitchen, Susan Maunding was organising cereals and fruit juice. Donna couldn't understand why she didn't employ a live-in housekeeper to do this sort of thing, rather than make do, as she did, with the thrice-weekly visits of their cleaner, Mrs Crohns. But Mother had always been a bit of a martyr, more fool her.

Although it was early on Sunday morning, Susan was already smartly dressed in a blue blouse and matching pleated skirt, set off by a string of Mikimoto pearls. Heidsieck the cat lay in his plush velvet basket, purring as he snoozed.

Derek Maunding sat in his chair, spreading butter on his toast.

"Susan!" He frowned towards the table.

"What, dear?"

"Look!" he boomed.

Susan bounced to her feet and fetched the small silver spoon, which was missing from its holder by the strawberry conserve.

"And where is Gail?" demanded Derek in his clipped, staccato tones. He tapped his watch and glowered at Donna. "Your sister gets lazier by the day."

"She must have overslept." Cringing from his gaze, Donna crept to the side table to fetch a boiled egg.

"Why are you limping like that?" asked Susan.

"I'm fine."

"What do you mean, fine? Your poor ankle's all swollen up." Susan started towards her for a closer look.

"Don't fuss, Mother." Donna risked a quick glance at her father, worried he might ask awkward questions, but he was gazing out of the window, in the direction of Clara's mine. Should she tell him what had happened? His nerves seemed stretched to breaking point as it was, and this new complication was sure to enrage him—if he even believed her, that was.

She needed to see Gail, agree a story with her. Eating her breakfast in silence, she consoled herself by imagining all the nasty things she would say and do to Gail when she finally did turn up.

"Go and get your sister," barked Derek Maunding,

151

stirring from his reverie. "I won't endure her tardiness a moment longer." His words dissolved into spluttering as he pulled a ginger hair from his toast. "Has that benighted moggy been on the table again?"

***

Gail groaned as she turned her head to peer at the dim circle above. It looked the same: a grey disc through which trickled a small stream of light. She tried to keep still, but every so often her body twitched from the tension, and there was a terrifying wrench as the root slid another millimetre from the wall. She closed her eyes, thinking that in seconds she would go hurtling down into the darkness. The gorse bush held. But for how long?

She had worn her voice hoarse from yelling. Now she was silent. She felt as though days had gone by. A dreadful idea wormed itself into her head. No one could hear her. No one was coming.

The disc of light grew dimmer. Night was drawing in. She thought about the hole beneath her and what might lurk down there. Her knowledge of Clara's land was sketchy, but even Gail had by now realised that the hole she was wedged in was a mine shaft. But which one? Had she gone in a circle? Was this the shaft they had been watching from behind that tree?

She didn't think so. That one had been on the open hillside. How many others were there? The whole area might be littered with them.

Gail shivered violently. Her hands, her legs, even her shoulders trembled. She thought she heard a sigh from below, from the bottom of the shaft, like the low note of an oboe. How many men might have died down there? Might their ghosts still be roaming the tunnels?

With her good hand, she reached for Clara's St Christopher medallion. It was supposed to be lucky, wasn't it? She struggled and strained until she felt faint, but she couldn't touch it. There were too many prickly branches in the way.

She could feel the chain against her neck, though, pulsing with heat, constricting her throat.

As she thought about the necklace, Gail felt the strangest sensation. Just for a split second, there was a burning white haze all around her. As it faded she saw thousands of stars.

She began to sob. She was losing her mind, trapped in this vertical tomb. Hadn't she always tried to be good? Tried to do what Father wanted? She didn't deserve to die in this stinking hole.

The gorse bush groaned, as if voicing an opinion.

She felt so cold. And terribly, terribly thirsty. She licked dry lips and yelled again. "Donna! Where are you?"

She no longer expected a reply.

CHAPTER 14

CLARA and Hayley sat in Miss Sitwell's Spanish class, practising in pairs how to buy things in the supermarket. It was Monday morning, the day after their visit to the future. It felt strange to be back at school. Clara had wondered if it was worth coming, under the circumstances. Yet, at the same time, she craved the normality of it.

Miss Sitwell pointed to a picture of a slice of ham. "Quiero un kilo de queso."

One or two classmates tittered.

"Queso's cheese, not ham," whispered Hayley. "What's on earth's wrong with Miss Sitwell today?"

Hayley was right. Their teacher had a distracted look, and she wasn't smiling the way she normally did.

But Clara had too much on her mind to take on Miss Sitwell's problems as well. She felt shaky and exhausted. What little sleep she'd managed to get had been plagued by nightmares. She hadn't even been able to rid herself of the last vestiges of tempoplas slime. Her hair felt sticky and matted, despite washing it twice. Time travel was a much messier business than she had imagined.

After class, the four friends met up outside the classrooms and headed across the yard towards their usual meeting spot.

As they rounded a corner, Miss Grundy came trotting towards them. At her side was Archie Rowlands, the science teacher who was seeing Clara's Aunt Iris. Both of them looked worried and miserable.

Clara glanced left and right for an escape. She wasn't in the mood for Miss Grundy's sourness, and she felt awkward about seeing Archie too. He and Aunt Iris had fallen out about whether to attend the Maundings' Christmas party at the end of the week. Archie wanted to take her as his guest, but Iris refused to set foot inside Pardeaux Hall.

Too late. Miss Grundy had spotted her.

"Clara Callenick, I want a word with you." Miss Grundy cocked her head and squinted. "Are you a friend of the Maunding girls? I've seen you together."

Clara's heart sank. "I certainly wouldn't say a friend, Miss Grundy."

"Aah." The teacher peered at Clara, as if trying to read her thoughts. "I see. You didn't see her at the weekend, then? Yesterday, perhaps?"

Clara shook her head. "No. Why?" What was Miss Grundy getting at?

"Oh, no reason."

Miss Grundy's pearly eye was twitching. Archie Rowlands, standing nearby, had now been joined by Gideon Pasternak, the head teacher.

Clara and her friends walked on.

"Mr Parsnip looks serious, doesn't he?" said Hayley.

Mick waggled a finger and grinned. "You should watch yourself, Hayley. One day you'll accidentally call him that to his face."

Hayley chortled.

On impulse, Clara ran back to Miss Grundy, who now stood alone, gazing towards a group of students huddled in the playground.

"Miss Grundy, wait ... Why did you ask me about the Maunding girls? Has something happened?"

Miss Grundy sighed. "I shouldn't really say. There'll be an announcement later."

"An announcement?" This sounded ominous. "Why? What's happened? Please tell me, Miss Grundy."

Miss Grundy clenched her hands, as though to stop them shaking.

"We might be able to help," persevered Clara.

Miss Grundy checked no other teachers were within earshot. "All right. It's Gail Maunding. She's disappeared. Her mother rang this morning in an awful state. Gail was missing all day yesterday and still hasn't turned up. The police have been called, of course. It's likely they'll want to talk to her friends."

"Disappeared? How?"

"Well, if they knew that, they'd be able to find her, wouldn't they, Clara?"

Clara reddened. Getting nothing more out of the teacher, she loped away to give her friends the news.

They were silent all the way across the playing fields. Standing behind the shed, they stared into the thicket of trees. The morning was cold and overcast, and Clara watched the breath condensing in front of her face, her insides twisting with unease.

"Those girls are really horrible," said Hayley at last. "We know that, but … I hope she's okay. D'you think she ran away?"

"Why would she?" Clara wished she could feel as charitably about it as Hayley. When she thought of her stolen St Christopher, of Gail's smirking face, she couldn't help hoping something bad had happened to her.

Rob had a wicked glint in his eye. "Perhaps old man Maunding murdered her and hid her in the cellar at Pardeaux Hall."

"Rob!" cried Hayley, giving him a push. "That's a terrible thing to say."

"Joke," Rob muttered under his breath.

Clara stamped her feet in the leaf litter. "I can't help thinking her disappearance is connected with us. It seems too much of a coincidence, don't you think?"

Mick nodded. "I agree. By going forward in time the way we have, and then coming back, we could already have affected things. It's fascinating to think about, isn't it?"

Mick had a glazed look, as though his mind was bursting with all he had seen and heard over the weekend. Clara, by contrast, felt numbed and horrified. She wished she could just forget about the future and get on with her life. But to Mick, she realised, it was wonderful. What he had read about in his favourite books was true. It was possible to travel in time.

Hayley grabbed Mick's arm. "You mean we might already be changing things, in ways we don't know about?" For the first time since Clara had known her, she had puffy shadows under her eyes, and looked like she hadn't slept a wink.

"Never mind all that," said Rob. "I know it's bad about Gail, but I'm sure she'll turn up. We've got other things to worry about. If the lottery idea's no good, how are we going to stop Maunding?"

Clara had been asking herself the same thing all night, lying awake, battling waves of hopelessness.

"What about Aunt Iris?" said Hayley. "Is it worth getting her up to the shaft? Try to explain things to her? Or Granny, even?"

Clara shrugged. "I've thought about it. But Granny's already fed up with me for meddling in her business. I'd never get her up there, anyway. She's too frail. As for Aunt Iris … She didn't believe us the other day, did she? I doubt Granny would take any notice of her, even if she did." The image of Granny's stubborn face filled Clara with despair. She gazed heavenward, banging her head back against the shed wall. "Oh it's useless! Who's going to listen to us? It's the adults who make the decisions. They always reckon they know best, even when they so obviously don't."

Rob and Hayley exchanged a glance.

"Come on, Clara," said Rob. "Don't be like that. How about … Could we raise the money another way?"

Mick snorted. "Last night I had a look at the house and land prices in The Bugle. Just out of interest, I worked out how long it would take us to save up enough if we pooled all our pocket money."

158

"You did?" asked Hayley. "And?"

"Don't get too excited. It came to ten thousand weeks. Yeah, that's around two hundred years."

Clara gave a wry smile. "Ah, that's out, then."

"Maybe we have to do something more drastic," suggested Rob. "Get Maunding out of the way, somehow."

Hayley sucked in a breath. "Rob! What are you saying? For God's sake, do we want to ruin our lives and spend the rest of our days in prison?"

Rob looked around the side of the shed to make sure no one was nearby. He turned back to them, his face grim. "Well, I'm not going to sit about doing nothing. All girls want to do is talk."

Clara and Hayley rolled their eyes. Mick gave an indignant huff, as though he had been lumped in with them.

Rob was still glaring at them. "So come on, get your brains into gear. What are we going to do?"

Clara's cheeks burned with sudden anger. "It's my problem anyway, not yours. It's my family's land and I've got to find the way."

There was a silence.

Hayley slid her arm through Clara's. "I know you're upset—but you're wrong. It's your land, true. But it's not only your problem. It affects us all. All of us and everyone we know. Besides, we'd never leave you to cope with it on your own. You don't know us, if you think that. We just wouldn't, would we, Mick?"

Mick cleared his throat. "No."

"Rob?" Clara swallowed hard, her green eyes blazing.

Rob sighed. "Of course not! I just want us to get on with it, that's all."

Clara felt guilty for doubting them. She couldn't imagine anything worse than trying to fight Maunding on her own. If she failed, she would have to watch her land fall into his greedy grasp. Then wait, wondering when the terror would start.

Rob took a couple of paces through the leaf litter and leaned back against a willow tree, facing them. "If anyone's interested, I've got a plan."

"Out with it, then," said Hayley. "'Cos I sure haven't."

Rob's eyes glistened. "All right. First off, Mick and I will go into town and see if we can find this research place. MORE, isn't it? It's worth checking that it really exists, don't you think? I mean, I know St Piran's like the back of my hand, and I've never seen it, have you?"

Clara, Mick and Hayley shook their heads.

"Okay, so the first thing is to make sure Zeno's right about all this," Rob continued. "That it's not some sort of, I don't know, mass hallucination we've all had."

"Hmmph," said Clara. "I thought we'd rejected that idea."

Rob stabbed a finger at her. "You and Hayley, you can go check out the Maundings' house. See if you can throw any light on anything."

Clara grimaced. "What, with Gail missing? They won't want to see us."

"We get all the good jobs," muttered Hayley.

160

"It's worth a try," said Rob. "If Gail's disappearance has anything to do with all this—with old man Maunding, say—maybe we could use the information against him."

"Blackmail!" Mick rubbed his hands.

"Or," cried Hayley, "If we can find Gail, maybe Maunding will have a change of heart and leave Clara and her wood alone."

Clara smiled. "Good thinking, Hayley. But I don't think that's likely. You always see the good in people."

Hayley lowered her gaze, her cheeks reddening.

"Definitely worth trying, though," added Clara brightly, worried that her compliment had sounded like a criticism.

Rob picked up his backpack. "Come on, then, let's get going."

"You mean miss school? All of us?" Hayley's eyes were round with shock.

Mick shuffled from foot to foot. "Hayley's got a point. My stepdad will be fuming if I don't get top marks in the end-of-term tests."

Rob seemed about to blow a fuse. "Don't you get it? This is the end of the world we're talking about! There won't be any schools if Maunding gets his way. There won't be anything. Come on, we don't have time to lose."

CHAPTER 15

ST PIRAN'S was a small, bustling town dominated by a twelfth century Norman church and a stone-floored market house. Rob and Mick fought their way along the High Street, dodging the hordes of Christmas shoppers.

"Where shall we start?" asked Rob.

"Dunno. You're the one making the decisions, apparently," Mick grumbled.

"Don't be like that—it won't help."

Rob halted abruptly next to a barrel organ, where a man was selling hot chestnuts. Rob sniffed and sighed with pleasure. "Now, some of those will help us concentrate."

"Not for me, thanks."

Noticing them, the wizened vendor broke into an operatic rendition of "Silent Night". Rob rolled his eyes at Mick, but Mick gazed into space, his chin raised.

"You from these parts, then?" the man asked Rob as he scooped chestnuts into a bag.

"Yeah. Lived here all my life. Parents moved down when I was small."

"'Tisn't like it used to be backalong, I can tell 'ee that for nothing."

"No. Er, I don't suppose you've heard of a place called More? M.O.R.E? The Maunding Original

Research Establishment? Run by Derek Maunding?"

The man sucked in his breath through two remaining teeth. "More? MORE? No, that I haven't, old chap. I've heard of old Maunding, of course. Who hasn't? One o' they from upcountry, he is, him and his swanky lot."

Rob thanked him as they walked away.

After a few moments of silence Mick said, "How about the library? We might be able to find something online, or in a book."

Rob bit into a chestnut, shell and all, then yelped as the steam rushed out. "Hergh, goo ide-ah."

After ten minutes they reached the steep road that led up to the library.

"My stepdad's restaurant is along here, don't forget," Mick pointed out. "Don't let him see us. He's usually there this time of day."

They crept carefully past "The Taj Mahal". There was no sign of Mick's stepdad.

"Phew," said Mick. "If he caught me out of school I'd get extra chores and no pocket money for a month."

The library was pleasantly deserted after the bustle of the streets. Mick went online at a computer in a corner booth, while Rob scoured the shelves in the local history section. The librarian, a sombre woman in a Santa hat, watched them with suspicion.

Mick wasn't long on the computer. "No luck," he said. "I've tried all sorts, but there's nothing here. You?"

Rob shook his head. "This is all older stuff, nothing about what's going on in the town now."

"Can I help?" The librarian craned her neck in their

direction, clearly curious to know why they were out of school.

Mick shook his head, but Rob charged over to her desk and beamed at her.

"Maybe you can. I'm trying to find a research centre called MORE. The Maunding Original Research Establishment. It belongs to Derek Maunding, and it's in the town somewhere, but we don't know where. We'd be so grateful for your help."

The librarian cocked her head to one side. "Oh, it's his daughter that's gone missing, isn't it? Terrible business. My neighbour Mr Trundle works up there mowing the lawns and stuff. Do you know the daughter?"

Rob nodded. "MORE? Heard of it?"

She shook her head. "No, sorry. Mr Maunding keeps himself very much to himself. Wait a minute, though. Doesn't he own the Wolf and Lamb up on Pydar Road? The pub old Monty Leghorn runs? Maybe someone in there would know."

Rob grinned as he hurried Mick out of the library. "Thanks. We'll try it."

"You should be more careful," Mick hissed. "What if Maunding finds out we've been making enquiries?"

"What choice have we got? Come on, I know where the Wolf and Lamb is. My dad goes there sometimes at the weekend."

The Wolf and Lamb was enjoying a brisk lunchtime trade. Noisy shoppers filled every table, surrounded by plastic bags, and a tired-looking woman in black and white bustled about carrying plates heaped up with steak and chips.

Behind the bar stood a rotund man with curling sideburns and a ruby-red nose, who glared at Rob and Mick as they approached.

"On the young side, aren't you?" he said. "The school uniforms are a bit of a giveaway. Go on, skedaddle."

"We're not here for drinks, sir, I mean Mr Leghorn," said Mick. "We, um …"

Rob jumped in. "We're looking for my father. He works for MORE, Mr Maunding's Research Centre. We're supposed to be meeting him there, but unfortunately we're not sure where it is. We hoped you might be able to help."

Mick frowned, puzzled. As he cottoned on, his face broke into a grin.

Leghorn chewed his lip. "Works for MORE, you say?"

"Yes," said Rob. "Mick here's going to be a scientist and my dad's fixed him up with a chat with Mr Maunding about, um, career opportunities at MORE. Dad reckons Mr Maunding hates to be kept waiting."

Monty Leghorn nodded. "Hmm, I do know that. Not the most patient of men, our Mr Maunding."

Rob raised his eyebrows. "Can you help us? Please?"

"Doubt he'll be there today. Haven't you heard the news about his daughter going missing? But 'tis up behind the church. Offices over the betting shop, Tregowan Road, d'you know it?"

165

"Thank you, sir. We'll find it."

Rob grabbed Mick and they raced from the pub. Rob's hand met Mick's in a high-five. "Piece of cake!"

***

Rob pointed to some windows above the betting shop. "Must be up there."

"Hmm," agreed Mick. "How do we get to it, though?"

They could see no separate door, nor a sign anywhere.

"Let's ask inside," said Rob.

Rob marched past a number of tense-looking men watching TV screens, and planted his feet firmly in front of the counter.

"We have an appointment with Mr Maunding,"

The thin young man behind the counter blinked.

"You do? And that should interest me—why, exactly?"

"Mr Maunding won't want to be kept waiting," said Mick, following closely behind. "Rob's father works for him, you know."

"So? Shouldn't you be in school?" The man folded his arms.

"We've been given special permission," said Rob.

This wasn't going so well. It was as though the man knew they were lying.

There was a howl of triumph as a race ended. Two men bounded up to the counter waving betting slips.

"Curly Sue, ten to one!" yelled one. "Put that in your pipe and smoke it."

"We're late," said Rob, taking advantage of the distraction.

"Who are you exactly?" asked the assistant, as a queue began to form. "Oh, never mind."

He pointed to a doorway in the corner of the shop. "Up those stairs. Shut the door properly, or it'll slam."

Rob and Mick climbed a scuffed wooden staircase with no carpet. At the top was an unmarked door. A high-tech security keypad shone in the dark hallway.

Mick peered at it. "Okay, we've established that MORE definitely exists. We don't need to go—"

But Rob was already jabbing at the buttons.

An imperious female voice rang out. "Yes?"

"We've an appointment to see Mr Maunding." Rob winked at Mick. "Might as well stick with the same story, eh?"

"Name?" said the voice.

"Rob Hocking and friend," said Rob.

Mick drew in a breath. "Couldn't you have made something up?"

The keypad beeped and the door opened. Inside, there was a remarkable transformation. The lobby was smart and light, with plush chocolate-brown leather sofas grouped around a glass coffee table. A scarlet orchid grew from a vase of pearly beads.

Rob nudged Mick and pointed to an enormous oil painting on the wall behind the sofas. It showed a man posing near a marble fireplace, in a wood-panelled room. He was depicted in profile, one eye glaring out at the observer. His dark hair gleamed, smooth and neat except for the trademark streak of grey curling into a question mark.

"That's him all right," hissed Rob. "I've seen him at Clara's. And look!" Above the reception area were four gold letters on separate silver plaques. M.O.R.E.

"There's nothing in the book," said the receptionist, a stony-faced woman with frizzy hair. "Who did you say you were?"

"Rob Hocking. Did you forget to write it in? I fixed it up last week. We're here to discuss, um, career opportunities. Mick here's going to be a scientist."

The receptionist pursed her lips. "Mr Maunding is very busy, as I'm sure you can imagine. If you're not in the book, you can't have an appointment."

"But—"

A bald man in a stained white coat came running out of a room behind her desk. He began to speak loudly, then noticed Rob and Mick and lowered his voice. The woman turned to him with a sigh.

"All right, Arnold. Don't panic." She scowled over her shoulder at Rob and Mick. "I will return shortly. Take a seat. Don't touch anything."

She followed the man named Arnold into his room. Rob and Mick craned for a glimpse of the interior, then nodded in agreement. It was a laboratory.

"She could do with working on her people skills," said Rob, flopping onto one of the sofas. "And I don't know how she can speak with all that make-up caked on her face."

"What do we say if we actually get to see him?" whispered Mick in a worried voice.

"Bluff it. Ask him some science-y stuff. Should be right up your street."

Mick stretched over the reception desk and grabbed a sheaf of papers.

"Hey, look. This is a report about what they've been up to in CERN lately. You know, the hadron collider place in Switzerland."

"Yeah, yeah, I've learnt some things, hanging around with you. Shhh! Can you hear voices?"

Mick put the report back where he'd found it and crept over to join Rob. Raised voices were coming from behind a door to the left of the reception desk. Rob and Mick stepped close to listen.

"Why don't you just try?" said a man's voice. "If you knew how important it was …"

"That's what you don't understand," a woman answered. "How important it is to me." She sounded furious.

"The mine's perfect. Unique. There'll never be another chance like this."

"How can you even think about business when your daughter is missing? Don't you care?"

"She'll turn up," said the man. "Attention-seeking, that's what Gail is. These girls are prone to things like that. She's always been difficult. There's always one problem child, isn't there? But thank you for reminding me, my dear."

169

The man sounded calm, his voice silky smooth. Rob and Mick struggled to catch everything he said.

"Well, my dear. It doesn't matter what you think. Victory hovers close. I can feel it in my bones … Always been a fool … feisty … Not yours anyway … famous man in history, can't you see?"

"It must be Maunding," said Rob. "D'you think he's having a row with his wife?"

There was the sound of chairs scraping. Rob and Mick sprang back.

The door burst open and a woman marched out of the office. But it wasn't Mrs Maunding. It was Clara's Aunt Iris.

She had her head down, the collar of her long coat turned up. Behind her they glimpsed Maunding, unmistakeable with his disobedient streak of grey hair. He sat at his desk, gazing thoughtfully at his departing visitor.

Iris came to an abrupt stop. "Oh! What're you two doing here?"

"Us? What about—?" began Rob.

The receptionist reappeared behind the counter. "They don't have an appointment," she sneered in a superior tone, as if they had a nasty disease.

Iris glared at her. "Come on," she said to the boys. "Let's get out of this place."

She whisked them out of the door.

CHAPTER 16

CLARA and Hayley tethered their bikes to the iron gates and crunched along the gravel drive. Up ahead was the ivy-clad stone façade of the Maundings' Elizabethan manor house, resplendent with its turrets and castellated towers. It was flanked on all sides by huge, immaculate lawns and neat walled gardens dotted with topiary shrubs.

"Wow! Wouldn't you like to live here?" Hayley's voice was hushed with awe.

"It's a lovely house. But think of the dusting. Wouldn't be my cup of tea." Clara had enough trouble helping to keep one caravan clean.

"Those repulsive girls don't deserve to live in a place like this."

"You're not wrong. But I'm quite happy in my caravan."

Towards the end of the drive, a low wall bordered the gravel. A large marmalade cat was eyeing a hole in it. Fearing for the mouse, Clara tapped the wall with her foot as she passed. The cat sauntered off, tail twitching.

They walked up the stone steps. "Wonder why they go to St Piran's School, with all their money," said Hayley.

"I reckon it's where their father wants them, don't

you? Helps him keep tabs on everyone. Come on, let's get this over with."

Secretly, Clara thought they were wasting their time, but it was thanks to Rob that she wasn't alone in all this, so the least she could do was try what he suggested.

She rang the doorbell, combing her mind for suitable words. What on earth could she say to the family of a girl she hated, but who might have met some grisly end? Her mind had gone completely blank.

A woman opened the door. Her hair was dishevelled and she had streaks of mascara running down her cheeks.

"Oh! I thought you might be the police, or—or even my dear girl. You've got news, have you? You know my Gail's missing?" She dabbed at her eyes, which were large and startled, like a frightened rabbit's.

Clara nodded. "We're very sorry to hear it, Mrs Maunding. I'm sure Gail will turn up soon." She tried her best to sound sincere, but had never been too good at hiding her feelings.

"Where can she be?" blurted Gail's mother. "You hear such terrible things these days. She's such a good girl, she'd never … Over a whole day since we've seen her. She wasn't in bed yesterday morning, and—" She stopped abruptly as her eyes narrowed. "So who are you, exactly? What do you want?"

Clara's throat went dry and she felt herself reddening. She glanced at Hayley for inspiration, but Hayley looked petrified, and obviously expected Clara to do all the talking.

"We wondered if we could see Donna," Clara began. "We're, um, friends of hers, and we thought we might be able to cheer her up. Maybe help her look for Gail."

Mrs Maunding stepped back. "Oh! That's very good of you, that is, if she ... I'll go and ... Come this way, I'll take you to her. She's in the games room."

They followed her along the oak-panelled hallway. It was the grandest Clara had ever seen, with magnificent oriental rugs and gilt-framed paintings of hunts and hounds. A stag's head watched them dolefully from a mounted plaque.

"That's disgusting," Clara hissed in Hayley's ear. "The only place it belongs is on the poor stag's body. My auntie's right, she always says money is wasted on the rich."

At last they reached the games room at the back of the house. Susan Maunding knocked briefly, then bustled inside.

"Donna, dear, a couple of friends of yours have come to see you. I'll fetch some mango juice." She scuttled off.

Dressed from head to toe in black, Donna was reclining on a peach leather sofa, her hand thrown across her forehead. She turned a wan face in their direction, then saw who it was and sat up quickly.

"What are you two doing here? Crazy Callenick and her doll. This I don't need." She flopped back onto the sofa.

"We heard Gail's missing." Clara clenched her fists, desperately trying to think of something to add. Her mind filled with the image of Gail's devilish eyes gleaming as she held a lighter to Clara's arm.

Hayley glanced at Clara's blank face, then swallowed and cleared her throat.

"What happened?" she squeaked to Donna. "Maybe we can help."

Donna stared into space, then sat up again.

"I don't need help from a wimp like you," she said to Hayley, then jabbed a long-nailed finger in Clara's direction. "Or a weirdo like you." Her face collapsed suddenly, as if she was about to burst into tears. "It's all your fault!"

Clara and Hayley exchanged puzzled looks.

"What's our fault?" asked Clara. "What's it got to do with us?"

Donna stood up and hobbled to the window overlooking the back lawns. "There we were, happily minding our own business and planning our Christmas party—which may have to be cancelled now—and Gail's gone and vanished."

She lowered her voice to a dramatic whisper. "I don't know what's happened to my sister, is that clear? If you talk to the police, you can tell them that. I haven't seen her since Saturday night when we went to bed. Why should I know anything about where she is? They keep asking me, but why should I know?" Her voice rose. "It's like they don't believe me, like they think I know something."

Susan Maunding tiptoed in, glancing nervously at her daughter. Without saying a word, she dropped a tray of

174

fruit juice and biscuits onto the table and scurried away.

"What happened to your foot?" asked Clara, noting Donna's swollen ankle.

"Mind your own business." Donna wiped away a tear, smudging black eye-liner. "Oh, get out. I can't stand looking at you two losers." She gazed out of the window.

Clara shrugged. "Suits me fine. Come on, Hayley, this is pointless."

Holding their heads high, they swept out of the room.

***

"I wonder why she blames us?" asked Hayley, as they walked back down the drive. "What have we got to do with Gail's disappearance?"

"That's what we need to find out. Donna's obviously lying about something."

"Did you ever get your necklace back? The one they stole?"

"Not yet. My mother gave me that before she died. It was a St Christopher pendant, for good luck on journeys."

"What did your mother die from?"

"Cancer."

Clara would never forget those awful final days. Her mother propped up on the sofa, thin and damp. Her father silent with desolation. Worst of all was the look her mother had given her the night before she died. A

175

pitiful smile, masking heartbreak. As though she knew it was the last time. Clara had hoped never to see a look like that again. But she had seen it only recently. In Zeno's eyes.

She noticed Hayley staring at her and turned away. "I'll have to get my necklace back as soon as I can. Not now."

Something was nagging at the back of her mind, something to do with the necklace. But the thought was gone before she could grab hold of it.

"Do you think Gail's dead?" asked Hayley.

"Dunno." Once again, Clara felt guilty she didn't feel more upset.

***

Donna was watching them from an upstairs window. Damn them. That stupid Clara in her raggedy clothes, that halfwit Hayley Shezell who looked like a feather could knock her down. No hopers, both of them.

If it wasn't for Clara and her ghastly land, Donna would be planning her party outfit and getting her nails done. This was the best chance she'd had all year of prompting Jean-Pierre Vaucluse to ask her out. She knew he was dying to. They belonged together. She with her golden curls, he with his sun-kissed good looks.

It was all wrong. Where was Gail? Up until last night, she'd convinced herself her sister would come through the door at any moment, gabbling some daft excuse. But as the dark hours of the night ticked by, her chest had tightened and fear had dripped into her mind like acid.

Donna hated to admit it, but if she'd told the truth from the beginning, she wouldn't be in this mess. She couldn't explain what she'd seen up on the Downs at Callenick mine and was convinced no one would believe her. But if only she'd told her father where they'd gone and why, the police would at least be looking in the right area. Her father would probably have been pleased they were trying so hard!

But as things were, she had denied seeing Gail at all yesterday morning, and no one had a clue where to start looking. She'd even padded out the tarpaulins in the shed, telling her parents their bikes were still there, and could only hope they'd be too preoccupied to check. First chance she got, she'd have to sneak out and get the bikes back somehow.

Why had she lied? It was the way her father had asked her about Gail, looking straight through her with his laser beam stare, as though he could see her thoughts. That way of his always made her grasp for a lie, when the truth would do just as well. She gripped the window sill as a tiny flash of yellow caught her eye.

"Mother!" she cried, scooting down the stairs. "Where's Trundle?"

"He's out, dear. Said he had something to do for your father."

"When he gets back, tell him there's a dandelion on the lawn. He'd better sort it before Daddy gets home."

Daddy had been so tense lately, the slightest thing out of place could catapult him into one of his rages. If her father spotted that, their lives really wouldn't be worth living.

***

Clara and Hayley pedalled furiously towards home.

"I still can't work out what Donna meant," said Hayley. "But then, she hasn't got the brain cells of an ant."

Clara laughed. "She hasn't got the brain cells of an amoeba!"

"Or a bacteria."

A vehicle came zooming past, forcing them to swerve.

Hayley paused for a moment, fanning her face. "Wow, that idiot could've killed us."

Clara glanced at the retreating car, which was muddy and nondescript. "I know that man's face. Where from? … Oh! Isn't he the chap who works for Maunding? Trundle or something."

"He's in a hurry, that's for sure."

As they set off again, Clara wrinkled her nose. "Can you smell smoke?"

"Yeah. Bit cold for a barbie, isn't it?"

They rounded the brow of a hill. Up ahead was Clara's land. With a rush of horror, she realised what was happening.

"The woods are on fire! I think 'tis Granny's place."

Clara was so shocked that her front wheel wobbled and she nearly ran into the hedge.

178

Hayley stopped dead. "Quick, ring the fire brigade."

Clara was already pulling out her phone, screeching to a halt by the roadside.

"Emergency," said the voice. "Which service please?"

***

They jumped back on their bikes and sped towards the mine. Up ahead, ugly black smoke billowed into the air. Clara felt the blood pounding in her veins as she turned into the tiny road leading to Granny's cottage, which was on the other side of the woods from the caravans. The image of her grandmother lying dead on the floor blotted out all other thoughts. She strained every muscle to get there before it was too late.

They threw down their bikes and pelted down Granny's driveway. Smoke was streaming through the half-open kitchen window.

Please don't let Granny be in there. Clara knew you should never go into a burning building. But what if Granny was inside? She couldn't just stand there.

She tried to look through the glass but was beaten back by heat and smoke. Then she remembered Granny normally had a lie-down in the afternoon while Coles watched TV in his room.

She raced around to the far side of the cottage, but couldn't see anything through Granny's thick bedroom curtains.

Clara banged on the glass. "Gran! Can you hear me?

Wake up!" She sped on to the window of the adjoining bedroom. "Len! There's a fire!"

Hayley was close behind. "Are they in there? What can we do?"

"Go round to the front and wait for the fire brigade. I'll try to get in the back way."

"No, Clara. It's too dangerous. They'll be here in a minute."

"I can't just wait. Go on, Hayley."

Clara ran to the back door. Granny never locked it, but it was seldom used, since rain had swollen the wood and jammed it tight. The handle was cool to the touch. Clara turned it and kicked. The door refused to budge.

"Gran, Len! Can you hear me?"

No reply. Clara kicked again. This time the door flew open.

Smoke was already darkening the hallway. Clara took a breath and plunged in. Fumes were coming through to this side of the cottage through the half-ajar door to Gran's sitting room. Wrapping her jacket over her hand, Clara pulled the door shut, halting the smoke's progress.

She burst into Gran's bedroom. Her grandmother lay on the bed, eyes closed.

"Wake up!"

Clara raced to the side of the bed and shook her grandmother frantically. Smoke was acrid in her nostrils and she already struggled to breathe.

Granny Callenick began to move. "Eh? Who's that? Wassa matter?"

Suddenly awake, her lips parted in a moan. She

180

fought to get out of the bed, coughing and spluttering as the smoke filled her lungs.

Clara held onto her, pulling her up and helping her stumble out of the smoke-filled room. They moved quickly along the hallway towards the exit. As they passed Coles's room Clara banged on the door. Letting Granny go, she opened the door and gazed inside.

Gran's carer lay on his bed, eyes shut, TV blaring from the top of a chest of drawers.

"Wake up!" shouted Clara. "Get out!"

Without waiting for a reply, she shot back to her grandmother's side. Together, they hurried out of the cottage. Len Coles staggered after them, coughing and hacking, his face white.

Hayley took Granny's free arm. Len fell against the wall of the cottage, trying to catch his breath.

"The fire brigade's here," cried Hayley, although Clara had already heard the sirens.

The small party moved around to the front of the cottage. Fire officers were already inside the kitchen. Another, in full protective clothing, held up his hand.

"Stand back! Is anyone else inside?"

"They're both here," Clara told him. "But there's a cat."

Smoke was still pouring from the kitchen window. Clara and Hayley lowered Granny onto a wooden seat. Two paramedics, a man and a woman, strode towards them. Clara and Hayley shifted out of the way while they took charge.

Clara noticed a nearby tree had caught fire. It was

one of the biggest, oldest oaks. She crossed to the water butt and threw a bucketful at the trunk. Half the flames fizzled out. Hayley found an old saucepan by the hedge and, together, they extinguished the rest of the flames.

The fire fighters had the fire under control within minutes. As they emerged from the cottage, Clara's dad, Tom, came hurtling down the path. Granny was strapped onto a stretcher, on her way to the ambulance.

"Mother!" Tom bent down and kissed her white hair. Granny gave him a watery smile, clearly too stunned to speak.

Coles stood off to one side. His room had escaped most of the smoke, and he appeared unscathed. "Where's Pickles?" he asked querulously.

"He's not out yet, Mr Coles," cried Hayley. "Was he definitely in there? Wouldn't he have escaped through the cat flap?"

Coles shrugged miserably. Tom came over to Clara and Hayley, and they were joined by one of the fire fighters and the female paramedic.

"Your grandmother will be fine," the paramedic assured them. "We're just taking her to the hospital to be on the safe side."

"The fire broke out in the kitchen," added the fire fighter. "It didn't spread far. The hall door was shut, thank goodness."

Clara didn't tell him it was she who'd shut it. No doubt she'd be in trouble—rightly so—for going in at all.

"How did it start?" she asked, fighting back the tears.

"Chip pan," said the officer. "Happens all the time. They should be banned. Chip pans kill fifty-odd a year. Still people won't give 'em up."

"But they were in their bedrooms, not the kitchen," protested Clara. "Why would they leave chips frying?"

She chewed her lip, hoping no one would enquire too closely about how she knew their whereabouts. The officer shook his head, as though he couldn't be expected to explain the actions of people as old as Granny and Coles.

An image flashed through Clara's mind: Maunding's assistant, Trundle, speeding towards them from the direction of the cottage. He could easily have slipped into Granny's kitchen and put the cooker on.

She glanced across to the tree. Part of the trunk had been burned away, and she didn't think it could survive. She had known that tree all her life. It had been growing for many years before she was born.

"That tree caught fire too," she said. "It must be a good ten metres from the house. How could that happen? And how come the trunk caught alight, not the smaller branches higher up?"

No one replied. Clara turned and marched away.

CHAPTER 17

HAYLEY slipped home for an hour to have her tea and ring Rob and Mick with the news. Clara met them later at the entrance to her lane. It was dark by now and a blanket of cloud hid the stars. They sat on the wall overlooking the road. The light from a nearby streetlamp threw shadows across their dazed faces.

"This is Maunding's doing," said Clara grimly. "He'll stop at nothing to get the mine."

"Is Granny home from hospital?" asked Mick.

"They're keeping her in overnight, but she and Coles are both fine. They didn't inhale much smoke. Granny's more shocked than anything. For all Maunding knew, though, they could've been killed."

"And Granny's cat?" breathed Hayley. "Is he all right?"

Clara smiled. "Pickles is fine. He soon turned up when it was time for his tea."

"Phew, that's a relief. I was so worried … You really think Maunding's behind it?"

"Don't you? I expect he gets other people to do his dirty work. Granny never locks her door and she and Coles usually have a rest in the afternoon. Trundle could easily have crept in and started the fire. We could never prove it, though."

Mick was looking at her with his arms folded. "You mean this Trundle brought a pan of burning oil with him?"

"No, of course not. Gran and Coles leave a chip pan on the stove. All he'd need to do is turn on the ring. Go look at the burnt tree if you don't believe me. That trunk would never have caught fire from so far away. I reckon someone threw petrol over it. They wanted to set the woods on fire."

"But why would Maunding do all this?" asked Hayley. "What would he have to gain?"

"He's trying to frighten Granny. Frighten all of us. She won't know it's Maunding who's done it, but it'll make her all the more keen to leave. She told me she's made up her mind to go, but I don't think she's told Maunding yet. He's trying to hurry things along."

Hayley exchanged a glance with Rob. "But Clara, think about it. If Granny had died, then he couldn't buy the land from her at all, could he?"

Clara was trembling, but whether from delayed shock or anger, she couldn't tell. Her friends didn't believe her! She took a few breaths, trying to calm herself. "I guess you're right. He probably just intended to scare her. But it could have gone wrong, all the same."

"How much damage is there?" Rob asked her.

"It looks like there's been an explosion in there. Everything in the kitchen is black as a crow. You'd never believe one chip pan could cause all that. The rest of the house isn't too bad. Good job the fire brigade got there when they did."

185

"Why hasn't she got a smoke alarm?" asked Hayley.

"She has," said Clara, bristling, "but she'd forgotten to replace the battery. She's going to stop with Aunt Iris for a day or two when she gets out of hospital. Coles is going over to Farmer Bolton's."

Rob leaned in close to Clara. "Speaking of which, we saw her today."

"Who?"

"Your Auntie Iris."

"You did? Where?"

Rob and Mick told Clara about their visit to MORE and what they had heard outside Maunding's office.

"So it's true, then," said Clara. "About MORE, I mean. I knew it would be. It's odd about Iris, though … Now you mention it, Dad said something about them going to school together. I expect she was trying to talk him out of buying the mine."

"Could be," said Rob. "She didn't say. But she's the only one besides you who doesn't want the mine sold, isn't she?"

Clara shrugged. "Yeah."

A bus thundered past. Two squirrels scooted up an elder tree. It was freezing now, as though it might snow. Clara felt exhausted. She just wanted to sleep for days and days, forget about everything.

"Anyhow," Mick said brightly. "MORE definitely exists. And wow, wouldn't it be great to work in a place like that? Imagine being able to spend your time exploring the secrets of the universe. So cool!"

Hayley put her hand on Clara's arm. "Are you okay?

I can't imagine how I would've felt if it was my gran's house."

Clara shut her eyes. "I'm fine. We've got to keep going. I mustn't let him win." She shook herself. *Focus.* "Okay, Rob, Mick, what else did you find out?"

"Um, well, not a lot," confessed Rob.

Hayley frowned. "You just went in, then came out again? Hmmm. Did you find out whether they were doing any experiments with time travel, at least?"

"As it happens," said Mick, "I saw a report about the latest research at CERN in Switzerland. That's where they've got that fantastic Hadron particle accelerator thing."

"Okay, not bad," said Hayley.

"And I managed to look past the old trout who was on reception," said Rob. "There was a room with people in it, wearing white coats. It definitely looked like a science lab, just a lot newer, with a lot better stuff in it than Zeno's."

Hayley laughed. "Okay, pretty good."

"I think we should do a bit more research. It might give us a clue how else we could stop this thing happening." Mick fished in his pocket. "And look, I've drawn up a timeline. I've been putting together everything I know, from bits and pieces Jed and Zeno said."

He jumped off the wall and showed them his sheet of paper. "I reckon the Disaster is set for a few years from now—maybe somewhere between ten and twenty."

187

Clara winced. With Maunding involved, they must all have realised by now that the Disaster was set to take place in their own lifetimes.

Mick continued, "And I think the time we went to—the time we were in the cavern—is about sixty years in the future. I've made a guess at Jed's year of birth, too. I've pencilled it in thirty years from now."

"Good work," said Clara, but Rob looked far from thrilled. Red in the face, he grabbed the sheet of paper from Mick's hands and waved it around. "This is all fine and good, but it doesn't help much, does it?"

Hayley's mouth dropped open. "Rob!"

A hurt look in his eyes, Mick snatched back his paper and stuffed it in the pocket of his parka. "Rightio, I can see I'm not needed here." Turning briskly, he strode off towards Polgrehan.

"Mick, don't go," pleaded Clara.

Mick didn't look back. Within seconds he had rounded the corner out of view.

Clara and Hayley stared at Rob, but he gazed stubbornly into the distance.

"Poor Mick," said Hayley. "That was mean."

"He just gets on my nerves sometimes," Rob said. "His brain never stops."

"You're just jealous," said Hayley, her eyes ablaze.

"Stop it!" cried Clara. "The last thing we need is to fall out." She had a horrible sinking feeling, as though the future were catapulting towards them, leaving no time to act.

No one spoke. Rob whistled to himself tunelessly for

a few moments, then cleared his throat. "Let's meet back here tomorrow morning. Decide what we're going to do next."

"But—" began Hayley.

"There's no time for school. Term finishes in a few days anyway."

"Rob's right," said Clara. "If only there was a—oh! I've just remembered." She rooted around in her jacket pocket and pulled out the tennis ball-sized sphere Zeno had given her in the Siri shaft.

"Wow," said Hayley. "The trilly thing. I'd forgotten all about it."

"Me too. Looks like it survived the journey okay." Clara held it up in the direction of the street light. "A trilloscope, wasn't it? Zeno said we might be able to contact him with it."

She stared at it for a long moment. Her skin prickled. "I'm going up to the shaft. I want to see if it works."

"Now?" Hayley shrank back. "Clara, you can't. You should get some sleep. You look awful."

"Thanks, that makes me feel a whole lot better," snapped Clara, though she knew her friend was right.

"What's the point, anyway?" Rob asked. "We haven't got anything new to tell Zeno. Shouldn't we save it for when we have? They haven't got many resources left, remember … You shouldn't go on your own. It might be dangerous."

"And Mick will be really cross if he misses anything," said Hayley.

Clara sighed. "Yeah, I know. There are lots of good

reasons not to go." How could she explain the crushing sensation she felt every time she thought about Zeno and Jed? A horrible uneasiness, a sense they were in danger. They had said she was sensitive. Was she picking something up? Some echo, a ripple from the future?

"I just feel I should." Her mind made up, she leapt to her feet and set off along the lane, not even saying goodbye.

Rob ran after her. "Clara, wait. I'll come with you."

"Me too," said Hayley. "Don't leave me behind."

***

Clara stopped outside her caravan. "Oh no, Zeno said we needed some sort of acid. Where'll we get that? Can anyone remember what it was?"

"Ethanoic," said Rob.

Clara and Hayley stared at him.

"Don't look so surprised. I do remember some things. Well, Mick was talking about it actually. He said vinegar might work. It contains this ethanoic acid, apparently."

"Okay, wait there." Clara dashed into her caravan and emerged clutching a small bottle of vinegar.

"I hope Mick's right," said Rob, glaring at it. "Seems a bit ridiculous, if you ask me."

Clara patted her jacket pocket. "I brought some water, too. All that smoke has made my throat awfully dry."

190

They plunged into the woods. The cloud cover had cleared and a feeble moon penetrated the darkness. There was a frozen look about everything, as though time had stood still. Clara glanced over at the water wheel lurking in the shadows. It looked woefully sad and neglected. Would there come a time, perhaps soon, when all this would be gone?

Hayley bumped into her. "Why've you stopped?"

Clara felt so choked with sorrow, for a moment she couldn't speak.

"Clara?"

"Oh, it's just that every time I come here now, I keep wondering if it'll be the last time. I can't bear the thought of leaving. There's nowhere else I want to go."

Hayley linked arms with her. "Don't be like that. You've got to stay positive. We'll beat them."

Clara wished she could believe her.

They left the woods along the gorse path leading to the Downs and the Siri shaft. Halfway along, Hayley stopped in the clearing by the overgrown track.

"That's the path that goes to the other shaft, isn't it? The one you were telling us about before?"

"That's right," said Clara. "I've spent ages trying to work out where everything is down there in the future, compared with up here. I think that shaft is the one they call the Skeleton Shaft."

Hayley shivered. "I don't like to think about it. Any of it. It's ... ooh, horrible. Like things could change at any minute. Like what we think is real might not always be real. If we do manage to change things about the sale of the mine, Mick said all sorts of other stuff might change, too." Her voice rose higher. "He said even what we know so far, what we're doing already, might change things. Jed might not get born!"

"Can we get on now?" asked Rob. "Please? Before we turn into icicles?"

Clara strode ahead, picking up a short, stubby stick by the path and beating back the brambles. About to throw it aside, she remembered another patch of brambles further on, and slipped it instead into the torn lining of her jacket.

"That was interesting what Mick was saying about the timeline," she said. "I've been trying to work out how many years into the future we went, as well."

"Jed said things started to go wrong a few years after Maunding got hold of the mine," said Hayley, "and that Zeno was working there, before he got the sack."

"Might that mean Zeno is already around?" wondered Clara. "Somewhere?"

Rob stomped past them, waving his arms. "Just stop thinking about it. You'll drive yourself nuts."

"You're right," agreed Clara. "But it's hard not to."

Out on the hill, by the Siri shaft, the wind was blowing fiercely, bending the trees on the horizon and playing them like a woodwind instrument. Soft rain began to fall.

"Hurry up," said Rob. "Let's see if it works, then we can get home and into the warm."

Clara could feel his irritation, and it began to rub off on her. She hadn't asked him to come, after all—yet wasn't sure herself what she hoped to achieve. She just had to know if the trilloscope worked. Would they be able to contact Zeno again, or were they now completely on their own?

Carefully, she withdrew the spherical white device and held it up to the faint starlight. It was too dark to see the tiny perforations she'd noticed before. She laid it on a granite boulder near the shaft.

"There, it's on the granite, like Zeno said. Trouble is, I don't know what we're supposed to do now. What do we do with the vinegar?" Wind whipped her hair across her eyes and rain seeped inside her collar and down her neck. They would get soaked.

"Dunno," said Rob. "Pour it on top? Seems a bit daft, but give it a go."

"Stand back," said Hayley. "He said it's only a proto-whatsit. It might be dangerous."

Clara hesitated. Rob swiped the vinegar from her hand.

"Hey!"

Rob tipped the vinegar over the ball. Clara and Hayley jumped back. The vinegar washed over the trilloscope and spilled onto the granite boulder. A sour tang filled the air.

The thing looked just the same. They waited a few moments. Still nothing happened. Clara felt a throb of relief. If it didn't work, it wasn't their fault, was it? For a second, she thought how wonderful it would be not to worry about that terrible future any longer, about Zeno and Jed and their awful lives. Then she shook herself,

193

angry that she'd been so selfish. They would have to carry on, Zeno or no Zeno.

Rob paced up and down. "Maybe it doesn't work with the vinegar. Maybe vinegar's too weak. And the rain won't have helped any. We might need full-strength acid …"

He took a step towards it. As he did so, it emitted a pulse of light. A wave of heat hit them.

"Ouch." Rob yelped and rubbed his forehead. "It's singed my eye brow."

The trilloscope shimmered and began to rotate.

"It's heating up," cried Hayley.

Within seconds it was as hot as a bonfire. Clara and Hayley stepped further back. Beneath the globe the granite boulder glowed red.

The vinegar smell turned to citrus, like the smell of the tempoplas. The sphere was spinning so fast it was a blur. Orange and scarlet clouds appeared inside, then it turned blue. Sparks flew as the spinning slowed and it came to a stop.

There was a loud crack, followed by sizzling and squeaking.

From the corner of her eye, Clara noticed a faint gleam. "The time portal—it's back!"

Sure enough, within the mine shaft, the orange disc was glowing. Firework lights began to fizz out of it.

Upon the granite boulder, a transparent globe rose up from the trilloscope, like a bubble being blown through. It hovered uncertainly, then grew in size until it reached the size of a beach ball.

"Look." Clara gazed, spellbound.

The bubble filled with a golden mist. The mist glittered and swirled, then grew thick and milky. Cloudy shapes came together to form a face.

A voice boomed, "Is that you, Clara? Rob?" The face looked like Zeno's—but not the Zeno they knew. As he spoke, dribbles of straw-coloured liquid oozed from the bubble and dripped onto the trilloscope beneath.

Clara knelt as close to the boulder as she could get. Heat blasted her face and the lemon smell was overpowering. "It's working, Zeno. The trilloscope works."

There were more squeaks and crackles, then muffled shouts.

Within the bubble, Zeno's face was clearer. He looked deathly pale. The voice boomed again. "Go home, Clara!" There was more shouting.

The trilloscope whirred as new shapes appeared inside the bubble. Zeno was in the lab. Behind him, people were rushing to and fro. The vision wobbled, as though he had been hit by something. Clara saw his face, screwed up in pain.

"You're too late! The Grammets—" Slime oozed from the bubble.

The image burst apart as another formed. People were running, screaming, falling. Clara glimpsed a girl, her skin covered in boils, her face contorted with loathing. Clara couldn't be sure, but she thought it might be the girl she'd seen climbing the windows of the cavern, that first time. The girl who looked like Donna Maunding.

"What's going on?" Clara shouted into the device, her voice high and scared.

Hayley ran to kneel beside her. Rob had crossed to the shaft and was gazing down towards the orange disc, his silhouette framed by blue and lilac sparks.

Jed's blurry image formed inside the bubble. His face was scrunched in terror as his voice crackled out of the device.

"Forget about us, Clara. You can't help us now."

There was a dreadful scream. The bubble burst. The trilloscope went dark.

After a second's pause, Rob stepped over the low fence. "I'm going in."

"Don't be stupid," cried Hayley. "You heard what they said. It's too dangerous."

"They need us."

Clara watched in alarm as Rob leapt onto the orange disc and began to sink through.

"Don't go, please." Sobbing, Hayley struggled to her feet.

"I'll try to stop him." Clara raced towards the shaft, Hayley following at her heels.

It was too late. Rob was already more than halfway through the tempoplas.

Clara turned to Hayley. "I'll have to go after him. I can't let him go alone."

Hayley's jaw was clenched in miserable determination. "I'll come too."

"No!"

"But—"

Clara grasped her shoulders and peered into her frightened eyes. "Why risk all of us? You must stay here."

Without waiting for an answer, Clara released Hayley, took a running jump and vaulted the fence. Rob had disappeared and the bright orange of the disc was fading. Any moment now it would vanish. With a yell, Clara sprang onto the tempoplas.

Hayley gripped the fence, her face chalk-white. "Clara! Come back!"

Swallowed by the disc, Clara heard no more.

***

The lift did not sink gradually as it had before. Instead, it swerved and dropped with terrifying speed, illuminated by fizzing purple lights. Rob was thrown against the walls and yelled in pain as his foot became squashed between the floor and the uneven stones of the shaft. Clara held onto him as he wrenched his foot back from the gap.

"It's gone wrong!" screamed Clara.

"Full … marks." Rob bent double, catching his breath.

"Why did you jump in? Look what's happened!"

"You didn't have to follow me."

The lift crashed to a halt. The purple lights went out, leaving them in darkness. Clara inched towards Rob, her mind numb with fear and disbelief. She reached tentatively for his hand.

The door slid open. A man stood staring in at them. But this time it wasn't Zeno. The eyes boring into Clara's were those of Derek Maunding.

CHAPTER 18

AT the bottom of the Siri shaft, the man scrutinised Clara and Rob, his mouth twitching in a grim smile. Clara would recognise those eyes anywhere: the colour of pond water, and icy cold. Up close, one of them looked slightly out of synch with the other.

"This must be the famous Clara Callenick," he said.

The silky, pleasant voice was also just like Derek Maunding's. Straight away, however, Clara realised it couldn't possibly be him. This man was a sorry parody of the imposing businessman, thinner and older, his hair short and grey with tufts missing where the skull was pitted. His face was a sickly yellow, marred by a smattering of purplish boils. One boil was like a teardrop beneath his left eye, which, together with his downturned mouth, gave him the look of a sad clown.

"Allow me to introduce myself," he said. "I am Patrick Maunding. I believe you may know my grandfather, Derek? And my mother, Donna?"

Clara did a quick calculation: the man looked to be somewhere in his late forties, which meant Mick's theory about this time being sixty years in the future could be spot-on.

"Yes, I see that you do," he continued. "But enough of this chit-chat. Carpe diem, seize the day, no?"

His voice hardened. "Take them to the cell."

From behind, two burly men stepped forward, younger than Maunding, but with the same sallow skin and boils on their faces. They wore black overalls above scuffed, sturdy boots.

One of them clamped Rob's shoulders. He had arms like ham hocks and legs as thick as tree trunks, half his face concealed by a greasy red beard.

"Get off me." Rob tried to struggle free, but though big and strong for his age, he was no match for this giant. He groaned as the man kicked him savagely in the shin.

"Leave him alone!" Clara rushed at the bearded man and pushed him. He let Rob go, but before she could blink, his meaty fist closed around her throat. Clara watched his muscles bulging as he squeezed. She gasped for breath, the pain sickening. Stars danced before her eyes.

"Clara!" As Rob tried to reach her, the second man grabbed him and twisted his arm up his back. This guard was taller than Redbeard, his skin pulled tightly across pointed cheekbones, giving him a skull-like appearance.

With a laugh, Redbeard tossed Clara aside. She sat on the ground, panting and clutching her throat.

Derek Maunding's grandson was watching with his arms crossed. "I wouldn't bother struggling if I were you. Unless you wish to witness the effects of a Desiccator. Do you have those yet, in your time? I don't think you did."

From the pocket of his black uniform he withdrew a small red object, shaped like a gun. He held it up to the green light and pointed it at each of them in turn, looking through a viewfinder on top.

"A very clever thing, this. One of my grandfather's more amusing inventions. A tiny object that can suck the water out of its victim in one-and-a-half minutes. Leaving nothing behind but, well, a dry biscuit!" He slipped the weapon back into his pocket. "Now, isn't that a sensible idea in a world without clean water? Clever, yet so much fun." He chuckled, a harsh, braying sound completely at odds with his smooth, commanding voice.

"What have you done with Zeno?" demanded Rob as Clara hauled herself to her feet. "Where's Jed?"

Patrick Maunding waved his hand. "Don't you worry your little head about them." He gestured to the two men. "Take them away. I'm so looking forward to hearing all about their adventures."

The men frog-marched Clara and Rob along the tunnel. The green light flickered, and occasionally snapped out for an instant, leaving them in darkness.

They were forced through the door at the end of the tunnel, now wedged open, and out into the cavern. A very different sight greeted them from the one they had seen so recently. Instead of people in odd clothes running to and fro, there were small groups of brutal-looking men, dressed mostly in black. They wove in and around the buildings, all of them armed. Clara saw two with rifles, one carrying a long knife, another with a red

201

Desiccator.

"The Grammets have taken over," whispered Clara. "What have they done with the others? Where are they?"

Rob groaned. "Dunno. You okay?"

"I think so." Clara saw that he was limping. "Rob, you're hurt!"

"I'm all right."

Scanning the scene, Clara spotted a girl with straggly, blonde hair. She was standing near the lab, her back turned towards them. Clara thought she might be the Grammet girl, the one who looked like Donna Maunding. But much as she craned her neck, she couldn't glimpse the girl's face.

Redbeard and Skullface shoved them across the cavern and into a tunnel to the left of the windows, the one which led to the sleeping cells. Not far along, they stopped in front of a cave-like room with a thick metal door.

"In you go," Redbeard said, thrusting them inside. Clara cried out as her head banged the stone ceiling. A stench of mould and decay filled her nostrils.

The door clanged shut and the bolt slid across. They were in pitch blackness. Neither spoke for a moment. Rubbing her sore head, Clara felt her way gingerly to the ground.

"I saw this place before," she said. "When Jed showed us round. It's where they put the mad people."

She sensed movement as Rob sat down beside her.

"Hang on," he said.

Clara heard a ratchety noise and saw a glimmer of light. "You've got your torch! That's something, at least."

Rob shone the beam around. The cell was a triangular hollow gouged out of the rock, the roof tapering to the floor at the back. It contained only a pile of old rags and boxes, and was too cramped for them to stand up.

"It's really s-small in here." To ward off her claustrophobia, Clara tried to fill her mind with images of wide open spaces, fields and oceans.

"You're not wrong." Rob was breathing heavily, and his voice came out in gasps.

"You are hurt. Is it bad?" Clara felt guilty that she'd been thinking only of herself.

Rob grunted. "It's okay. Twisted my ankle in the Siri shaft, when my foot jammed … Then that bruiser kicked me. I think he's got half a ton of steel in his boots. You're sure you're all right? I thought he was going to strangle you."

Clara rubbed her shoulders. "I'm fine."

Rob pulled up the leg of his jeans and shone the torch onto his shin. There was a big swollen weal, splattered with blood.

"Oh no," cried Clara.

"It's not deep. Don't worry."

"Oh, Rob, we should never have come."

"I know … But they needed us. I'm sorry."

Rob's apology made Clara feel worse than ever. It was her fault they'd gone up to the shaft in the first place. Now they were trapped here in the future, and if they didn't get back, they'd have no chance whatsoever of keeping Callenick mine out of Maunding's hands. Despite all their efforts, they had achieved precisely nothing. They had failed—spectacularly.

Clara couldn't take much more. She felt dizzy and there was a rushing in her ears, as though she might faint. "I can't stand it. I've got to get out of here." She leaned forward and banged on the door. "Let me out!"

Although there was a resounding clang, her fists made no impression on the thick metal.

Rob gripped her arm and pulled her back beside him. "Keep calm. We'll get out. We need a plan."

"You know I can't stand small places."

"I gathered."

There was a noise beside Clara, a bit like a groan. "Aaahf."

Clara stopped wailing and listened. "What was that?"

Rob shone the thin beam of his torch past Clara onto the pile of boxes and rags. It began to move. Someone was there!

Clara gasped. "Zeno!"

Slowly, Zeno raised his head and stared at her through glazed eyes.

"Oh no, what have they done to you?" asked Clara.

With shaking hands, she pulled out the bottle of water she'd brought with her and did her best to pour some into Zeno's mouth.

Zeno spluttered. "Clara? You came! You thun-der-head." His words trailed off into wheezing.

"Drink, Zeno." Clara held the bottle to his thin blue lips.

He managed to swallow a few sips. "Water? Real water?"

"That's it. Real water."

Zeno whimpered, struggling to sit up. "They know everything. It's the worst that could have happened. They even know ... You see, Jed and I, working with the tempoplas, it makes you aware of time's mysteries. And ... We've had dreams. As though things have already changed, since we brought you to our time."

"He's rambling," said Rob, his voice hushed.

"Zeno, where's Jed?" cried Clara. "What have they done with Jed?"

Zeno slumped and was silent.

It was several moments before he moved again. "I dreamt our Sun Shaft used to be called the Skeleton Shaft. Do you know anything about it? Is it really true, dear Clara?"

"I ... I don't know." Clara tried to keep the confusion from her voice. "Zeno, please don't give up. We'll get out of here and go back. We will change things."

She wished she could believe it. In truth, Clara had no idea what Zeno meant, and doubted she could do what she promised.

"What's he talking about?" she asked Rob. "What's the Sun Shaft? Does he mean the Skeleton Shaft?"

Rob didn't answer. Clara placed her hand on Zeno's old, wizened one. It felt cold, despite the sweltering heat of the cell. She encircled him with her arms and tried to warm his bony shoulders.

Suddenly she remembered what Jed had called the Farrula Effect. "Rob, why can I touch him? There's no tingling when I touch him now … It's as though he's slipping away. I think he's ill, Rob. I think he's dying." A tear rolled down her cheek.

Zeno's chin fell forward onto his chest. His breathing became more regular.

They could get nothing more from him after that. He stirred only once and cried out one word: "Siri." Then he slumped forward, seemingly asleep.

Cautiously, Clara tried to get comfortable against the sloping roof of the cave. She offered Rob the water bottle and he drank a couple of sips. Clara knew he was trying to save it for her and Zeno.

"I don't understand," she said. "Is he saying the Skeleton Shaft is now the Sun Shaft? And how come those horrible people know my name? Is Zeno saying what I think he is, that they've learned the secrets of time travel?"

Rob shrugged and shook his head.

"Oh, Rob, what do they want with us?"

"Dunno. But they want something, or chances are they would've killed us. We'll find out soon enough."

**

Up on the ground, Hayley knelt for a long time by the granite boulder. Tears ran down her face, mingling with drops of rain. She wondered what on earth she should do, praying for Clara and Rob to reappear. They were so brave. So stupid!

The rain stopped, but Hayley was already drenched. By the hazy glimmer of the moon, she could just make out the hands of her watch. Six o'clock. She pulled out her mobile phone, then remembered there was never any signal here on the Downs.

She had to do something. Should she fetch help? Clara's dad? Aunt Iris? Who would believe her? Mick. Mick would know what to do.

Decision made, she set off down the hillside. Above all else, she must keep calm and concentrate on the route. Everything looked so different in the dark.

Remembering she had a small penlight on the end of her key ring, she pulled it out and shone it along the path. It wasn't much, but it was better than nothing.

At last she found the gorse track. Although it was December, the gorse bushes still had coconut-scented yellow flowers. They glowed in the moonlight like beacons on an airport runway.

"They say kissing will never go out of fashion while the gorse is in flower," Clara had told her, whatever that meant. Clara and her family had lots of Sayings.

In among the gorse bushes there were other trees. Clara had told her their names but she had forgotten them. Festooned with lacy lichens, they stretched out knobbly twigs towards her face, like old ladies' fingers trying to stroke her.

Hayley hated it here on her own. She wasn't like

Clara, who liked nothing better than to charge about on the Downs. Hayley preferred the indoors, she liked to feel safe and warm and clean. She'd give everything she owned to get out of here, now, and into the light.

She kept heading in the direction of the wood, which she could make out dimly in the shadows ahead. Halfway along the path she came to the clearing. Sure enough, once again she caught her foot in the snake-shaped root. She thrust out her hands, but was unable to stop herself falling flat on her face.

"Oof."

Not again! She got up slowly and wiped the mud from her nose. About to set off, she realised she had dropped her penlight. Bending to pick it up, she noticed something glinting in the little beam near her feet.

It was small and round, partially covered in mud. Attached to it was a slimy, broken chain.

Screwing up her face in concentration, Hayley brushed off the mud and examined the object by the light of the torch.

She caught her breath. Engraved upon it was a man crossing a river, holding a crooked stick and carrying an infant on his shoulder. Could that be St Christopher? Hayley's eyes widened. This had to be Clara's necklace!

What was it doing here? The Maunding girls had stolen it. Hayley had asked Clara about it only this afternoon, at Pardeaux Hall. She knew Clara hadn't got it back.

Hayley shone the beam around. A small track led off to the second shaft Clara had told them about. The

Skeleton Shaft.

I wonder if … surely not.

Blood thumped in Hayley's ears as ideas tumbled over themselves. Things started to make horrible sense. Gail wearing Clara's necklace … Gail disappearing … Had Gail come along this way? Could she have injured herself? Might she still be here, dead or alive?

Hayley shone her torch along the tiny track, barely visible in the gloom. She wanted to run as fast as she could in the opposite direction. But she knew she'd never forgive herself if she didn't at least have a quick look.

She stepped along warily between the brambles, glancing left and right for Gail—or Gail's body. She had no idea how far along the shaft was, and might not be able to find it.

After she'd followed the track for a minute or two, she spotted a low fence, similar to that around the Siri shaft. Beside it, a little sign had been knocked into the ground.

"Danger, open shaft," she read in the torchlight, daubed in paint the colour of blood.

Hayley slowed her steps, the impulse to turn and run almost overwhelming. She stopped a few metres back and shone the beam in the direction of the hole. Although she peered and strained her eyes, it was no good. She couldn't see enough from this distance. She'd have to step over the fence.

Her body ached with tension as she raised one leg and then the other, taking care not to get snagged in the wire. Once inside the fence, she crouched down and shuffled slowly towards the edge of the shaft. Her knees quaked and she shivered from the cold. One false move and she'd meet the most grisly fate she could imagine.

The hole looked like a hungry mouth opened to the sky. Hayley shone the beam inside.

All was still within the shaft. A damp, musty tang hung in the air. The tiny light glanced off the stone and she couldn't see far down. Pointing the torch into the centre of the hole, she peered along the length of the beam.

Where the light ran out, she could make out a shape. The shaft appeared to be blocked. But that wasn't surprising, was it? Stones and things would be falling in all the time.

Feeling dizzy, Hayley sat back on her heels. Then she leaned in again, shining her penlight. "Hello?" Her voice was thin and shaky. "Is anybody there? Gail?"

Despite her fear, she began to feel silly. Her imagination had run away with her—Mum was always teasing her about that. Gail had probably turned up by now and was at home watching her enormous TV.

Hayley had better get home. If she didn't watch out, she would go missing as well. She wriggled carefully backwards, away from the shaft.

As she got up to retreat across the wire fence, she thought she detected a noise. A small noise, far away. Coming from somewhere below.

"Gail?" She turned and crawled back to the hole. "Gail? Is that you?"

The noise came again. Hayley peered into the gloom. It was a voice. Indistinct, but definitely a voice.

"Urgh. Help! Don't go. Get … me … out of here."

CHAPTER 19

IN the tiny rock cell, hour after hour crept past. Clara shifted painfully. Her limbs had long since gone numb, and every bone in her body ached. There was no point in trying to sleep. She was far too frightened and miserable, overcome with feelings of dread worse than anything she'd ever known before.

She thought about her home, her family and her beloved woods. They seemed unbearably far away, as though on another planet. She might never see any of them again. More importantly, she was further than ever from stopping the sale of her mine. Her actions had only made things worse.

The air inside the cell was putrid. It made her feel sick and light-headed. She wanted Rob to talk to her, to take her mind off the cramped, narrow space of the cell. But whenever he spoke, she could sense what it cost him. He was clearly exhausted, and in pain.

Every so often they tried to move the door. It wouldn't budge a centimetre. The other walls were solid rock, so there was no chance of moving them. Eventually, they gave up and waited in the dark.

"I wonder what Hayley and Mick are doing," said Clara. "They'll be worried sick. And my poor dad! What's he going to think when I don't come home?"

She groaned and put her head in her hands. Her face felt greasy and her hair was still slimy from the tempoplas.

She ran her hands carefully over her skin. What if Jed was wrong about the spots? What if they weren't just a by-product of travelling through the tempoplas? The thought of getting the same disgusting boils as the Grammets, on top of everything else, was almost too much to bear.

She searched her mind for new ideas. "Zeno said the same amount of time will pass back home as it does here. I reckon it must be night-time by now, don't you, Rob?"

Rob was silent for so long, Clara thought he must have fallen asleep. Either that, or he was so fed up with her rambling he had decided to ignore her.

"Hard to tell," he said at last. "My phone doesn't work here at all. Neither does my watch."

The bottle of water was empty. They hadn't eaten in hours, but neither of them mentioned it. Zeno moved occasionally, but when they tried to speak to him, he only moaned.

Clara was terrified that Zeno would die here, sitting next to her in a pitch-black hole.

"What have they done to him?" she asked Rob for the tenth time. "Is he ill? Or is there something wrong with his mind?"

"Be quiet, Clara!" cried Rob. "I'm trying to think."

"What? Oh, sorry, Rob. When I stop talking, I start panicking."

There was a long silence, then Rob's voice sounded again, much softer this time. "I didn't mean to snap … If only we had a weapon of some sort."

Clara caught her breath. "I've got a stick! I was using it for brambles on the way to the Siri shaft. 'Tisn't much, but …"

Due to the heat, she had long since thrown off her jacket. Reaching behind, she fished inside the lining and retrieved the stick. It was as thick as a broom handle and a foot or so long.

Rob sounded exasperated. "A stick? Why didn't you say?"

"I didn't think. Sorry. You can have it if you want."

"No. You might need it."

"You can do more damage with it than me," insisted Clara. "Though I hate to admit it."

Rob's voice was quiet and resigned. "Okay. Guess you're right."

Clara held out the stick and felt Rob groping for it in the dark.

"Thanks," he said. "Better than nothing. You hid that in your jacket? I'm impressed."

Clara laughed ruefully. "My jacket's seen better days, as I'm sure you've noticed. There's a hole in the lining, and you can wiggle things inside. Being poor has its advantages, you know."

"That's something, then. Here, Clara: you take my torch."

"Are you sure? Thanks." Clara slipped Rob's wind-up torch into her pocket. Though neither of them was saying as much, Clara felt sure Rob feared the worst, the same as she did.

"Put the stick in your jacket lining, Rob, like I did. They won't know it's there."

Rob's jacket was a lot newer and tougher than Clara's, but at last he managed to work a hole in a loose seam and poke the stick inside.

Just as he'd finished, there was a scraping noise. Someone was drawing back the bolt.

Cursing, Rob slipped quickly into his jacket.

A sliver of light grew as the door was dragged slowly open. Clara blinked, disorientated after so much darkness. As her eyes adjusted she made out a pale face.

It was the blonde girl. She was flanked by the two guards who had brought them here, Redbeard and Skullface. The three of them were talking, sharing a joke.

Rob gasped. "Wow, you were right," he whispered. "She looks just like Donna."

"She's a Maunding too," hissed Clara. "Another descendant, she's got to be."

"Quiet!" the girl barked.

Close up, Clara could see that she was taller than Donna and more athletic, also older, perhaps fifteen or even sixteen. But she had Donna's sharp features and piercing blue eyes.

She wore a plain uniform of tunic and trousers, and the skin of her face and arms was livid with boils. Over her shoulder she carried a quiver of arrows, also a small wooden bow, one end of which was carved into a vicious spike.

"We're ready for you now," she said with a smirk. "Get up."

Neither Rob nor Clara moved. The girl sprang forward, holding out the spiked bow. "I said, get up."

Clara and Rob got stiffly to their feet, Rob wincing as he pitched on his bad foot. Together they stumbled out of the smelly, confined space.

The girl poked Zeno with her bow. "You too, old man."

"Leave him alone," cried Clara. "He's not well. He needs rest and food."

Pulling back her lips, the girl prodded Zeno again. At last he grunted and began to move.

"You people make me vomit," she said. "You leave us out there, with no clean water, scraps and rubbish and poison for food ... But Father kept us going. He always said our day would come."

Redbeard jabbed Rob and Clara with the end of his rifle as he pushed them along the tunnel. Skullface escorted Zeno, who was shuffling forward, stumbling over the tatters of his old robe.

"It's nothing to do with us," Rob cried. "We didn't leave you out there. We don't belong here at all."

"Shh!" warned Clara, worried Rob might give too much away.

The girl laughed. "We know all about you. You and your cosy, safe time, your clean water and your glutton food, your soft beds. Well, you're not the only ones who can play at that game."

However much she hated the Grammets and what they had done, Clara felt a stab of pity. For a brief moment she looked at things through the girl's eyes, and saw the horror of her life.

The door at the end of the tunnel had been jammed open so the Grammets could move easily to and fro, without the need for codes. Clara and Rob emerged into the cavern and were thrust forward. The dim lights flickered horribly, making Clara's head throb.

The girl led them through the buildings in the direction of the lab. Her hair might once have been the same golden shade as Donna's, thought Clara, but now it was matted and dull, secured at the back of her head by a grotesque bone comb in the shape of a skull. She stopped outside the open door of the building Jed had called the processing room.

Looking beyond her, Clara realised with a shock where the cavern people had gone. Some were crammed against the rock face, pouring hissing liquid onto the rock. Others operated the crushing machine or funnelled dusty powders into tubs on trolleys. The rest stood around the vat, pounding the mixture within and stirring it with poles.

It was a similar scene to the one they had witnessed before, on their previous visit. But with one crucial difference. This time, the workers were watched over by a group of Grammets, some with whips, all carrying weapons.

The cavern people looked exhausted. Sweat dripped from their glistening skin, and their ragged clothing was shabbier and dirtier than ever. Several had metal bracelets around their wrists, chained to iron rings in the ground. Any sympathy Clara had felt for the Grammets evaporated.

The Donna-lookalike spoke to Redbeard, who nodded and went across to the nearest guard. "Prepare two more chains and lumpenhammers," he said imperiously. "The boss has two more bodies for you later."

Clara and Rob exchanged an uneasy glance.

Just then, a blood-curdling yell came from the end of the room. One of the men working at the rock face was shouting and staggering, pulling at the chain which held him. The Grammet guard nearest to him leapt forward and lashed out with a whip.

A bloody weal appeared on the man's naked back. He kept going, shaking his fist and screaming, despite the fact that two rifles and a red Desiccator were now trained upon him.

The worker chained next to him grabbed his arm and whispered furiously in his ear. The man threw him off.

"Go on, shoot me," he shouted to the guards. "What do I care? What's it matter?" He was foaming at the mouth, drops of spittle flying out.

Redbeard raised his rifle. Clara's heart stopped. Redbeard fired. The man fell to the ground, a patch of blood at his shoulder. The other workers barely glanced over, or if they did, they pretended not to.

"They've shot him!" cried Clara, stupefied.

218

Redbeard grabbed her and pushed her on past the door.

The blonde girl chuckled. "A feeble lot, our ancestors, weren't they?" she commented to Redbeard. Turning back to Clara she said, "Haven't you seen a bit of blood before, you bunkerton?"

She was still laughing as they got to the lab. Then her lips twitched in a scowl.

"You don't know what it's like to have nothing but poisonous scraps to eat, do you? Or even bits of dead people?" She rolled her eyes as Clara recoiled. "Well, I do."

She banged on the door. "Open up. We're here."

CHAPTER 20

"AH, there you are, Flavia. Having fun?"

Patrick Maunding, grandson of Derek, stood leaning against a bench. Nearby, Jed sat working quietly at a computer. At the far end of the lab, two more scientists sat at terminals, each with a burly Grammet guard watching over them. The room was sweltering and smelled caustic, like bleach.

Jed glanced up, but it was not the Jed Clara knew. His eyes were dull and glazed, and he looked back to the screen without speaking. A metal bracelet on his wrist chained him to the floor.

Clara broke free from Redbeard and ran to him. "Oh Jed, what have they done? Don't you recognise us?" She tugged desperately at his sleeve.

Jed lowered his gaze. Redbeard strode over and dragged Clara away.

Patrick Maunding folded his arms and wrinkled his sad clown-like face into a smile. He was smartly dressed, his black uniform distinguished from the others by a narrow band of red at the neck.

"Come and see, Flavia. We've got nearly all the information we need." He indicated a sheaf of papers behind him.

"I couldn't sleep last night. Is it really like you said?"

The girl skipped across to him, clapping her hands in delight.

Clara found her sudden gaiety even more chilling than her anger.

"Oh yes," said Maunding with a smile.

"They eat whatever they want, whenever they want? They have a thousand different things to drink and spend their time just enjoying themselves? Is it really true that their air has no poison? They even go in the sea? For fun? I'm so looking forward to it, Father."

So Clara had been right. This girl was another Maunding descendant, Patrick Maunding's daughter. But how much did they know? According to Zeno, they already knew too much.

"Have a haba, Flavia." Patrick Maunding offered her a bowl filled with the little lozenges everyone ate.

"Why, thank you, Father." Flavia tossed one into her mouth and made ghastly slurping noises which turned Clara's stomach.

Out of the corner of her eye, she thought she saw Jed wince. Was he aware of them after all? Clara scanned his face, but saw no sign of recognition.

Zeno and his guard, Skullface, arrived at the door of the lab. Skullface pushed Zeno inside and he leaned against the wall, breathing raggedly, his eyes blank. Skullface's gaze strayed with longing towards the bowl of habas in Patrick Maunding's hand.

Flavia crossed the room to peer at Clara. Clara glared back, trying not to gag at the smell of Flavia's breath, which stank like rotten fish. So this girl was Patrick

Maunding's daughter, and his mother was Donna Maunding. Clara struggled to take it all in.

"You're Donna's granddaughter?" she said, trying to sound confident. "That makes sense. You've got the same nasty, spiteful face. They're two peas in a pod, aren't they, Rob?"

Flavia slapped her face. Clara gasped as a stinging pain flared through her cheek. Before she could respond, Redbeard and Flavia gripped an arm each and dragged her to the centre of the lab.

Rob sprang towards them. "Leave her alone!"

In a second, Patrick Maunding pulled out his red Desiccator and trained it on Rob. "I wouldn't do anything rash, if I were you."

Redbeard and Flavia threw Clara down on a chair by the table.

Rob made another move towards her. Redbeard rounded on him and pounced. There was a horrible crack as he kicked Rob with his steel-capped boot. Rob staggered and fell to his knees.

"Rob!" cried Clara.

Before Rob could get up, Redbeard struck again, this time with a punch to the jaw. Rob's face contorted as the colour drained away.

Skullface left Zeno leaning against the lab wall. Together, he and Redbeard pulled Rob to his feet.

Rob's mouth was bleeding. He swore loudly, language Clara had never heard him use before. The guards marched him to a bench near the door and jerked him down between them. Clara watched

222

impotently as he tried to wriggle free, sweat beading his brow. He had no chance.

Flavia looked at her father. "What shall we do first? Tell them about the work they will do? I can't wait to see how they enjoy pounding the rocks all day."

Patrick Maunding brushed his lips with his forefinger. "All in due course, dear Flavia. First, there are still things we must find out from this Preedee girl. Then we'll have everything we need."

What was he calling her? Pretty? Ugh! Then Clara realised what he meant. She was Pre-D. Pre-Disaster. She had heard Jed use the term before.

She tried to stand up, and was instantly pushed down again by Flavia. They had now been joined by one of the other guards from the opposite end of the lab.

Clara felt sick, her palms clammy. The Grammets were clearly ruthless. How did she and Rob fit into their plans?

"I'm telling you nothing," she said, in as tough a voice as she could manage.

The beefy guard prodded her with his rifle. Rob moaned and thrashed, but Redbeard and Skullface restrained him with little effort.

"Whether or not you intend to cooperate is of no interest to us," brayed Maunding. "How d'you think we know about the time tunnel in the Siri shaft? How d'you think we know about you? Zeno and Jed were just falling over themselves to tell us all about it."

Clara glanced at Jed and over to Zeno, who was still leaning against the wall by the door. Neither seemed aware of what was going on.

"Flavia dear, fetch the Truth Juice, will you?" Patrick Maunding hauled himself onto the table, so that he sat right in front of Clara's face.

"With pleasure, Father." Flavia crossed to the shelf near the cockroach cage, picked up a transparent jug and dipped it into a bucket. There was a hiss as the bucket gave off black steam. The jug emerged full of foaming purple liquid.

Flavia brought the jug over to Clara. Maunding clicked his fingers and the Grammet guard grasped her arms from behind the chair.

Squashed between Redbeard and Skullface, Rob continued to struggle.

"Let her go!" he yelled, his voice cracking.

Clara's head was yanked backwards as someone tried to force open her lips. She clenched her teeth, but it was no good. Slowly, her jaws were prized apart, and the hot liquid trickled between them. She gagged and tried to spit it out, but couldn't prevent some of it going into her mouth. It smelled corrosive, and there was a ghastly sizzling as it burned her tongue.

Her throat felt as though it had been ripped open. She tried to scream, but only a grotesque gurgling came out, along with black steam.

Terror engulfed Clara. She couldn't survive this. If she did, she would be scarred for life.

All she could see was Flavia's face, her eyes glittering like black olives, lips curved in a cruel smile. The girl raised the jug and poured more liquid into Clara's mouth. Clara spluttered as it burned.

She swivelled her eyes as far as she could around the room. Rob was staring at her with his mouth open. She had never seen him look so pale and horrified.

The room around Clara grew blurry and vague. Colours ran into each other, as though she were in a watercolour painting. A cloud of darkness descended, like thousands of blackbirds filling the sky.

Flavia's face disappeared. Patrick Maunding hovered over her, staring into her petrified eyes.

"This is fantastic, isn't it, Flavia?" he said. "Like fate. I'm sure we could get all the information we need from that bunkerton Jed. But how nice to have the horse's mouth."

"Clara, don't taste it! Don't tell them anything." Rob's voice sounded faint and distant.

The guard had let go of her arms while he held her head in place, but Clara felt too weak to do more than grip the edge of the table. As Flavia stopped pouring the liquid, Clara's head fell forward. She blinked rapidly. As her vision cleared, she became aware of an appalling change.

Looking down at her hands, she could see her own bones.

Her hands were like a skeleton's, poking out of her sleeves. The image was shadowy, like an X-ray. Around the bones, arteries glowed purple amid nets of veins like fine green wool.

"Rob, what's happening to me?" Clara struggled to look at him.

Rob said nothing. The shock on his face spoke for him.

Maunding laughed. "Your friend is much too shy. He doesn't want to tell you that you're now translucent! Look at her skull, Flavia. You can see her fuzzy brain inside. Small, isn't it? Nice teeth, though. You can tell she looks after them."

Maunding took her skeleton hand and patted it. "See, dear people, we have not been completely idle out in the world. These clever chaps in here seem to think they're the only ones still achieving anything. However, we do have some things to show for our paltry existence."

Clara tried to pull away from Maunding's grip, but her arm had gone completely numb. This Truth Juice must be what they'd given Zeno and Jed, to prise their secrets from them. Whatever it took, she must stop herself telling them anything.

"Now then, dear Clara," said Maunding. "Are you ready? This is going to be delightful." He leaned towards her, a finger on his chin. "I would say the first thing we need to know is this. What has Zeno asked you to do? We know he has brought you here from the past. Why?"

Clara felt like someone had cracked open her skull and was mashing her brain into sludge. Her mouth fell open and a deep, guttural voice came out, not like her own clear tones at all.

"Change the past. Change the future."

She heard Rob's voice: "Fight against it. Don't tell them any more."

Maunding continued with his interrogation. "Change the past? How?"

"Tin mine ... In my family ... Full of Lux ... Luxulyanite."

"We know this, bunkerton. Go on." He leaned even closer so that his face was just centimetres from hers.

"Stop Maunding. Stop him getting the mine." Against her will, the words flowed out of her mouth.

"I thought as much!" Patrick Maunding thumped the table. "How?"

"Don't know. Try to ... find Gail."

There was a pause. Clara heard Flavia's voice. "What's that supposed to mean? Find Gail? Is that the Gail you told me about? Your mother's sister, who disappeared? The one who—"

"Give her some more," barked Maunding.

"No!" cried Rob.

Clara's head was yanked back again and she retched as more of the foul liquid slipped into her mouth. Steam hissed from between her lips. She knew she'd lose consciousness soon, and that when she did, she would never wake up. She blinked hard, tried to keep her vision clear.

Rob swore.

Flavia removed her bow from her shoulder and pulled an arrow from the quiver. "Don't try anything, boy. I could do with some target practice. I have a wonderful new toxin in this arrow."

"Wait!" Rob sounded desperate. "Surely you don't want to stop us changing the past. Surely you know what happened. You can't want it to happen. We can stop it, we can prevent the Disaster. That's the best thing for everyone, isn't it?"

Maunding laughed and shook his head. "See how stupid they are, Flavia." He tapped his teardrop boil, his voice icy. "We might have our crosses to bear, but our brains are far superior. Ask yourself this: what will the Disaster matter to someone who can control time? Someone who can live wherever and whenever he wishes? Exactly. I see you understand."

They don't care, thought Clara. The world means nothing to them. They care only about their own selfish place in it.

Fury welled inside her as she jerked her head forwards, swinging her hair across her face. Through the tangled strands she glimpsed Rob. His eyes were half closed, his mouth twisted.

She scanned the room, her face still partially hidden. Zeno leaned against the wall, his face pale and vacant. Jed worked silently at his computer. Clara's eye was drawn to a glow.

On a shelf near the door was a tray of spherical objects, the size and colour of apricots. They were vaguely familiar, resembling orange eyeballs. Clara had seen them before. Zeno had called them lightballs— he'd told Rob off for touching them. But what had he said about them? Clara couldn't remember.

Rob started as their eyes met. She flicked her gaze over to the shelf. Rob scrunched his face and mouthed a silent *what?* Clara tried again, her strength failing.

Helplessness washed over her. Even if the spheres might help, there was no way Rob could get to them. The guards still held him in their crushing grip, and the lightballs were a long way out of his reach.

"Can I fetch another jug, Father?" wheedled Flavia. "She hasn't had enough yet, I'm sure."

"Enough for now," said Maunding. "I fear you may have overdone it again, Flavia. You know what happens when they aren't strong enough. I haven't forgotten you killed one of them yesterday. Very clumsy of you, dear. Think how useful these two are going to be, with their young, fit Preedee bodies. Or do you want to be working at the rock face yourself?"

"It wasn't my fault, Father! How was I to know he was such a weakling? He would have been no use to us anyway." She dug Clara viciously in the back with the sharp end of her bow.

Clara gasped as stars danced in front of her eyes.

"Relax," Maunding said to Flavia. "Just think what a dobzha time we will have in their world."

Flavia laughed. "Will we have that money stuff you told me about?"

"Oh yes." Maunding stroked his chin. "We will have all the money we want. Stop worrying, dear child. With all the secrets of these bunkertons under our control, we will have everything."

Flavia pulled Clara's head up by the hair and sliced a black fingernail down her cheek. "I want my skin to be like hers."

"It will be. We'll have clean air on our faces, and all

the medicines of the Preedee days. But you are lovely to me as you are, Flavia, you have no need to fear."

Clara's eyes sought Rob's. He gazed back at her, trapped and helpless.

Then came a loud boom.

CHAPTER 21

AT the sound of the boom, everyone jumped.

"Father?" Flavia's voice was small and terrified.

The sound had come from the far wall. Halfway up, a yellow cone-shaped object was fizzing and crackling like faulty electrical wiring. It went silent for a few seconds, then a voice came out of it, so loud that Flavia covered her ears.

"Clara? Rob? Can you hear me?" Dribbles of slime spewed out, accompanying the words.

Although distorted, the voice sounded familiar. With a shock, Clara realised who was speaking.

It was Mick!

Clara's heart pounded. Another voice, high-pitched, bellowed out of the sphere: "Hayley here. Is anyone there? Oh, say something, please."

Clara felt too dazed to understand what was going on. She turned her head just in time to see Rob make full use of the distraction.

Wrenching his arms free of the guards' grasp, he leapt to his feet. Skullface and Redbeard tore after him, but Rob was too quick. He rushed to the shelf and grabbed one of the orange lightballs from its compartment on the tray.

Patrick Maunding launched himself from the table

and darted towards him. Rob held the ball as high as he could stretch. Then, with a grin, he dashed it to the ground.

An explosion of light turned everything orange. Clara was blinded by the brilliance. A smell like burning hair filled the laboratory, so intense she could scarcely breathe.

The papers on the shelves burst into flame. Clara fought desperately to keep her eyes open in the dazzling light. She blinked and squinted, but the pain was too intense. Against her will, her eyes jammed shut. Someone shook her.

"It's me," cried Rob. "Fight it!"

She felt a body close by. Forcing her eyelids open, she glimpsed a stick whipping through the air. There was a high-pitched squeal.

Rob pulled Clara to her feet, jabbing at the guards who rushed to stop them.

Maunding appeared behind Clara's shoulder. As she thrust her chair at him, Rob managed to stab him in the ribs with the stick. Maunding doubled over with a howl.

Rob grabbed Clara's arm and together they staggered towards the doorway. Shouting and screaming erupted all around them, punctuated by shrieks of agony.

"Call me a bunkerton, would you?" hissed someone.

"Father? Father, where are you?" whimpered Flavia.

A meaty fist swam into view and clamped Clara's free arm. She glimpsed a skull-like face, twisted in fury. She kicked out with every bit of strength she possessed, but her legs felt numb, and the hand held on.

Rob released her for a moment and gave an astonishing karate kick. There was a satisfying yell as the hand let go.

The fire from the papers had spread with alarming speed, and a roaring blaze now surged across the room.

Clara blinked frantically as heat and light scalded her eyes. It was impossible to see clearly, like looking through a burning orange fog. Rob whacked left and right with the stick, brandishing it like a sword as he dragged her towards the door.

They made it out of the lab. Light poured through the doorway into the cavern, but it wasn't so blinding now. Clara shrank back as a face reared up in front of her. Rob raised the stick, then gasped in relief.

"Jed!"

"Quick." Jed's eyes were round and frightened, but the glazed look had gone.

With Rob on one side and Jed on the other, Clara stumbled towards the tunnel leading out of the cavern. Her legs dragged, making only rigid, mechanical movements. When she tried to speak, gurgling noises issued from her throat.

An explosion sounded behind them.

Clara struggled to look back, her head like a stiff tap. Weak and groggy, she could barely make out what was happening.

Light still pulsed from the lab, but now the fire had escaped. There was a gaping hole in the lab's roof and flames licked at the collapsing walls. Wisps of burnt paper and plastic swirled all around. Heat rolled towards them as they battled to outstrip the fire.

"We can't save anyone," wheezed Jed. "We must get to the Siri shaft."

People ran in terror as the fire raged out of control. Clara saw a man screaming in agony as flames curled up his back. There was no time to think about what she was witnessing. She forced herself to concentrate on getting away.

"Hurry!" Jed gasped, not yet recovered from his ordeal.

"What's going on?" puffed Rob as they raced up the steps and ducked inside the tunnel. "I heard Mick's voice. I heard Hayley."

Jed spoke with an effort. "Your friends must have … used the trilloscope, back in your time. That cone is the receiver."

"How did you get free?"

"Wrist … thin … managed to slip out of the chain."

"Was that you I heard fighting?"

"Dad taught me."

Clara's feet were moving more quickly now, and she could almost support herself. She glanced down at her hand, to see if she was still see-through, but her vision was distorted and blurry.

"Great thinking with the lightball, Rob," breathed Jed. "The effect won't last long, but the fire might hold them back. We've got to get to the shaft before they catch us."

"T-trying," managed Clara. Her mouth was still burning and her lips felt like rolls of rubber.

"It's worse than I ever imagined," cried Jed. "They know about the tempoplas, how it works. They want to go back to your time. God only knows what would happen then."

Rob groaned, limping on his bad foot. "They can't, though, can they? You said you could bring us forward, but not send anyone back. And they'd need more Luxulyanite, wouldn't they?"

"There's enough for—"

A shot rang out from the direction of the cavern. The screams grew louder amid the roar and popping of the fire.

Up ahead, Clara made out the entrance to the Siri shaft, its keypad flickering in the green light.

Rob cursed. "There's someone there! I don't believe it. How could they get here before us?"

Jed's steps faltered. He peered into the gloom, then shrieked. "It's Dad. Dad! He must have managed to slip out before we escaped." His voice cracked. "Oh, well done, Dad."

Zeno stood with his hand raised, beckoning them urgently.

Clara was running almost unaided, staring about, straining to make sense of things.

As they reached Zeno, he slumped and put out a hand to steady himself. "Project Gigi," he gasped. "We've been trying … Now we must …"

Clara barely recognised him. His eyes were lifeless, their beetle glint gone.

"That Maunding man won't be able to do it, will

he?" repeated Rob. "He can't go back?"

"We'll destroy the shaft," said Jed. "Then he can't. They mustn't get control."

"Take this." Zeno pulled a small wooden box from the folds of his robe and tossed it towards Rob.

Rob caught the box and stuffed it into his jacket pocket. There was no time for questions.

Another gunshot sounded, much nearer this time. Clara felt something whip past her ear. A plume of powdered rock flew out of the wall beside her.

"They've found us," cried Jed. "They're in the tunnel."

Clara heard shouts and terrified voices. She smelled smoke on the air, felt the acrid dust burn her nostrils.

Jed sprang towards the control panel. "We must get you both away. Then I'll destroy it. I can do it … I can … I can …"

Further back in the tunnel, Patrick Maunding and Flavia were advancing towards them, guards at their side. Maunding had his Desiccator trained on them. Flavia's bow with its poisoned arrow was raised.

Jed's fingers darted over the keypad. The door to the Siri shaft slid open. Before Clara had a chance to move, Zeno grabbed her and thrust her inside. Rob leapt over the threshold and stood beside her on the platform.

With sudden strength, Zeno gave a tremendous roar and ran full pelt towards Maunding and Flavia.

A shot rang out. Zeno froze. He opened his mouth—but the cry died on his lips. With unbearable clarity, Clara watched his body shrink and darken as the life force drained away.

Zeno's clothes fell loose as his body collapsed in on itself. His arms withered and cracked. His legs evaporated into twigs, then snapped beneath him as what was left of his body sank to the ground. A pool of dark liquid gathered where he lay.

Clara screamed. She heard laughter. Patrick Maunding and his daughter were racing towards them.

"One down, three to go, Father," cried Flavia. "Oh, this is unbelievable fun!"

Jed didn't even turn to look. He pounded the keypad, trying to make the door shut. It was stuck.

"Go, go!" Jed kicked the wall in frustration. At last the door started to move.

Rob shoved his hand through the gap and seized Jed's arm. "Come with us. Don't stay."

Jed shook him off, continuing to work at the panel.

"It might work," urged Rob. "You've got nothing to lose!"

A cool female voice issued from the controls. "You have launched the self-destruct sequence. Z-X1877. Please confirm. You have launched the self-destruct—"

Flavia was just metres away, her arrow drawn. A grotesque smile twisted her lips. Patrick Maunding raised the Desiccator again. Both weapons aimed directly at Clara.

Flavia chuckled. "Boom boom! Bye bye."

The door was only half shut and moved unbearably slowly. Rob threw Clara behind him as a ball of fire smashed into the back of the shaft. Black smoke mingled with the stench of burnt metal. At the same time there was a whipping noise, followed by the sound of an arrow clattering to the floor.

"Murd." Flavia pulled another arrow from her quiver.

Clara heard rather than saw something whizz to one side of her, the side where Jed stood.

"Jed!" She gazed through the gap.

"You have launched the self-destruct sequence," intoned the passionless voice. "Z-X1877. Please confirm."

Jed hunched over the panel, his face contorted, his arm stretched above him as he slid to the floor.

An arrow protruded from his back, above a trickle of blood.

It was clear there was no help for him. With a yell of anger, Rob kicked the door twice, three times. It snapped shut. The lift began to rise.

Too weak to stand, Clara sank in misery to her knees. The floor lurched and swayed. Rob held onto her to stop her getting thrown against the moving walls.

The orange disc formed above them. It looked far away, like a small sun in a dark sky.

"There are thirty seconds remaining before self-destruct." Clara heard the voice, then a moan from Rob.

"We're not going to make it." He sounded almost resigned.

"We must!" She could hardly speak, and her words were slurring.

The disc grew in size, yet still seemed miles away. It

was almost as if they were in the outer reaches of space, instead of inside the shaft. There was rumbling as the platform trembled. Clara covered her ears. Her teeth chattered. Was this how it was going to end for them, crushed to death amid the stones of the shaft?

"There are twenty seconds remaining before self-destruct."

The disc was above them at last, close enough to touch. But something was wrong. It was fading, no longer a rich orange, but greenish brown, like slime from the depths of a pond.

"Get up!" Rob tried to hoist Clara to her feet, but her legs wouldn't work. "Mick and Hayley used the trilloscope," he shouted. "They might still be there. They'll help us. Reach!"

Clara shut her eyes and plunged her head into the tempoplas, stretching until her shoulders screamed. The platform reeled below her as she forced her way upwards. Unlike previously, the tempoplas didn't sting. It felt sticky and hard, like treacle.

"Ten seconds remaining before self-destruct."

She felt Rob shoving her from beneath. The tempoplas closed around her and sucked her in.

"PUSH!" Rob commanded. With her last morsel of strength, Clara reached out her hand …

… And felt it grabbed from the other side.

Her head burst through the disc. Gulping fresh air, she saw an amazing expanse of blue, then recognised Hayley's face. Her friend was leaning towards her from the ledge of the shaft, clinging for dear life onto her hand.

Mick seized her other hand.

"Get Rob," she tried to say. It came out like "Gerrov."

She felt herself being pulled from the treacly mass and hauled aside onto the ledge.

"Get Rob," she cried again, though there was no need. Mick and Hayley had already turned back to the disc. For one heart-stopping moment, there was no sign of him. Then a hand burst through. Mick tried to grab it, cursing as it slipped from his grip and disappeared.

"Rob!" screamed Clara.

The hand appeared again. This time, Mick managed to hang on. Rob was disgorged from the disc until he stood on top of it.

An ear-splitting boom sounded as the disc shook violently. A crack appeared across the centre. Around its edge, stones loosened and fell into the darkness beneath, taking clumps of dried tempoplas with them.

Rob was thrown from Mick's grasp and screamed as his leg vanished into the crack. Grimacing in terror, he was pulled downwards. He struggled furiously as he scrabbled his way back towards his friends. Kicking out with all his strength, he succeeded in hooking one foot over the ledge. Clara and Hayley tugged at his shoulders while Mick grabbed his legs.

The shaft glowed white. Sparks shot out in their hundreds, white, orange, lemon, scarlet.

"Three, two, one." The voice in the shaft spoke its final words.

As the disc split wide open, they dragged Rob clear.

He stared at them. "Run!" he yelled. "RUN!"

They bounded away from the hole, their feet catching in the fence as they threw themselves over.

Half running, half falling, they tumbled down the hill. Behind them, the remains of the disc spluttered and bubbled as sparks shot into the air.

Above the hole, the sparks merged and spun together to form a tornado. All around, loose debris was sucked into the vortex—twigs, leaves, even stones and plants. There was a tremendous whooshing, like wind through a thousand trees. Then a deafening crack as an explosion ripped the sky.

CHAPTER 22

HARDLY aware of her actions, Clara stumbled down the hill towards the woods. Mick was at her side, helping her along. She looked back at the explosion and stared in disbelief at the blue sky dyed black by billowing smoke.

The sharp scent of the woodland rushed into her lungs, making her giddy after the rank air of the cavern below. Its purity filled her eyes with tears.

Everything became blurry after that. She lay lifeless on the sofa in her caravan. Faces swam in and out, but she couldn't recognise them. Her mind felt woolly. Words formed but were all jumbled up, and when she tried to speak, nothing came out.

Patrick Maunding had accused Flavia of overdoing the Truth Juice and killing one of the cavern people. Had Clara had too much, too? The thought of dying now, before she'd managed to stop the nightmare, threw her into a fresh bout of despair.

Terrified of finding herself translucent again, she raised an arm in front of her face. Her hand felt like an iron bar, so heavy she could barely lift it. To her relief, it looked normal enough, although the skin was bluish and there was a tracery of violet lines.

She felt tired, bone tired, as if she were ninety years

old, not twelve. With a sigh, she leaned back and closed her eyes. Then there was nothing but silence.

***

When she awoke, she found herself in bed. Aunt Iris's kind green eyes were gazing down at her. She held a strange-smelling liquid to Clara's lips.

"Drink this."

Clara didn't ask any questions. She had known her aunt's herbs cure various ailments which had defeated normal medicines. Struggling to sit up, she coughed and retched as she tried to force the liquid down.

Iris made her drink a few more sips, then took her pulse. "Thank God. I thought I was going to have to get the ambulance for you."

"How—how's Granny?" croaked Clara, wincing at the pain and dryness in her throat.

"She's fine. She's back from hospital. You know Granny, strong as an ox." Iris chuckled suddenly. "I made her lunch today, one of those cup-a-soups she likes. Coles normally makes it in her favourite mug. She said she never realised you could have it in a bowl!"

Clara tried to smile. "Has she said anything more about the sale of the mine?"

"Huh. You think she'd give me any details? It's definitely happening, that's all I know. She wants it settled by Christmas."

"Oh Auntie, no." Clara grabbed her arm. "Talk to her, please! You don't realise how important it is."

Aunt Iris pulled back. "Clara, stop this. Sometimes you have to accept that you can't have things your own way. What on earth's going on? Your friends said you had food poisoning, but it's the weirdest food poisoning I've ever seen. And what were you doing up on the Downs? There's a load of smoke up there. Farmer Bolton said he saw fireworks … Well?"

Clara flopped back on the bed, too weak to argue.

"Where are they?" she asked, ignoring all her aunt's unanswerable questions.

"Your friends? I've sent them home." Iris didn't sound sympathetic now. She sounded angry and confused. "Why aren't you all in school, anyway? And where were you last night? Hayley told your dad and me that you were stopping with her. But my head's not buttoned up the back. She's a useless liar, your friend. I smelled a rat and phoned her mum. Her mum didn't know anything about it! What have you got to say for yourself, Clara Callenick?"

"Please don't ask me any more, Auntie. You wouldn't believe me if I told you."

Iris shook her head and sighed.

***

That evening, Clara's friends arrived to find her propped up in bed reading a book and drinking sweet tea. Most of the bed was taken up by Jess, who lay sprawled on her back, paws in the air.

Rob, Mick and Hayley piled round the bed, barely

fitting into the tiny room. Hayley had brought some shortbread biscuits, and Rob handed Clara a jelly bear. Jess's bootlace tail flapped in a frenzy as she wriggled the right way up, hoping for a treat or three.

Rob had already told Mick and Hayley about what had happened down in the cavern. Everyone was reeling from the news.

"How are you feeling now?" Hayley asked Clara, her eyes round with concern.

"I'm loads better, thanks. My throat still feels like it's been coated with tar. But apart from that, even those spots have gone. Yours have, too." She smiled round at them.

"Jed was right about that, thank goodness," said Hayley. "It was just a side effect of travelling through the tempoplas." Plonking herself on the edge of the bed, she examined Clara's face. "Your colour's better. You were pale as death. Oh, Clara, it must have been so frightening."

"I don't remember much about it." Clara passed around the biscuits. "It's all a horrible blur. I remember Flavia coming at me with a jug of purple liquid, but after that, not much, except … Rob was brilliant. Has he told you what he did? His fighting was amazing—with a bad leg and all. It was like in a film." Clara was convinced she owed her life to him. One day, she hoped to repay the favour.

Rob went bright red, and Clara felt her own cheeks glowing too.

"Thank God Mick and Hayley tried the trilloscope

again," he said, avoiding Clara's eye. "It was a great distraction. Gave me the chance to make a grab for those lightball-thingies. But for that …" He shrugged.

Clara smiled. Rob and Mick's brief squabble was clearly forgotten. Glancing out of the window, between the trees, she could see a trail of smoke in the distance, hanging in the air above the Siri shaft.

"Is the shaft really destroyed?" She turned back, unable to suppress a glimmer of hope, but the look on their faces left her in no doubt.

"It's totally collapsed," Rob said. "We sneaked back up there after your Auntie sent us home. The stone's all fallen in. It's just as well, I suppose. At least it means that brute of a Maunding and his disgusting daughter can't use it to get back here to our time."

Hayley shuddered. "Ugh, just imagine. I thought our own Maundings were bad enough."

Mick's voice was thin with disappointment. "We couldn't even find the trilloscope. We looked everywhere."

Tears gathered in Hayley's eyes, which were already red from crying. "Poor Zeno. I know he wasn't always that nice, but you could understand why. He had such a horrible life, and so much to do."

"And Jed," said Mick quietly.

"Yes, poor dear Jed." Hayley stood up, clasping her hands together.

"The last thing he did was destroy his entire life's work," said Clara.

"He had to." Rob spoke firmly, yet his eyes had a

246

faraway, velvety look.

"You're right," Clara agreed.

Those final moments in the cavern would haunt her forever. Zeno struck down, the life sucked out of his body. Jed, sinking to the ground, the arrow in his back. She felt sick and hollow at the thought.

Silence fell. How did you grieve for someone who wasn't yet born? Instinctively, Clara knew that Jed and Zeno would want them to put their deaths behind them and carry on.

She changed the subject. "So, what happened while we were away?"

"Haven't you heard?" asked Mick, his pale face unusually bright.

"Heard what?"

"Hayley's only gone and found Gail Maunding!"

"She has? Wow!"

Hayley and Mick told Clara all about their own adventure of the night before.

"It took hours for the fire brigade to get her out," said Hayley with relish.

"There were quite a few of us who went to watch," added Mick. "Hayley's mum came up, and Iris and your dad."

"How did Gail look?" asked Clara.

Hayley's eyes sparkled. "Dreadful. She wasn't speaking. She was blue, and her arm was sticking out at a funny angle. I think she's broken it. We haven't heard anything today, of course, because we've been skiving, but the last we saw of her, she was being air-lifted to the hospital. The helicopter landed on the Downs. It was all very dramatic."

Clara threw a biscuit to Jess, who caught it in her jaws and crunched daintily, pulling back her lips and showing sharp little teeth.

Hayley absent-mindedly brushed the crumbs from Clara's bed. "I felt terrible, lying to your Auntie, though. We didn't know when you'd be back, or even if you'd be back. It was so awful. But we knew there was nothing we could do. So we told Iris you were spending the night with me—"

"And we told Rob's dad that he was with me," finished Mick.

Clara decided against telling Hayley that her fib had been rumbled. "What was Gail doing up there anyway?"

"We've been asking ourselves the same thing," said Mick. "My guess is that Gail and her repulsive sister were up to no good on the Downs and she fell into the shaft."

A memory from the depths of Clara's mind finally came to the surface. "Of course! I'm such an idiot. They were spying on us! They heard us making plans, by the school shed. They must've followed us up to the Downs. That's how she fell in."

Hayley bristled. "Followed us? What a cheek."

Mick shook his head with impatience. "It's not important how she got there. The important thing is …"

Everyone looked at him.

"What?" asked Hayley.

Mick cleared his throat. "My theory is that Gail was—would have been—the skeleton in the Skeleton Shaft. In the future we've seen."

Hayley frowned. "But the necklace! Gail wasn't wearing it in the shaft. I only found her because I found Clara's necklace. And Jed told us the skeleton had a chain around its neck. Remember?"

"Yes," said Mick. "That's true. But I believe we have already started to change things. I think, because we've been to the future, we've already changed something back here. Somehow. In the future timeline, Gail kept the necklace, and became the skeleton in the shaft. In our timeline, the necklace dropped off before she fell in, and Hayley found her."

"Mick, you're doing my head in," said Rob. "I really wish you'd stop saying stuff like that."

Clara tried to think it through. "Mick's right. Don't you remember, Rob? In that prison cell, Zeno called the Skeleton Shaft the Sun Shaft. Things had changed. Not the things we've been trying to change, unfortunately. Not the sale of the mine. But some things, at least."

Rob gave an enormous sigh. "If you say so."

Clara shut her eyes. Then flicked them open again.

"Rob, didn't Zeno give you something down in the cavern? A little box?"

"Er ..." Rob frowned.

"He threw it at you as we were leaving."

"Oh yeah! I forgot all about it."

He grabbed his jacket, rummaged in the pocket and pulled out the box.

"Wow," said Hayley. "I never saw anything like that down there. I reckon they saved it from the Disaster. It must be really special."

Hayley had a point. Unlike most objects of the cavern, which were rough-shod and utilitarian, the little box was striking. It looked ancient, and was cleverly made, with dovetailed joints. It had been sanded down carefully, bringing out the grain of the pale wood. Tiny perforations speckled the top of it.

Clara's heart raced as Rob slid back the lid. Maybe it contained something that would help them in their fight against Maunding.

"Aaargh!" Rob dropped the box. It landed on its side and a blur of carapace and tiny legs shot across the room and vanished under Clara's chair.

Hayley shrieked and jumped onto Clara's bed. Jess yelped and jumped off.

Mick darted over to peer beneath the chair by the wardrobe.

"It's—I think it's those two cockroaches of Zeno's."

"Get them back in the box!" squeaked Hayley. "Now!" She fanned herself frantically with her hand.

"I'm trying," said Mick. "Don't just stand there. Give me a bit of biscuit or something."

Rob grinned as he handed Mick the packet. "They aren't birds, you know."

Ten minutes later, Felix and Fido were back inside their box.

Clara didn't know whether to laugh or cry. "Poor Zeno. He wanted to make sure they had a good home."

Hayley patted her arm. "We'll make sure they get one. They're not my favourite things in the world, but it was Zeno's last wish, after all."

Clara thought about Zeno's love for insects which were universally despised. After what she had witnessed in the future, she could understand his attachment to them. There was nothing else to love.

She looked down at the intricate little box in her hands. "They can stay with me. I've got an old fish tank somewhere. I'll tell Dad they're tropical ladybirds."

Mick took his glasses off and began cleaning the lenses. "Isn't it interesting that they survived?"

Rob raised his brows. "Interesting?"

"You do realise what it means?"

Mick's friends stared at him blankly.

"They came back," he explained. "They're living things—and they came back in time. Zeno didn't think it was possible. Felix and Fido are living proof. It can be done."

Last thing that night, Clara's dad poked his head around the bedroom door. "Feeling better now?"

Clara lifted her aching head. "Not so bad."

"You still look pale." Dad sat down awkwardly on the bed. He had just returned from the Flea and Feather, and Clara could smell beer on him.

"Sally popped in to see Iris, has she?" he asked.

Clara's sister Sally had promised, reluctantly, to keep her company while Dad was out, but Clara hadn't seen anything of her all evening.

"I expect so," she said carefully. Most likely Sally had

crept off somewhere to meet her new boyfriend, Jamie. But although Clara and her sister didn't get on, she would never give her away.

Tom was peering at her, an odd look of melancholy in his eyes.

"What's up, Dad? I'm okay, honest." Clara wondered briefly if this might be a good time to have another go at him about stopping the sale of the mine. But something else was on his mind.

"Oh, it was just—you looked so like your mother then."

"I did?"

Tom laughed wistfully. "You do, more and more, as you get older."

"No, really?" Clara smiled, unconvinced. Her mother had been very beautiful.

"Sometimes, I just wish …"

"Don't start that, Dad. There was nothing you could have done."

"I suppose. But if we'd caught it sooner … She said she had these pains, but she never wanted to bother the doctor. She was like that. I should've made her go."

He gazed past Clara towards the window, his face bathed in moonlight. For a fleeting moment, she was reminded of Zeno.

Clara's dad wanted every bit as much as Zeno to go back and change the past.

She patted her father's hand. "Go to bed, Dad. 'Tis late."

Tom left the room. Clara fell asleep in an instant.

CHAPTER 23

DESPITE how tired she was, Clara spent a bad night. At one point she woke up to find Sally in her room, shaking her.

"You were screaming," Sally wrinkled her nose, seeming almost concerned.

"It was just a nightmare. Sorry." Clara had dreamt Flavia's arrows were poking out of Rob's body, so many of them that he looked like a hedgehog.

In the morning she felt exhausted, as if she hadn't slept at all. Her neck was stiff and she ached all over. She dressed for school, where she had promised to meet her friends, but the thought of going seemed an unbearable effort, like climbing a mountain in flip-flops. For a split-second, she considered returning to bed with some toast and a cup of tea. None of this was her fault. Maybe she could just forget about it, let the future take care of itself, at least for a day.

But she knew she couldn't. The time portal was destroyed, Jed and Zeno dead. There was more reason than ever not to waste any time.

During the night, the temperature had plummeted below zero. Despite the forecast of snow, Clara cycled to school with Hayley. The crisp morning air would do her good, she decided.

They arrived to find school buzzing with the news of Gail Maunding's rescue. Hayley was greeted as a hero, and throughout the morning, classmates hugged her or patted her on the back, showering her with hearty congratulations. Everyone agreed Gail could never have survived a second night in that shaft.

Even the teachers wanted to know the grisly details, and Hayley's story helped them to overlook the fact that Hayley and her friends had all missed school the previous day and no one had rung to explain.

Clara felt delighted for her brave, modest friend, who was so easily overlooked. "Well, you did save Gail's life. Let's just hope she remembers it. I don't suppose she's around today?"

"Haven't seen her," said Hayley. "I expect she's still at the hospital. I must admit, I'm a tiny bit interested to hear what she'll say to me."

"She's bound to be grateful. Who wouldn't be? She might even agree to talk to her father for us." Linking arms with her friend, Clara felt a surge of hope. "Just think, Hayley—you might've done it. You might be the one to prevent that horrible future."

At break time Clara, Hayley and Mick were waiting in the school yard to meet Rob, when they spotted Miss Grundy tottering in their direction.

"Oh no, what does she want?" Clara shrank into the shadows behind a wall. "I'm not here. You haven't seen me, right? I can do without old pasty-face right now."

Hayley and Mick grinned.

"I hear you're quite the Heroine of the Hour,"

boomed Miss Grundy to Hayley as she came within range.

Hayley looked down at her feet. "Anyone could have done it, Miss. I was lucky, that's all."

Miss Grundy pursed her lips. "Well, it was very brave of you to go looking for Miss Maunding like that in the dark … Or stupid, perhaps, I'm not quite sure which."

Clara watched from the shadows. Miss Grundy looked especially unwell today, her complexion yellowish and her eyes pink. She's been at the booze again, thought Clara, remembering the bottle of gin Miss Grundy was reputed to keep in her store cupboard.

The teacher made to move off, then hesitated. "By the way, have you seen Clara Callenick? She's a friend of yours, I believe. I haven't had any homework from her in weeks. It's really not good enough."

Hayley fiddled with a butterfly slide in her hair. "No, Miss, um, I haven't seen her. I think she's got a tummy bug. No. No, it wasn't. Um, it was food poisoning." She pulled her lips to one side as her cheeks turned crimson.

From her hiding place, Clara cringed. Aunt Iris was right. Hayley was spectacularly useless at telling fibs.

"I need to talk to her, urgently," continued Miss Grundy, her whiskery nose quivering. "Can you get a message to her?"

"I'll try, Miss."

Miss Grundy shifted from foot to foot. She glanced at Mick, as though seeing him for the first time. "Well, if either of you see her, tell her I'm looking for her, will you?"

Hayley nodded. "Will do."

The teacher jumped nervously at the sight of Gideon Pasternak, who was bearing down on her, humming as he marched.

"Have you got a minute?" he asked, raising a hairy eyebrow.

Miss Grundy moved off with the head teacher. When they were out of sight, Clara emerged from the shadows.

"Phew, thanks. That woman. I wish she'd leave me alone."

"If she only knew," Mick said ruefully. "Homework is the least of our problems right now."

Gail Maunding surfaced on Friday, the last day of term. Despite coming within sight of Hayley several times, she made no effort whatsoever to come and talk to her. Hayley insisted it didn't matter, but Clara felt her anger mounting.

Just after lunch, they spotted both sisters amid a cluster of gabbling students. Gail was leaning against the playground wall, her left arm in a blue plaster-cast. As she spoke, she waved it about dramatically, clearly proud to show it off.

"I nearly died," they heard her saying as they came within earshot. "I was balanced on this tree-thing and it was coming out of the wall. I thought I was a goner. I don't remember much about it, though. I think I must have, like, fallen asleep. Though it was like being awake at the same time. Like being awake … and asleep. The hospital said I was hydrofoiled, but luckily it rained and

I drank some of that."

Hayley grinned as she whispered in Clara's ear. "I think she might mean dehydrated, don't you?"

Gail thrust her arm in Jean-Pierre Vaucluse's handsome face. "Here, sign my plaster-cast … You will be at our party tomorrow, won't you? It'll be the Event of the Year, I promise. Got your invitation? Ghouls and Vampires is the theme, don't forget."

Jean-Pierre smiled vacantly.

Clara gasped, her fists clenched. "She's not even going to thank you, Hayley! All she thinks about is that stupid party."

She took a step towards the group.

Hayley tugged at her sleeve. "Oh, Clara, don't."

Pulling away, Clara marched up to Gail Maunding and tapped her on the shoulder.

Gail's eyes widened. "What do you want? Keep away from me."

Donna stood at Gail's side, nose in the air. The rest of the students shrank back like a parting sea.

Clara swallowed. "That's Hayley over there, the one who saved your life, remember?"

"So?" said Gail with a shrug.

Clara was taken aback. She didn't know what she'd expected, but Gail's complete lack of gratitude floored her.

"So—so aren't you going to say thanks, at least?"

Gail shrugged again, a bored look on her face. Several seconds ticked by.

"That all you got to say?" asked Donna.

"No," said Clara, ploughing on. "You can give your father a message."

"Oh yeah?" Gail exchanged a smirk with Donna. The other students stood watching, some with rapt, shining faces, others looking tense and nervous.

Clara hesitated. Now that it came to it, she didn't have a clue what to say. It was Hayley who'd found Gail, not her. Why would Maunding want to do the Callenicks any favours?

"Tell your father we're on to him," she said uncertainly. "We know about the fire. His bullying doesn't scare us. We'll never sell. Tell him to leave us alone."

She could feel her cheeks glowing hot. She wasn't being truthful, and she didn't sound convincing, even to her own ears. Why should any of them listen?

Malice glinted in Donna's eyes. "And he's got a message for you, ain't he, Sis?"

"Sure," agreed Gail. "He said to thank you."

"Thank me? It's Hayley he should be thanking."

Gail sneered. "Daddy says he's got a grid-iron case against you and your poxy family. Leaving death-traps lying about like that."

Clara started to feel faint. "What d'you mean? You were trespassing. It was your own stupid fault you fell in the shaft."

"Doesn't matter. It's against the law. Daddy reckons he'll get your land dirt-cheap now. Maybe even for free."

The two sisters ambled off, laughing.

"What if she's right?" Clara trembled as Hayley tried to calm her. "What if Maunding won't even give us any money for the land? We'll be homeless. Apart from the awful future, we'll have a horrible present as well."

"No, Clara. That mustn't happen. Has Granny said anything more? How is she, by the way?"

"She's not bad, no thanks to that awful man. Dad and his friend have redecorated the kitchen, and she and Coles—and Pickles—are back in the cottage."

"Gosh, that was quick."

Clara smiled. "Yeah. Dad calls it Speed Decorating. You're right, Hayley. I mustn't panic. Maunding can't have spoken to Granny about paying less for the land. Even she would have mentioned something like that. Auntie Iris said her mind's on Christmas. Granny loves Christmas."

The school bell rang. They headed inside for the final lessons of the year.

***

On Saturday morning, Clara looked out of her bedroom window and saw a dazzling white woodland. There was a narrow strip of snow balanced on the washing line and Xavier the psychotic cockerel was chasing the hens through powdery flurries.

Clara sighed. If the snow continued, they would have a white Christmas. Normally she'd be thrilled, but the beauty was lost on her today. What sort of a Christmas was it going to be? She was about to lose her home, and it wouldn't only be disastrous for her. It would be a Disaster with a capital D—for the whole world.

She made herself a peanut butter sandwich and flopped onto the sofa. Desperate for inspiration, she gazed through the window at the snowy white skeletons of the bare trees and the fluffy fat shapes of the evergreens. At least term had ended and they were now on holiday. That would give them more time to think.

Mid-morning, she received a phone call from Hayley. "Clara, you'll never guess what I got in the post this morning."

"Just tell me." Clara wasn't in the mood for games.

"Go on, guess!" sang Hayley. "You'll never guess in a trillion years."

Clara sighed. "A gorilla?"

"Don't be silly. It wasn't a gorilla. No, it's an invitation to the Maundings' party tonight. It says my gracious presence is requested at Pardeaux Hall. Mind you," she said with a laugh, "it's got a strip of tape across the middle. I think it's been ripped in half, then stuck back together again."

"Not everyone is keen to have your gracious presence, then," said Clara.

"It's probably come from their mother. I can't imagine they'd invite me themselves. Of course I shan't go. I'd rather stick pins in my eyes."

Clara weighed it up. "You should go. Mick'll go with you. You might be able to find something out, something that could help."

"Thanks a lot. You're asking me to step into a nest

of adders."

Eventually, though, Hayley agreed to go.

Over the afternoon, the snow fell more heavily. Clara took an excited Jess for a run on the Downs, hoping the exercise would cheer her up. On her return, Rob dropped by to see if he and Clara could cook up a new scheme. Unfortunately, Clara's dad distracted him with his old Triumph Twenty-One motorbike, which was rusting away outside the caravan.

"I keep meaning to order the parts I need on the internet," said Tom.

"Cool," said Rob. "Shouldn't you cover it up, though, Mr Callenick? The snow's getting inside."

"Yeah, better had, I suppose."

"Cool motor, too," said Rob, eyeing up Tom's battered red Ford Capri Ghia.

Clara watched them through the bay windows. She was hiding it well, but she had never felt more miserable. It was wonderful to be back in her own time, to have escaped from that dreadful future. But despite all their efforts they were no nearer to stopping the sale of the mine. Her family wouldn't listen to her. What could she actually do? Her head was throbbing and there wasn't a single idea in it.

Tom came indoors, leaving Rob tinkering with the motorbike. He sat reading The Bugle, then leapt up and began pacing to and fro.

"Er, Clara. I've got something to ask you."

She looked up. "What is it, Dad?"

"Well … Your teacher, that is, Amelia Sitwell, your

Spanish teacher … Ahem, she's invited me to come over for Sunday lunch tomorrow. I met her through that boyfriend of Iris's—Archie. You don't mind, do you?"

Clara thought how good it was to see her father look happy for a change. "'Course not."

"That's grand. What should I take her, do you think? Flowers or chocolates?"

"She'd like either, wouldn't she?"

"Come on, Clara. Help me out here." He fished a pound coin out of his pocket. "Heads or tails?" He threw the coin up in the air.

"Heads for chocolates," suggested Clara.

Tom looked at the coin on the back of his hand. "Heads it is. 'Tis chocolates, then. Good, that's decided."

Rob came in and flopped onto the sofa beside Clara.

"Gotta nip out for a bit," said Tom. "That okay? Iris is around somewhere."

"You go ahead, Dad. But on second thoughts, I think you should get her flowers. She's too slim to eat many chocolates."

Tom grinned. "You're a good girl. Here!" He tossed her the pound coin. "Get yourself some chips."

Chips cost more than a pound, but Clara didn't like to say.

As Tom was racing out of the door, he popped his head back in. "Aw, by the way, some teacher was here looking for you earlier, while you were out. Can't recall her name now. Seemed a bit cross, something about homework. Stout woman, short grey hair?"

Rob and Clara looked at one another. "Miss Grundy," they both said at once.

"That's the one. See you later." Clara's dad scooted off.

"I feel like I'm being stalked," said Clara. "Can't she leave me alone? She must have got other things to worry about, besides me."

Rob shrugged. "Don't worry about old Grundy. We've got bigger fish to fry. Bigger fish than whales, in fact."

"Whales aren't fish," said Clara. "They're mammals."

Rob went across to the shelf where Clara had created a home for the two cockroaches. She had unearthed the old fish tank and filled it with margarine tubs, straw and cardboard tubes. The cockroaches had settled in nicely. Felix waved his antennae at Rob, as if greeting an old friend.

"What do your sister and dad make of them?" Rob asked.

Clara laughed. "I don't think they believed me when I told them they were tropical ladybirds. But we're getting quite fond of them, actually. They've got a lot of character when you get to know them. Fido's quite shy, but Felix is a real show-off. He comes when I call his name. Like to see?"

Rob rolled his eyes. "No, you're all right."

Clara couldn't shake off a jittery feeling, a sense of time running out. She glanced at the clock on the wall. It was five to six. Five fifty-five, a time which always made her uneasy nowadays. Outside, it was already dark.

"Wonder how Hayley and Mick are getting on?" she said. "The party will be starting soon."

"I'd love to see Mick's costume. I spoke to him earlier. He was very cagey about it. I don't think he'd thought of anything. Wonder what they'll be having to eat? I couldn't care less about being invited, but I reckon they'll have some fancy grub."

"You and your stomach! If you're hungry, why don't we stroll into Polgrehan? The walk will do us good. Get our brain cells ticking. What do you fancy? Pasty or chips? Better than caviar any day, I reckon."

Rob grinned. "Proper job."

Clara fetched her jacket and they set off through the snow.

CHAPTER 24

AT Pardeaux Hall, the air crackled with excitement.

The banqueting room looked splendid, aglow with silver tinsel and golden lamps. At one end shimmered an enormous Christmas tree covered in white lights and hand-painted bells. Beneath it lay a mountain of beautifully wrapped presents, which were to be handed out at the end of the evening.

A table ran the full length of the room, heaving with gourmet delights: sausages and pâtés, a fabulous cheeseboard, plates of venison and Serrano ham. There was a chocolate fountain, three tiers high, with rivers of creamy chocolate cascading down.

"This is going to be the best party ever," breathed Donna.

"I reckon Jean-Pierre's going to ask me out tonight," said Gail. "He's been so concerned about me since my terrible accident."

"Don't be stupid. It's me he wants."

Donna was completely fed up by now. For the past few days she'd done nothing but run around after Gail, attending to her every whim, while Gail draped her arm over the sofa cushion like a crown jewel.

Things would be different tonight. It was she, Donna, who would be the star of the show. Gazing in a

265

full-length mirror, she basked in self-admiration.

She couldn't deny it, she was the image of perfection, from her crimson silk gown right up to her golden curls, pinned up with diamante clips which twinkled like stars. The vampire princess effect was completed with the palest foundation and violet lipstick.

Gail, by contrast, wore a Count Dracula black robe and—rather unnecessarily, Donna thought—little vampire caps on her canine teeth. Her hair was slicked back with gel and she had a stripe of dark eye-liner beneath each eye.

Donna strode across the room to check on the food. Yes, the good stuff was all there, the chicken nuggets, the turkey twizzles and of course … Her eyes swept the table. No, it couldn't be!

She ran off screeching to find her mother.

Susan Maunding sat in the kitchen beside an empty sherry bottle, ticking items off the list for the adults' meal, which would be served in the dining room. "Crab soup. Salmon—smoked, hare—jugged. Krug, Rioja, Chardonnay. What is it, Donna?"

"The chips, Mother! Where are the chips?"

***

When Hayley and Mick arrived, the party was already warming up. They claimed a vantage point in the corridor, from where they could watch the various comings and goings. Their plan was to find a moment when all the Maundings were downstairs at once, so

266

they could risk a bit of snooping upstairs. But although Mrs Maunding was very much in evidence, flapping around like a shot duck, there was no sign of her husband.

"Some good costumes, aren't there?" said Hayley enviously as she gazed around at the collection of ghosts, wizards, gnomes, vampires and werewolves.

"Don't rub it in," came Mick's muffled voice from within his disguise. "I know I stick out like a sore thumb."

Mick was dressed in an old sheet with jagged eyeholes cut in it. It didn't quite cover his gangly frame, and someone had spilt cranberry juice down the front, so it looked like he had been stabbed.

Hayley's chin dimpled as she tried not to laugh. "Well, my outfit's not much better. We didn't have much time to think about it, did we?"

Hayley had come as a witch. She wore one of her mother's black dresses, which was much too long for her, together with a witch's hat like a traffic cone which kept falling over her eyes.

Mick sighed. "I so hate parties. The things we do to save the world, eh?"

"Well, I'm going to have some food. I love the look of that chocolate fountain."

"We're not here to enjoy ourselves," Mick pointed out, but Hayley had already vanished.

Gail soared past, her plaster-cast held aloft like an Olympic torch. "Huh, very original costume ... not," she cackled, eyeing Mick up and down.

267

In the banqueting room, Hayley found herself standing next to Jean-Pierre. He towered above her, dressed in a flowing black cloak lined with purple silk, lilac streaks glistening in his blonde hair. He speared a marshmallow and twisted it within the flowing chocolate, then took a bite, eyes half closed in pleasure.

"Hi. You're Hayley Shezell, aren't you?" he asked, glancing in her direction. "The one who found Gail in the mine? Can I get you a marshmallow?"

"Yes please." Hayley really wasn't used to all this attention.

He coated another marshmallow in gooey chocolate and handed it to her with a flourish. As his eyes lingered on hers, Hayley couldn't help noticing how lovely they were, shiny and purplish-blue, like the skin of a plum.

"Come on," he said. "I'd love to know. How did you do it? How did you find her?"

Over his shoulder, Hayley spotted Donna glowering at her. Hayley stuck out her tongue, then beamed at Jean-Pierre.

"Well, what happened was ..."

Eventually, Mick succeeded in prising Hayley away from Jean-Pierre. They slipped along the hallway to look inside the dining room, where the adults were shortly to be seated.

"Jean-Pierre says they're going to have a five-bird roast," Hayley told him. "Each bird is cooked inside the next biggest one, like those Russian dolls. The smallest one's a dinky quail."

"Yuk. Sounds horrible to me. Macabre."

They peeped inside the room.

"Wow!" Hayley cried.

The dining room was lit with hundreds of tiny white lights, reflecting off glittering chandeliers. In one corner, a tuxedoed musician played classical music at a grand piano. Logs blazed in the massive hearth. The long oak table was dominated by a huge ice sculpture, a reindeer with spectacular ice antlers.

The school governors, some of them quite ancient, were already seated. A handful of important-looking men and women wearing suits and dresses were dotted around the room, drinks in their hands.

Hayley pointed to a small group huddled by the fire. "Who are they, d'you think? Business colleagues? Or Maunding's staff? Scientists and that?"

"That woman with the frizzy hair and the make-up—she's the receptionist we met at MORE, the one who was so horrible."

"Really? Huh, does she call that a skirt? More like a scarf."

"And that's the chap who runs the Wolf and Lamb, the pub Maunding owns." Mick jabbed a sheet-covered finger in the direction of Monty Leghorn, who stood by the window, looking awkward, almost crushing the tiny glass in his hand.

The teachers from St Piran's were clustered together. Archie Rowlands, the science teacher, had come to the party without Clara's Aunt Iris. He stood deep in conversation with head teacher Gideon Pasternak, dapper as ever in his pinstripe suit, a triangle of cherry-red silk at his breast pocket.

"Ah yes," he boomed in Archie's ear, "But in my day, we had a thing called Discipline."

Amelia Sitwell was chatting to PE teacher Barry Fender, who hobbled about on crutches, having broken his ankle taking his karate class.

The doorbell clanged. One of the maids who had been hired for the evening ran to answer it. Hayley and Mick shrank back against the wall. They could hear a voice coming from the doorstep. It was a shaky, nervous voice, and sounded like an old lady's.

"Mr Maunding's expecting you, Mrs Callenick," said the maid. "You're to come with me."

The lady stepped over the threshold and shook the snow from her black coat and white hair. She followed the maid towards the stairs.

"Mick! Is that—?" Hayley nearly choked on her third chocolate marshmallow.

**

Clara and Rob left the caravan and set off down the lane towards the nearest shop, which was a mile away, in Polgrehan village. They had almost reached the road when Clara heard a car pull over and spotted someone emerging from a taxi.

Instantly alert, she peered into the darkness. As the figure crossed beneath a street lamp and turned into the lane, Clara made out the stocky frame of Miss Grundy. Behind her, on the road, the taxi slipped away.

"Oh no," hissed Clara. "Quick, Rob." Half feeling, half seeing their way, they climbed over the stone wall bordering the woods and dived behind an oak tree. They peeped around its trunk as Miss Grundy sauntered unsteadily in their direction.

"What's she doing here?" whispered Clara.

Rob shrugged. "I didn't realise teachers were as dedicated as this, did you?"

Miss Grundy was wearing a long black cloak—perhaps a school gown—and a triangular hat with a feather in it. Her face looked green in the shadows, and her small eyes were almost hidden within the folds of her eyelids.

As she reached the point in the lane where they were hiding, her footsteps slowed. She squinted into the woods.

"Clara?" she called. "Clara Callenick? Are you in there? Come out, girl. For pity's sake!"

A stick cracked beneath Rob's foot. Clara held her breath, tense and embarrassed. She didn't know whether to brazen it out and carry on pretending she wasn't there, or crawl out and face the consequences. Miss Grundy must have spotted them leaping over the wall, but she couldn't possibly be sure who it was, could she? It was too dark.

Miss Grundy let loose a stream of curses, then, muttering to herself, she turned and trudged back towards the road. Clara thought she heard something about what Miss Grundy had seen over the years and how infuriating it was to let people down.

Clara and Rob waited until she was well out of earshot before they emerged from behind the oak. They stepped over the stone wall and crunched through the snow. From their hiding place they'd been unable to see which direction their teacher had taken, but there was no sign of her now. They turned out of the lane and set off along the road to Polgrehan.

"Do you think she's going to Polgrehan too?" wondered Clara. "I don't want to catch up with her. The taxi left without her, and we walk a lot quicker than she does."

"I think she lives in St Piran's," said Rob. "Most likely she's gone back that way. Quite a long walk for her though."

"What on earth was she talking about, anyway? Something she'd seen over the years? What's that to do with homework? Or anything?"

Rob hesitated. "It didn't sound like 'seen over' to me, but I can't have heard what I thought I did ... that would be too ridiculous."

"No, me neither, but ..."

They walked on a few paces.

At the same moment, they clattered to a halt. They were silent for a few seconds, then both spoke at once.

"Oh my—" said Clara.

"She can't have," cried Rob.

"Zeno! She didn't say 'seen over'. She said Zeno! Quick, we've got to get after her."

CHAPTER 25

SKITTERING on the ice, Clara and Rob raced back the way they'd come. There was no sign of Miss Grundy. She had completely vanished.

"Perhaps she was going to Polgrehan, after all?" said Rob.

They turned around again.

Tears of frustration stung Clara's eyes. "It's useless! She could be anywhere."

Hampered by the ice, it took them over a quarter of an hour to get to Polgrehan's corner shop. They stopped outside and peered in all directions. The glow from the shop illuminated the swirling snowflakes.

"Maybe the pub?" suggested Rob. "Probably the best bet."

As he spoke, the shop door beeped and Miss Grundy stomped outside.

"Miss Grundy!" cried Clara.

Their teacher looked up and scowled. "Clara Callenick. As I live and breathe. What a merry dance you've been leading me."

Clara didn't know what to say. Nothing made sense any more. She opened and closed her mouth a few times, like a floundering mackerel. At last she found her voice. "Do you know? Do you know about Zeno and the future?"

"Are you here to help us?" asked Rob.

Ignoring them, Miss Grundy slapped her forehead and turned back to the shop. "Why, I've got a mind like a colander." She patted her pockets. "Damn, has anyone got a couple of pounds? I've only got a twenty pound note. I don't want to break into that."

Clara and Rob looked at one another. Reluctantly, Clara fished in her pocket and drew out the pound coin her dad had given her, along with one she already had. She handed the money over, and Miss Grundy stalked back inside the shop.

"What's going on?" asked Rob. "Do you think Miss Grundy's actually in touch with the future? Do you think she knows about the Siri shaft?"

Clara stamped in the snow. "D'you think that's why she's been chasing me all this time? It's not just that she hates me?"

The shop door beeped again and Miss Grundy stepped out. She tottered a few paces and grabbed hold of a lamp post to stop herself falling.

"Ice or booze, d'you reckon?" muttered Rob in Clara's ear. Clara felt so anxious, she didn't even giggle.

Miss Grundy's face wore a pained expression. "I don't know why you're both looking at me like that. I can't tell you much. I didn't really intend for you to find out about me at all." She looked longingly in the direction of the Flea and Feather. "In fact, I'm still not sure … If you knew how I've agonised over this …

Interfere, don't interfere … So hard to know what's for the best."

She edged away from them.

"Now wait a minute," demanded Rob. "You can't just leave it at that. We deserve an explanation after all we've been through."

Clara stepped towards her. "Please, Miss Grundy. Tell us what's going on."

Miss Grundy gave an elaborate huff. "You know the rules. The less you know the better. You should realise by now how complicated time travel is. Everything you do, everything you say, can have the most dramatic consequences. The stability of time, et cetera."

"Yes, but—" protested Clara.

Mick was always saying stuff like this. He'd even said it might be a bad thing Hayley had rescued Gail Maunding from the mine shaft. Clara had to agree that she didn't deserve it.

"Why have you been chasing Clara all this time, if you don't intend to help?" asked Rob.

Miss Grundy took off her triangular hat and ran a hand across her moleskin head. She replaced the hat, pulled a tissue from her gown pocket and gave her nose a hearty blow.

"We already know more than we should," said Clara. "A bit more won't hurt, surely."

Miss Grundy sighed. "I've run it through my head a thousand times. I'm sick of it. Nevertheless, I suppose you're right. Come on, I'll walk you home to your caravan, Clara."

They made their way back, Miss Grundy's stubby legs struggling to keep up. Clara felt desperate for answers, but Miss Grundy refused to speak until their excitement had died down.

"Remember Project Gigi?" she began at last.

"You know about Project Gigi?" asked Rob, his eyes wide with disbelief.

"Hmm, you could say that."

"Zeno mentioned it," said Clara, "and Jed was involved in it too, wasn't he?"

Miss Grundy nodded. "Correct."

Clara tried to remember everything she could about Project Gigi. It seemed a long time ago now. She had to remind herself that it hadn't actually happened yet.

"Were—are—you in touch with Zeno and Jed?" asked Clara. "Do you know about them?"

Miss Grundy came to a halt and leaned against another lamp post. Snowflakes dotted her black gown. She looked at Clara.

"I not only know about them. I was there. I am Project Gigi!"

Miss Grundy let this sink in for a while as they crunched along the snowy road.

"I was the one chosen," she added, puffing out her chest.

Clara realised she was shaking. What on earth was the woman talking about?

Rob cleared his throat. "And Project Gigi was …?"

"Why, the next stage, of course! Zeno had worked out how to bring you forward—and since you belong to this time, you were able to get back. We were pleased about that."

"We weren't unhappy about it ourselves," muttered Rob.

"Well, Project Gigi was the next step. To send one of us back. It's harder, you see. It upsets the equilibrium more."

She slid on a patch of ice and started to fall. Rob reached out and grabbed her. She patted her chest while Clara and Rob waited impatiently.

At last they set off again, Rob holding onto Miss Grundy's arm. Clara couldn't believe what she was hearing. All this time she had been avoiding the one person who might have been able to help.

"But Project Gigi didn't work," Rob said. "Zeno said they'd nearly cracked it … but not quite."

"That's right." Miss Grundy shook off Rob's arm and attempted to walk by herself. "Goodness, this air's cold."

"Tell us what happened!" Clara had to force herself not to shout.

Miss Grundy gazed at the sky, snowflakes speckling her nose. "Be patient, girl. I'm getting to it … So, yes, Project Gigi. I was the experiment. But as you rightly said, Project Gigi didn't work. We tried again and again. Then there was a breakthrough."

Rob leaned in close to Clara. "They said something about that in the lab," he whispered. "Remember?"

"We tried again, as soon as we could," went on Miss Grundy. "This time, the experiment worked. But it wasn't one hundred per cent successful. Life's not like that. Something went wrong. Maybe it was just the slip of a finger on the keypad. Zeno was getting on a bit, after all. I doubt Jed and Zeno even realised the experiment had worked. You see, I did get back here—but ten years too soon."

Clara struggled to take this in.

"You mean ... You've been here for ten years?"

Miss Grundy nodded, holding a hand to her throat, stroking her chin. "Ten—long—years. Yes indeedy. And all I had was Clara's name and the approximate date when all this would happen. At first I was delighted. I thought it would give me all the more time to stop Derek Maunding getting hold of your mine. But, as I soon discovered, that was easier said than done."

Miss Grundy stopped. Rob held onto her arm once more, and they set off in tandem.

"Did you try?" he asked her.

"Well, I ... Of course."

Clara's footsteps had slowed almost to a halt, she was so engrossed in Miss Grundy's words. Things began to fall into place. She remembered the scientist in the lab, the one dressed in green, who looked like an apple. The one who'd first brought Jed the trilloscope.

"I remember you!" she cried. "But it couldn't have been you. You look so ..." She stopped mid-sentence. She couldn't possibly tell Miss Grundy how much different she looked from the vivacious, curly-haired scientist in the cavern.

Miss Grundy hesitated. "Ye-es? Look so what? It

was a long time ago, you know. For me, anyway."

A group of teenage revellers passed them in the opposite direction, singing and swaying as they walked. No one spoke until they were out of earshot.

"So … So what have you been doing all this time?" Clara asked, her mind spinning. Could her dreary, monotonous teacher really be a visitor from the future?

Miss Grundy swallowed. "Well, once I got here, I couldn't communicate with Zeno. I had no life here, remember, no money. In due course I managed to establish an identity. I travelled around Europe for a while, picking grapes, oranges, that kind of thing. More fun than teaching, let me tell you."

Rob's voice was harsh. "Yes, all right. But what about the mine? You had ten years to think about it. Didn't you do anything to try to change things?"

"I said I did, didn't I?" snapped Miss Grundy. "I went to see your Granny, Clara, a year or so ago. I tried to warn her that she mustn't sell the mine."

"You did?" Flabbergasted, Clara cast her mind back. "Granny never said anything."

But then, why would she mention it? She hated strangers. Clara could already guess what her reaction would have been.

"I did," said Miss Grundy. "Your delightful grandmother sent me away with a proverbial flea in my ear. I believe she thought it was a scam, or that I was campaigning for a political party. I mean, I admit I've embraced the pleasures of your time with rather a lot of gusto—your wonderful food, your exquisite drinks. But

279

I ask you! Do I look like a politician? Anyhow, she was having none of it."

"Okay, so what else?" demanded Rob.

She gave him a sour look. "Next, I thought about buying the mine myself. I soon discovered I couldn't raise anywhere near enough money, even if I could persuade Granny to sell. Teachers don't get paid a hill of beans, you know."

A car slithered by, its snowy tracks blue in the moonlight. They had almost reached Callenick mine. Clara shivered, her fingers numb in her thin jacket.

"What about Maunding?" asked Rob. "Did you go to see him?"

"Well … I thought of tackling him directly, but decided against it. After all, history had shown me the kind of man he was. I couldn't imagine he would listen to me. I was convinced I would only alert him to my intentions."

"So what was your plan, then?" asked Rob, clearly unimpressed.

Miss Grundy paused. "About six years ago, I managed to get a job at your school, teaching history. I thought that was the best way to get to meet Clara and follow what was going on."

Clara peered at her, eyes narrowed. "You knew I'd go to St Piran's?"

"Not for sure. I thought it was a fair bet, since it's the nearest school to your home."

They trudged along in silence.

"But if all that's true," said Rob eventually, "why

have you been giving Clara such a hard time?"

"I would hardly say that," huffed Miss Grundy. "Though I must admit, I find it rather galling that such an important mission rests with a slip of a girl who can't even hand her homework in on time."

"But—" said Clara.

Miss Grundy raised a hand. "I was harsh, I admit. I thought you needed toughening up, Clara. But my intention was always to help, in whatever way I could."

"Why didn't you tell me all this before? I wouldn't have kept running away from you."

"It's easy to say that now, young lady. Why do you think I've been hounding you these past days? You've been like a fox gone to earth. There was no point in acting too soon. Can you honestly say you would have listened?"

"So instead, you left things rather too late," said Rob.

Miss Grundy spoke ruefully. "You're right. I haven't handled it at all well. I can see that. Try to imagine how things have been for me. Frankly, your world is incomprehensible. People have so much, yet appreciate so little. I found things … hard."

Rob shook his head. "You turned to drink, you mean?"

"Rob!" said Clara.

Miss Grundy took his comment in her stride. "There's another thing, too. For the past ten years, I haven't known if things would turn out the same way. The simple act of my coming here—where I don't belong—might have changed everything. At first, I didn't know if I'd be able to interact with people, if they'd even see me. Going back might have been a whole different can of worms from bringing you lot forward. People could see me, of course. Shame in a way. I rather fancied being invisible."

At that moment, Clara's phone buzzed. She stopped in surprise. A few steps further and there would have been no reception. She fished it out of her pocket and looked at the illuminated screen.

"It's Hayley." Clara put the phone to her ear and listened for a moment. Her legs almost gave way.

"We'll be there as soon as we can," she said. "Do what you can to put them off. You're right, there can only be one reason why she's there."

She rang off and turned to Rob and Miss Grundy.

"We've got to get to Pardeaux Hall. It's Granny. She's gone to Maunding's. She's signing the mine away."

CHAPTER 26

CLARA, Rob and Miss Grundy stared at one another.

"I'll call a taxi," said Miss Grundy, pulling out her phone.

"No," said Clara. "It could be ages. And there's no bus due either. Maybe Auntie Iris can drive us."

"What, in this snow?" said Miss Grundy as they turned into Clara's lane. "You must be mad."

The caravans stood in darkness. There was no sign of Iris or her Mini Clubman, and Tom wasn't back yet from wherever he'd gone—possibly they'd gone out together. Clara stamped her feet in frustration. There was nothing else for it. She ran inside her caravan and flicked a set of keys off the hook.

"We'll have to take Dad's car. Get it started while I scribble him a note."

The future of the world might be at stake, but Clara dreaded to think what her father would say if his car disappeared with no explanation. She held the keys out to Miss Grundy. Miss Grundy shuddered and veered away.

"I haven't driven a car in years. I don't really do driving."

"It's insured," said Clara. "Dad's been teaching Sally."

"You've got to," cried Rob. "Unless you prefer me to drive. I worked for a bit at Farmer Bolton's in the summer—he taught me how to drive his tractor. It can't be that much different."

Miss Grundy frowned at him. "You're not old enough."

"So what d'you suggest?" asked Rob in an exasperated tone.

Miss Grundy sighed. "Okay, okay, I'll do it." She took the keys from Clara's outstretched hand and headed towards the car.

Clara scrawled a note and put it by the kettle. They got inside the old Capri Ghia, Clara in the back seat, Rob in the front next to Miss Grundy. Miss Grundy turned the key and the car sprang to life. She gripped the steering wheel, a look of fierce concentration on her face.

"Now then … Hmm." She fiddled with the gear stick, hummed and hawed some more, then pressed the accelerator.

The car jumped backward. There was a sickening crunch as it crashed into the dustbins. The engine died with a rattle.

Clara blanched. "Dad's going to kill me."

"She put it in reverse! Oh, let me do it." Rob jumped out of the car, stormed around to the driver's side and heaved Miss Grundy out. Cursing, she stomped past the bonnet and got into the passenger seat.

The car pulled away smoothly as Rob manoeuvred it through the snow. They reached the end of the lane and turned in the direction of Pardeaux Hall.

Clara tried to ask more questions, but Miss Grundy remained tight-lipped. She stared grimly ahead, her teeth clenched, her hands locked together.

"Let's just get there, shall we?" she said. "Or all this effort will have been in vain."

Under Rob's careful handling, the old Capri negotiated the snow without a single skid. Rob turned into the driveway at Pardeaux Hall and sailed past the vehicles parked along it. Clara shut her eyes as he inched between two frighteningly expensive-looking cars, stopping as close to the front door as he could get.

Clara and Rob jumped out, followed slowly by Miss Grundy on wobbly-looking legs.

"Thank the Lord we didn't bump into the police," she said. "You'll be the death of me, you children."

Clara and Rob raced up the steps. Miss Grundy hesitated and turned towards the lawns.

"You don't mind if I wait outside? I feel rather faint. I'll be here if you need me."

Rob marched back and grabbed her arm. "Oh, no you don't. You're coming with us."

Trembling all over, Clara tried the door handle. It was locked. She pressed the doorbell three or four times.

"Come on, come on," she hissed through gritted teeth.

At last, the door was opened by a girl dressed in a black and white maid's uniform.

"Yes?" She eyed them up and down suspiciously.

As Clara went to push past, the girl put up her hand. "Invitations, please."

"I've got to see Maunding," demanded Clara. "It's urgent. Where is he?"

The girl bristled. "Mr Maunding is busy. What d'you want?"

At that moment, Mick and Hayley came running down the stairs behind her. Mick was tripping over his white sheet, and Hayley's witch's hat bobbled about furiously. Hayley ran towards them.

"Come quickly! They're up here."

She turned back the way she'd come.

Thrusting the maid aside, Clara dashed after her.

Rob gave a confident smile as he stepped inside the hall.

"Mr Maunding's waiting for her," he told the maid. "It's, um, it's a surprise for his daughter."

Miss Grundy grinned ingratiatingly, slipping in after him.

Clara took the stairs three at a time, followed by Rob. Miss Grundy laboured up behind them, clinging to the statues of lions and tigers sprouting from the banister.

"You've got to stop her," breathed Hayley as they reached the top of the second flight. "She's in a room along here. We heard them talking. There's another chap in there, too. We think it's Maunding's lawyer."

They halted outside the furthest room. Clara signalled everyone to be quiet. Putting her ear to the door, she heard a faint, querulous voice coming from inside.

"You didn't say anything about lowering the price, Mr Maunding. That's not fair play."

"It's Granny all right," confirmed Clara, heart pounding.

Derek Maunding's tones were silky. "Ah, but what's fair about my darling Gail falling into your death-trap of a mine shaft? Hmmm? A death-trap, Mrs Callenick."

"The daft mare shouldn't have been there. 'Tis my land. What was she doing?"

"Well, well, Mrs Callenick. Just sign the papers as agreed, and we'll say no more about it. I can't say fairer than that, can I?"

"Hmmph. Half the price 'tis worth? I don't call that fair myself."

A different voice sounded, that of the second man. "It's still a considerable sum. Very generous, I'd say, in the circumstances ... There you are, Mrs Callenick. You just need to sign here ... and here."

There was a pause.

"All right, then," said Granny with a sigh. "I suppose I've no choice."

Clara twisted the handle and burst into the room.

Three amazed faces turned towards her.

Maunding was the first to recover.

"Don't they have bad manners these days, the children?" He glared at Clara. "Who are you? What do you want? Whatever it is, I'm sure my wife can sort it out."

Clara was taken aback. He didn't even recognise her. But then, she'd never actually met him until this moment. She'd only glimpsed him from a distance.

He was standing behind his desk at the window, framed by the snowflakes whirling outside. His curling streak of grey hair, the unasked question, shot into the air, refusing to lie flat. Clara's interruption had barely rattled him. Nothing could diminish the sense of triumph blazing from his cold, arrogant eyes.

The shifty-eyed lawyer lurked at Granny's shoulder. Granny sat at the desk, papers spread before her. Her gnarled, arthritic hand was poised above them, holding a silver pen.

She peered at Clara in astonishment. "My dear life and days! Is that you, Clara? What're you doing here?"

Maunding started.

"Aha! So this is the famous Clara Callenick." He crossed his arms, a smug look spreading over his face. "How delightful. You're just in time to witness my acquisition of Callenick mine, including a cottage, the ruin of an engine house, two caravans and all the surrounding acres. Your home, I understand. Or should I say, your former home?"

"No!" Clara turned to Granny. "You haven't, have you? Please don't say you've signed."

Granny's hand hovered over the document. Clara felt close to fainting. But she saw a blank space beneath her grandmother's hand. There was no signature yet.

"Don't do it, Gran," she cried. "Don't sell our mine."

Maunding grimaced. "Get out of here."

Clara ran across the study and threw her arms around her grandmother. "The future of the world depends upon it. We've seen it, Gran. I can't explain it, but we have."

Granny stiffened beneath Clara's embrace. "What're you going on about, girl? Have you been eating too many o' they E numbers?"

"Oh, Gran, why won't you listen? You must not sell our mine."

Pulling away, Granny shook her head. "'Tis true, I'd hoped for a lot more money. What he's offering me now isn't going to cover all I planned. But I've no choice, my bird."

"You have. There's always a choice."

Clara's gaze fell on the little chunk of Luxulyanite on Maunding's desk. With a swift motion, she swiped it and held it up.

Maunding gasped.

The stone felt cool in her hot hand. As it caught the light, mesmerising shafts of turquoise, sapphire and violet rotated about the room.

"You see this, Gran? See the crystals in it? They're Time Crystals. He needs them for his experiments. But it's going to go wrong, horribly wrong."

"Put that down," barked Maunding.

Granny Callenick frowned. "That's enough, Clara. You're being a nuisance, now. 'Tis only a bit of land, after all. Not the end of the world."

"NO!" A cry of rage erupted from Clara, so loud that her friends shrank into the doorway. She slammed the rock onto the desk. Maunding grabbed it and replaced it on its silver plinth. He stared at the small mark left behind on the wood.

His voice was a savage whisper. "What an ignorant hooligan you are."

With a sinister smile, the lawyer strode over to Clara, seized her and pushed her towards the door.

"Leave her alone," yelled Rob.

Clara shook the man off and ran from the room. Rob fled after her.

"Where's Miss Grundy?" she cried. "I've got to find her. She's a teacher. They'll listen to her."

"She's just here." Rob peered around. "Oh! Well she was, a minute ago."

Clara rushed past him, darted down one flight of stairs and raced along the hall.

Miss Grundy was halfway down the lower staircase, heading away from Clara.

"Miss Grundy, you've got to help! Help me convince them. Even Maunding won't want to do it, surely, not when he understands."

Miss Grundy stopped, but kept her back to Clara.

"You must tell them," pleaded Clara. "Please! Tell them it's true what I say. They'll believe you."

Miss Grundy held onto one of the carved lion heads lining the banister. "I don't know …"

She turned and held Clara's gaze for a split second. Her eyes looked watery, the make-up smudged. She looked almost as if she'd been crying.

"You can't just go," said Clara, on the verge of tears herself.

As the teacher released the statue and edged away,

Clara noticed how furtive her movements were.

"What's that in your hand?" Clara narrowed her eyes.

"Nothing," Miss Grundy said quickly, pulling her arm inside her cloak. She pressed her lips together and gave Clara a bold stare.

Clara glared back, searching the teacher's face. *I wonder* ... Once again, she recalled what Zeno had said about her being sensitive. She could feel it now: an inexplicable sense of knowing.

"You're hiding something."

Clara made a grab for her hand, and the two of them did a strange little dance.

At last Miss Grundy gave a muted laugh and held up a slip of pink paper.

"All right, all right. It's nothing ... just a lottery ticket. Satisfied?"

"A lottery ticket?" Clara felt the hair prickling on the back of her neck. There was something else in Miss Grundy's eyes, something she was trying her hardest to conceal.

"I do it every week," she said. "You've got to be in it to win it." She bared yellow teeth.

Clara thought quickly. "You just bought that, in the shop?"

"That's right. Now, if you'll excuse me ..." She took a step down the stairs.

"Then it's my ticket," said Clara.

"What drivel are you talking, child?"

"It's mine. It was my money you bought it with, wasn't it? So it's my ticket."

291

Miss Grundy fluttered her eyelids. "Yours? No, I don't think so."

"Give it to me." Clara stretched out her palm.

Miss Grundy gave a sour laugh. "Surely you don't think there's anything special about it? Yes, I remember you in the lab, I heard about your little plan. But Zeno told you—there was no way. This is just an ordinary ticket, bunkerton. No more chance of winning than the other millions sold."

Miss Grundy was probably right. Clara's hand wavered.

"You've nothing to lose, then," she said firmly. "Come on Miss Grundy. Give me my ticket."

Beneath the triangular hat, Miss Grundy's pale eyes bored into Clara's. Finally, she gave a long sigh.

"All right, Missy. But I'm telling you, it's no different from any other. It will lose just the same."

Clara grabbed the ticket and tugged it from her teacher's grasp. She sprinted back along the hallway towards Derek Maunding's study.

Only a minute or two had elapsed, but Clara knew it might already be too late. Inside the study, her friends were huddled around Granny Callenick, jabbering inanely, doing their level best to distract her from the documents.

"That's enough," Maunding shouted. "GET OUT."

Donna followed Clara into the room. "What's wrong, Daddy? What's she doing here?"

Clara pushed through to her grandmother's side. "Gran, I've got a lottery ticket. Remember what you

292

said? You said, if I had the money I could buy the mine instead. Instead of him."

She glowered at Maunding.

Granny shook her head.

"Hmm, fat chance 'o that. Reckon I got more chance o' winning one o' they daft dancing programmes."

Her hand, clutching the silver pen, was still hunched over the papers.

"Why not give it a chance?" said Rob. "The lottery draw will be on the telly any minute."

"Huh?" Hayley exchanged a glance with Mick.

Mick shrugged, clearly equally confused by the sudden appearance of a ticket.

"Come downstairs with us, Mrs Callenick," Rob coaxed. "You did make a promise, after all."

Derek Maunding smiled and shook his head.

"This is ridiculous, Mrs Callenick. Surely you're not going to listen to these misguided children? I must congratulate your granddaughter on her overactive imagination, although her behaviour leaves considerable room for improvement."

Granny Callenick licked her lips. Then she harrumphed and heaved herself to her feet.

"All right, Clara. We'll see what happens with your ticket. But if it loses—as it will—that's enough of this nonsense. You'll let me see to my own business."

Clara had no choice but to agree. They all trooped out of the study.

CHAPTER 27

CLARA, Rob, Mick and Hayley hurtled downstairs and along the hallway.

"Go in the games room," said Clara. "There's a TV in there, I saw it the other day."

Hayley bumped into Gideon Pasternak, who was heading for the dining room.

"Sorry, Mr Parsnip," she trilled as she ran on by.

Donna plummeted down in their wake. At the bottom of the stairs, she threw herself around the corner and collided with a young waiter carrying a drinks tray. Several crystal glasses crashed to the floor.

In the games room, Mick wrestled with his cranberry-stained sheet and tore it off over his head. He grabbed the remote control, turned on the TV and searched frantically for the correct channel. "It's got to be here somewhere. We haven't missed it, have we?"

At last he found it. The programme had already begun. A suave-looking presenter in a red sequinned coat was whipping his studio audience into a frenzy.

Clara sat sandwiched between Hayley and Mick on the peach leather sofa. Rob went to close the door against the noise of the party.

Clara had hoped they might watch the programme quietly by themselves. But just as Rob got to the door,

Jean-Pierre Vaucluse poked his head inside.

"What's going on, dude?" he asked.

"Er, nothing," said Rob. "Nothing at all."

Inferring the exact opposite, Jean-Pierre turned and shouted into the hallway. "Come on, everyone. There's a mega-telly in here and stuff." He sauntered towards the trio on the sofa. "Someone got a lottery ticket? Cool."

To Clara's alarm, a group of nine or ten trooped in behind him. Donna and Gail brought up the rear, their eyes like icicles.

"Oi, what're you doing with my telly?" snapped Gail as she marched across the room.

"Hey, chill," said Jean-Pierre. "Hayley's friend's got a lottery ticket. I love the lottery, don't you?"

Gail rolled her lips in a constipated smile.

"Quiet," yelled Rob from his position on the sofa's armrest. "It's on."

Silence fell. Clara held the ticket in clammy hands, her heart galloping like a racehorse. Was it just an ordinary ticket? Every shred of common sense she possessed told her it must be. Zeno had been certain he couldn't provide the numbers. In a few moments, she would look a prize idiot, that was all. To make things worse, Donna and Gail were here to witness her failure. She felt sick to think how they would gloat when their father took possession of the mine. Not to mention how disastrous it would be for the future of the planet.

She looked round for Granny and spotted her jammed in by the window, a slice of chocolate cake in her hand. Several more adults had entered the room by now—including Clara's father and Aunt Iris.

"Oh, no," said Clara.

Tom strode towards her, waving her scribbled note, his face thunderous.

"Clara, I can't believe this. You stole my car!"

Clara cringed and opened her mouth, but nothing came out. Hayley hid her face in Clara's shoulder.

"Well?" demanded Tom. "I've seen it outside. There's a dent in the back."

"Dad, I'll explain later. Please."

Tom searched her face, then muttered something under his breath.

"Later then," he said ominously. He pushed his way across the room towards Granny Callenick.

On the TV screen, the presenter had brought his audience to boiling point. There was a roll of drums as the balls skipped about. One fell into the slot.

"We have a twenty-two," the presenter crowed.

The audience in the TV studio gave a deafening cheer.

"Twenty-two," echoed the viewers in the games room at Pardeaux Hall. All eyes turned to Clara.

Hayley ran her hands through her hair, like a hamster grooming itself. "Have you got it? The suspense is killing me."

Clara scanned the ticket. "Yes. It's there."

"Ooh, that's a good start."

Clara remembered to breathe. It was only one number. There were a whole five more to go.

The second ball rolled and fell into the slot.

"And now we have twenty-one," said the presenter. "Key to the door. Twenty-one."

On the TV, the studio audience went wild.

Clara skimmed her ticket once more.

"I've got that too!"

She felt quite nauseous. Yet despite the awful worry, excitement started to bubble in her veins, like lava in a volcano.

Jean-Pierre let out a whoop. "Clara's got two numbers. Cool. One more and she gets twenty-five quid."

His comment brought Clara down to earth. She needed a lot more than twenty-five pounds. Sweat was trickling between her shoulder-blades. It was as hot as a sauna in here.

The third ball rolled.

"Thirty," cried the presenter as the ball fell into the slot. He sounded as though he had never heard anything so amazing.

A hush fell over the games room as Clara studied the ticket.

"Well tell us," croaked Hayley, craning for a glimpse.

Despite the heat, Clara went cold all over.

"Oh no! I haven't got that one … I haven't got it, Hayley."

"Look again," Hayley pleaded. "You must have."

Clara looked down. Her eyes widened and she shrieked.

"I've got it! I've got thirty!" In all the confusion her

thumb had been over it. "I've got thirty," she confirmed. "Sorry everyone."

The room erupted in cheering, mingled with groans of "Oh Clara."

"What's all that noise?" Gideon Pasternak poked his head into the room. "Is something happening?"

Clara whipped her head round and was horrified to see that the games room was now full to bursting. Her father and Iris had been joined by Archie Rowlands and Amelia Sitwell. They were surrounded by party guests who had been enticed into the room by all the cheering.

Even Derek Maunding was there, his face livid, his daughters glowering at his side.

The fourth ball rolled. Clara held her breath as she willed it to be one of the three remaining numbers: two, eight and nine.

It was a nine. Clara screamed, leaving no one in any doubt that she'd hit another target.

Cries rang out across the room. "Nine. She's got nine. SHE'S GOT NINE!"

Clara glanced behind. Granny's hand, holding the chocolate cake, was frozen halfway towards her open mouth. Tom Callenick's face was scarlet, his eyes shining like bluebottles.

The next ball was an eight.

"I've got that," screeched Clara.

Hayley squealed and stamped her feet. Clara's insides were like twisted wires. But she hadn't won yet. The last number might still be different.

"That's five out of six in the bag, isn't it?" Jean-

Pierre shouted. "What number have you got left?"

Clara's throat had gone dry. Hayley peered at the ticket and answered for her.

"She needs two. Number two."

On the TV, the presenter gabbled on, spinning out the suspense. The balls ricocheted into the air and rolled for what seemed an eternity. Clara shut her eyes and covered them with her hands.

The ball fell into the slot.

Clara removed her hands and forced her eyes open. This was it. Her fate—the fate of everyone—rested with this one little number. She stared at the screen.

It was a seven.

Clara kept looking at the television, as though somehow she could change things by sheer effort of will. Then, as reality sank in, her head fell forward.

Her voice was a murmur. "I haven't got that one … I haven't got it. It—it was supposed to be a two."

No one spoke. Hayley's head flopped onto her shoulder. Clara blinked in misery as tears stung her eyes. Her hunch had been wrong. It was just an ordinary ticket after all. It was over.

Now she would have to face her father and her grandmother. Then Maunding and his daughters. She shook her head, wishing she could vanish.

The silence was eerie. No one so much as murmured, and even the Maunding sisters remained quiet. Clara looked up slowly, and her gaze fell on Donna. Donna's china blue eyes gleamed as her mouth twisted into a malevolent grin. Clara, unable to bear the

299

sight, looked again at the treacherous ticket.

The numbers seemed to mock her. The five correct ones, and the last one, the two. The number that ruined everything.

Derek Maunding stood with his arms folded, a sardonic smile curving his lips.

"Right, show over." He nodded to Granny. "So, Mrs Callenick. We'll continue with our business, shall we? Your granddaughter has had her fun. I think we've wasted enough time for one day, don't you?"

Clara avoided his gaze. Hayley rubbed her arm in an effort to console her.

"I needed a seven," Clara mumbled. "Oh, Hayley, it went wrong … Something must have changed."

As the room fell silent once more, Clara lifted her head to see her grandmother making her tortoise-like way through the crowd. Derek Maunding, his eyes glittering with the anticipation of victory, waited for her just inside the door.

"See you later," Granny called to Clara. She sounded sorrowful, yet resigned.

Hayley leaned in close. "You got five numbers. That's brilliant. I think you'll get quite a lot of money for that."

"It won't be enough." Clara's tears dripped onto the ticket. "You need to get all six."

"May I see?" asked Hayley, holding out her hand.

"What's the point?"

Hayley's palm remained outstretched, so Clara shrugged and gave her the ticket.

Hayley stared at it as she mentally ticked off the numbers. She smoothed away Clara's tears, which had wet the paper.

Then she started.

"Wait a minute …"

She sat bolt upright, squinting at the ticket. She held it up to the light, then rubbed it again, her eyes round with astonishment. Her scream was so shrill that she almost splintered the window panes.

At the doorway, Granny turned back in surprise. Maunding cringed from the sound.

"Clara, look!" cried Hayley. "That's not a two. It's a seven! There was a smudge."

Clara grabbed the ticket and stared. Hayley must be imagining things. It couldn't be. Then an image flashed into her mind: Miss Grundy on the stairs, the watery look in her eyes, the smudged make-up … her fingers holding the ticket.

"It was eye-liner!" Clara said. "A smudge made the seven into a two."

Hayley was laughing. "But it's gone now. You can clearly see that it's actually a seven." She gazed round at everyone. "Clara's got the seven!"

Cheering erupted all around. Strangers whirled one another about the room. Clara and Hayley sprang to their feet, held one other's shoulders and jumped up and down. Jean-Pierre leapt across and threw his arms around both of them. Tom and Iris hugged one another and screamed. Rob and Mick slammed their hands together in a high-five.

At the back of the room, Derek Maunding slumped.

Clara was hoisted up on someone's shoulders. She had never experienced such joy. She waved the ticket in the air and cried at the top of her voice.

"WE'VE WON!"

CHAPTER 28

LOTS of things happened very quickly after that. Clara felt light as air as she skipped over to her family and fell into her father's arms. They stood locked in an embrace as, around them, people checked and re-checked the ticket numbers, roaring and shrieking as though they had all won something too.

Aunt Iris glowed as she turned to face Derek Maunding. "Seems we won't be selling after all, Mr Maunding."

Ignoring her, Maunding glowered at Granny.

"I don't see how this changes anything, Mrs Callenick."

Granny frowned, saying nothing. Then, a beatific smile transformed her face. Like a dragon unfurling its wings, she stretched herself up to her full height.

"Don't you? Well, Mr Maunding, I do. You see, to my mind, you called the deal off yourself, when you tried to change the price." She beamed at Clara. "My granddaughter here has made me realise what sort of a fellow you are. I should have seen it before. And I don't know how on earth she's done it, but I did tell her she could buy the mine herself, if she had the money. The mine's Clara's now."

Clara squeezed her grandmother's arm.

Maunding seemed to have aged ten years.

"We'll sue," he snarled, his face white. "There's still the fact of my darling Gail's misfortune to consider."

"Grow up, Derek," Iris spat. "Gail shouldn't have been there, and you know it. We have signs by the shafts, it's all above board. You'll just have to accept 'no' for an answer. For once."

Clara stifled a giggle. Maunding peered down at her, quivering with loathing.

"You've lost," she said, smiling sweetly. "You won't be getting the Luxulyanite. It's ours."

"You'll be hearing from me."

Maunding turned and marched from the room.

Clara and her friends followed shortly afterwards. Out in the hallway, they found Donna and Gail locked together in a fight.

"It's all your fault," squawked Donna. "We could have stopped her. Daddy would have got the mine by now if we'd kept her out of the way. But oh no! You were too busy chatting up my boyfriend."

"Your boyfriend? Dream on. It's me he wants. Get over it."

Donna yanked Gail's hair. "Don't be so stupid. How could he possibly prefer you to me? Look in a mirror, why don't you?"

"Why should you always get everything?" Gail dug her nails into Donna's cheeks. "I'm the one who nearly died!"

"Died? I wish you had! And how dare you tell those lies to Dad. Saying I knew where you were all along.

You stirring little—"

Donna gave her sister a vicious kick. Gail kicked back. Struggling and writhing, they tumbled to the ground.

Jean-Pierre and Hayley stepped around them. Jean-Pierre shook his handsome head and smiled at Hayley.

"Fancy coming surfing tomorrow?"

Clara strode jubilantly from Pardeaux Hall. Just outside, the sweet tones of a piano melody drifted on the air. Clara glanced back through the open dining room window.

Susan Maunding lay slumped over a deserted table. Heidsieck the cat munched happily astride the five-bird roast. One antler fell off the reindeer ice sculpture.

***

For days afterwards, the town of St Pirans and the village of Polgrehan were buzzing with the news of the lottery win at the Maundings' Christmas party. Everyone who had been there said it was a night they would remember for the rest of their lives.

In their favourite corner by the crackling fire at the Flea and Feather, Granny Callenick's lodger Coles and his neighbour Farmer Bolton chewed the story over many times, washing it down with a few pints of Tribute.

"And I'll tell you the funniest part," said Bolton. "I heard it from Old Leghorn at the Wolf and Lamb, who was there himself. He told me 'twas almost like she knew she was going to win. Knew she had the right numbers, like."

"Geddaway!" Coles blinked his sorrowful eyes. It was exactly what Granny C had told him, but he'd put it down to her age and her fanciful ways.

As if the lottery win weren't excitement enough, the town had been rocked by the news that Susan Maunding had vanished on the night of the party. Coles had heard three separate rumours. One said she had jumped off the cliff at Blackhead. Another that she had gone back to the Isle of Wight, where her parents lived. The third one, Len's favourite, said she'd been very friendly with the classical pianist who'd been playing at the party, and that both of them had disappeared together.

"Apparently this same feller's been coming down every year, all the way from Bristol just for the one night!" revealed Coles, tapping his nose. "Now what does that say to you?"

Farmer Bolton almost choked on his pickled egg. "Gedda-way!"

Len smiled. He liked nothing better than to share juicy gossip. It would see Granny C through many a dark winter's night to come.

"Been a lot of funny things going on around here lately," said Bolton. "Did you see those lights over the Downs the other day? Like fireworks … And then last week I found two bikes dumped behind a hedge. Not cheap ones, neither."

"Some people got money to burn. It'll be one o' they

from upcountry, no doubt. Couldn't be bothered to take the bikes home."

Farmer Bolton wiped the froth from his lip. "So, Len, you shan't be moving on for a bit yet?"

"Nope, I told Granny C all along what a silly idea that was. Moving house at her age, I ask you. She is eighty-two after all. Clara's promised to see us right. The lottery win will have to be in her father's name, of course. She isn't old enough to claim it herself."

"Should be a good ole Christmas for you then." Farmer Bolton raised his glass to his friend.

***

At first, Clara's dad refused to believe that her ticket had actually won. She had to prove it to him by showing him the results online, on Iris's computer, and in black and white, in the latest Bugle.

"Look, Dad. Those are my numbers. It's really true."

Tom stared at the newspaper, shaking his head in disbelief. But at last he felt confident enough to ring up the lottery company and get the sensational news confirmed. The wheels were in motion, and before long they would be presented with Clara's prize.

Clara could scarcely believe it herself. There was no way it could have been coincidence—the odds against it were just too phenomenal. That ticket must have been special. But if it was, why hadn't Miss Grundy wanted her to have it? Why hadn't she simply given it to Clara? Most importantly of all, how had Miss Grundy discovered the numbers?

It seemed that Clara would never know. For Susan Maunding wasn't the only one to disappear on the night of the party. Miss Grundy hadn't even waited for the numbers to be called. When they looked for her afterwards, she was nowhere to be found.

***

On Christmas Day, there were still patches of snow on the ground, although most of it had melted away. At Callenick mine, Clara and her family gorged themselves on an early Christmas lunch, then crowded into Granny's sitting room for yet more food and the Queen's Speech at three o'clock.

Clara hovered restlessly near the door, sipping at a glass of blackberry cordial. Hayley, Mick and Rob were due to arrive at any moment, and the wait was driving her crazy. She had quite a surprise for them.

This Christmas gathering was certainly different from the previous one, she thought, gazing round at the flushed, excited faces. Last year they'd had a rather sombre get-together in a damp, chilly room. This year, Granny's cottage was filled with holly boughs and sparkling decorations—and with warmth and laughter.

Aunt Iris had brought Archie Rowlands along—they had made up their quarrel about attending the Maundings' party. And Amelia Sitwell, Clara's Spanish teacher, had come as Tom's guest. The four of them sat chatting to Granny while Coles meandered up and down with nibbles.

In the corner, Clara's sister Sally had crammed herself into an armchair next to her boyfriend, Jamie. Jess posed beside them like a sphinx, fixing them with her gimlet stare.

"You should have seen those Maunding girls," Jamie told Sally as he threw Jess the last of his sausage roll. "The fight went on for hours. Gail ended up with a black eye."

Clara hadn't noticed in all the confusion, but Jamie had been a waiter at the party.

"And Donna?" enquired Sally breathlessly.

"That's even funnier. Her sister bit half her earlobe off. Serves them both right. I used to think they were okay till I heard about how they've been treating your sister."

"Yeah, selfish cows," said Sally.

Clara's heart swelled. She and Sally had been getting on much better since Clara's win.

It had been a good night for the lottery: a rollover in the run-up to Christmas, and only two winners. Clara's ticket had won over two million pounds.

It was an incredible thought—and Clara had plans.

First off, despite their objections, she would split the money four ways with Rob, Hayley, and Mick. They were a team, after all, and it was never Clara's intention to be rich for the sake of it. Besides, although Derek Maunding had gone quiet, he was still at large, not to mention his obnoxious daughters and henchman Trundle. Anything could happen in this un-trodden future, and there might yet be more to do.

After much discussion, instead of buying the land, Clara had persuaded Granny to let her pay for the work needed on the cottage, and settle various bills. On condition that Granny didn't sell up, she was to live out her days here and pass Callenick mine on to Tom and Iris.

In time, Clara hoped to buy a couple of Farmer Bolton's fields, where she might create a brand new wood. She still had nightmares about the bare, ashy landscape she'd seen outside Zeno's cavern, and would have covered the whole county with trees if she could.

Her aims weren't all lofty, of course. At home in her wardrobe hung a brand new school uniform, the best St Piran's had to offer. And outside Granny's cottage, where she had just parked it, stood a fantastic new mountain bike, which Dad had bought her on account of the riches to come.

It was time for her old bone-shaker to be retired. One wheel had just fallen off, anyway. Clara had taken this as a sign.

Clara's dad jolted her from her reverie, brushing past on his way to set up his eighteenth-century cannon on the lawn—a Callenick Christmas tradition.

"I suppose you'll be buying a house now, eh, Tom?" Len Coles's mournful voice wafted towards them.

Clara held her breath.

Tom laughed and shook his head. "Gah! Live in a normal house? Not for us, eh, Clara?"

"Too right, Dad!" said Clara, beaming. She hoped

he'd use some of the money to set up a new business. He'd always fancied putting a few goats up on the Downs.

Coles paused in front of Archie, holding out his tray. "Go on, Mr Rowlands, try a slice of ye olde Cornwall."

Archie surveyed the dish on offer, wrinkling his brow. A shoal of glassy-eyed pilchards stared back at him from an ocean of pastry.

"Er, what is it?" he asked in his gentle Scots brogue.

"Starrey gazey pie, o' course. Haven't you had it before?"

"I don't think so. Um, thanks." Archie accepted a slice and took a bite. "So, Mrs Callenick, have you heard any more from Derek Maunding?"

Granny froze. "Not a bean."

"Don't worry." Archie made a lopsided face as he crunched on a fishtail. "He doesn't have a leg to stand on. It's private land after all. He's lost a lot of friends in this town over the past few days."

"No wonder his wife left him," said Iris.

"Hmm, indeed." Archie turned to Amelia Sitwell. "Any sign of Miss Grundy?"

"Not a trace. Normally we do a bit of Christmas shopping together. She's a funny old stick, but all right really. I've rung and rung. I've even been round to her house. No one's seen her since that night at the Maundings'."

"Gone on holiday, perhaps?" suggested Archie.

"She would have mentioned it, surely."

Clara sidled across and whispered in her aunt's ear.

311

"Auntie … You knew Derek Maunding at school, didn't you?"

"Yeah."

"He quite liked you, did he?" Clara asked, testing out a theory she had.

Iris smiled mysteriously. "Maybe."

Clara suspected she'd get no more.

"Full cream or semi-skilled?" Granny interrupted, taking orders for tea and coffee.

Trying not to giggle, Clara followed her grandmother into the tiny galley kitchen.

"It's semi-skimmed, Gran!"

"Is it?" Granny said vaguely, rounding up mugs and spooning leaves into the teapot. Maud Callenick was the only person Clara knew who refused to use teabags.

Clara searched her mind for a good way to put what she wanted to ask.

"Granny …"

"Yes, my bird?"

Granny's eyes were brighter and livelier than ever.

"I was just wondering … Do you remember a woman coming to see you, about a year ago? Short with grey hair, a bit like a mole?"

Granny fetched the milk from the fridge.

"Mole … No, don't remember anyone like that."

"She advised you not to sell the mine. You sent her away."

"Hmmm. Aw! Yes, that does ring a bell. Market research, indeed. Busybodies sticking their oar into your business. Or was she campaigning about something? I

312

didn't wait to find out."

Clara nodded. She wasn't sure why she felt the need to check everything Miss Grundy had told her.

Granny poured boiling water into the teapot.

"How's that friend of yours from school—Rog, wasn't it?"

"Rob," corrected Clara, looking at her watch. "He'll be here any minute."

"Odd you came to see me that afternoon."

"Oh? Why's that?" asked Clara, remembering their joint attempt to change Granny's mind.

"Well, my decision was made by that time. In fact, I planned to go and see Mr Maunding that afternoon, to sign the documents."

"You did?" Clara's mouth fell open.

Granny spoke quickly. "It isn't that you talked me out of it, that day, not at all. 'Tis my affair, like I said then. But you did persuade me to wait a bit longer, think it through again."

Clara tingled all over. So it had been that close. She felt a glow of triumph. It was another piece of evidence that they'd really changed the future. Because they had, hadn't they? Of course they had ...

There was a knock at the door. Clara rushed to open it and Rob, Hayley and Mick piled into the cottage.

"I've brought some chocolate truffles," said Hayley. "First time I made them, but they're a bit yummy, if I say so myself."

Mick's normally pale face was red from the cold.

"Sorry we're late, Clara. I thought I'd never get away.

My mum and stepdad have got relatives staying, and they don't like any of them. They're squabbling over the remote control like a load of pigeons over a crust of bread." He looked round. "Wow! What a lovely cottage. I love those old beams."

Rob homed in on the sideboard and heaped up his plate.

"That starrey gazey pie is great, Mr Coles," he said, helping himself to the last pilchard.

Clara rolled her eyes. "I don't know where you put it all."

Rob rubbed his stomach. "Don't nag, Clara. I'm a growing lad."

Silence fell for the Queen's Christmas message. When it was over, Clara leaned towards her friends, lowering her voice so no one else would hear.

"I'm going out for some air. Anyone coming?"

"Ooh, yes, let's," said Hayley. "I've got about five trillion calories to burn off."

They jumped up and followed Clara from the room. As she shut the front door, she heard her grandmother's seal-like bark.

"'Tis only an old wood," Granny said. "I don't know why Clara gets so aeriated about it. I could understand it better if the mine was full o' gold and the trees were made o' silver. But then, a frog is a diamond in a duck's eye."

Clara smiled to herself. The mine was safe. That was all that mattered.

CHAPTER 29

THE four friends set off through the wood.

"Where shall we go, Clara?" asked Hayley.

"How about the Siri shaft? I've been going up there every day. I can't help wondering ..."

Despite her happiness at the lottery win and the saving of Callenick mine, Clara was haunted by the vision of that tangerine sea, so beautiful and yet so deceptive, containing nothing but poison. It had forever changed the way she saw the world. If I could only know, she thought, know for sure that we achieved what Zeno wanted. That we've stopped that terrible Disaster.

"What will be, will be," said Rob, kicking aside a bramble. "We need to forget all that."

"I disagree," said Mick. "I haven't been able to sleep for thinking about it. What will Zeno and Jed be doing in the new future? Will they even exist? Or will they exist, but live very different lives?"

Rob clasped his hands about his temples and gave a mock sob. "Oh, Mick, please stop frying my brain."

They emerged from the wood onto the gorse path. Two buzzards sliced through a sky of cobalt blue. The air was cold, but smelled like wind-blown washing, fresh with the elusive tang of the sea.

"You've heard there's no sign of Miss Grundy?" asked Clara.

"I know," said Hayley. "I'm still trying to take it all in."

Mick shook his head. "Imagine what it must have been like for her, being marooned here, waiting to see what would happen."

"It doesn't bear thinking about," Hayley replied. "But where is she now?"

"Haven't any of you considered the obvious?" Mick's lips twitched in a half-smile.

Hayley stopped dead. "What d'you mean?"

"Here we go," muttered Rob.

"The obvious," repeated Mick, stopping too. "What have we been trying to do all this time? What have we succeeded in doing?"

"Well …" Hayley cast a hopeful glance in Clara's direction, but Clara remained silent, gazing beyond the Downs towards the line of hazy grey sea on the horizon.

"We changed the future," said Hayley. "Is that what you mean?"

Mick spread his hands. "Exactly. So maybe the future's changed in other ways, too. Ways we can't foresee. Don't forget, technically, Miss Grundy hasn't been born yet."

"Oh no!" Hayley's eyes grew wide. "You're saying she might never get born. She no longer exists."

"The penny drops," said Mick. "It's a theory, isn't it?"

"You mean we've killed our teacher?" said Hayley in

a hushed voice. "Oh my word, I'm never going to forgive myself."

"Well, not killed exactly," said Mick. "You mustn't think of it like that. It's also possible that, because we changed the future, Miss Grundy will still get born, but she won't be sent back to our time—there won't be any need, d'you see? So when we changed the future, the Miss Grundy who got sent back here, well, she ceased to exist."

Hayley's mouth dropped open. "Oh my goodness, that's even worse."

Mick turned to Clara. "You're quiet. What do you think? Have you got a theory?"

"Me? About Miss Grundy?" Clara patted her jacket pocket, savouring the moment. Should she tell them now? No, she would wait until they got to the Siri shaft. She couldn't wait to see their reaction.

Mick was peering at her. "What's up?"

Clara gave what she hoped was an enigmatic smile. "Tell you later."

They walked on in silence.

Mick cleared his throat. "By the way, can I ask you all something?"

"What?" asked Rob. "Why the funny look?"

Mick was blinking rapidly, his lips set in a firm line.

"It's just … It sounds silly. But, well, did Zeno remind you of anyone?"

Hayley wrinkled her nose. "No, don't think so."

"Me neither," said Clara. "Why d'you ask?"

"Oh, no reason."

They passed an oak tree, scattering a pair of squirrels.

"Like who?" Clara asked Mick.

"I dunno … Like me, for example?"

Everyone stopped again. Clara laughed. "You? Of course not. Why would Zeno remind us of you?"

Mick shrugged. "I don't know. It's just—there was something about his eyes. And according to what I've worked out, Zeno must exist somewhere in our time. If I'm right that we were roughly sixty years in the future, that would make him about our age, here and now. And what about the connection with MORE? I can't stop thinking about how I'd love to work there."

Clara felt stunned.

"That's the silliest thing I've heard in ages."

Hayley fiddled with the butterfly slide in her hair. "Besides, Mick, if you were Zeno, Zeno could've just explained it all to you. You would be involved in all the experiments, later on in your life. So you could have stopped things going wrong yourself. If that makes sense."

Rob mumbled something under his breath.

"Good point," admitted Mick. "Unless … Maybe there's some rule that prevents you contacting your earlier self."

"You spoke to Zeno stacks of times," Clara pointed out. "We found it hard to prise you away from him, in fact. And think what a coincidence it would've been, that you happened to become my friend."

The four of them set off again along the gorse-lined path.

"Yeah, you're right." Mick smiled ruefully. "I'm just being silly."

Hayley patted his arm. "Your imagination's gone into overdrive."

"Yeah, it tends to do that."

They reached the clearing where the little track led to the second shaft. Hayley stepped carefully over the snake-shaped root which usually tripped her up.

"You're not getting me this time!" she said, turning and waggling her finger. She rushed to catch up with the others. "I still don't really get it, though, about Gail Maunding. I mean, is that the Sun Shaft we passed back there? Or the Skeleton Shaft? Any ideas, Mick?"

Mick gazed into space. "I think … I don't know, but I would guess that in our timeline, Gail Maunding fell into the shaft, but she was found. In the other timeline, the one we went to, she died in the mine."

"Yes but—but," spluttered Hayley, "she wouldn't have been following us in that other horrible timeline. We wouldn't have been going up there in the first place. So how would she be there to fall in?"

Mick's eyes glowed with a fierce intensity. "I'd guess that when Rob and Clara went down the Siri shaft, little things began to change. When they were captured by the Grammets, Hayley was busy finding Gail Maunding … and so in the future, things changed. The Skeleton Shaft became the Sun Shaft."

Hayley waved her arms around as she spoke. "But what I'm trying to say is … In their time, how did she come to fall in? She wouldn't have been following us,

319

would she? We wouldn't have been there. Chances are, we wouldn't have been involved in any of this."

Jess appeared suddenly and shot past them after a white-tailed rabbit. The rabbit vanished down a sandy burrow and Jess sniffed the hole, tail wagging.

Mick's steps slowed. "I've been giving it a lot of thought. I think that in their timeline, Gail was here for another reason when she fell in the shaft, instead of following us. My theory is that there is a sort of overlap between the two different futures. A blurred moment, when one timeline becomes another."

Rob huffed. "You're frying my brain again. It's not that I don't get it, but there's no point worrying about it. Gail didn't die. End of story."

Clara avoided catching anyone's eye. She didn't know who to side with, being both fascinated by the repercussions of time travel, but also sympathetic with Rob's view—that its paradoxes were too tricky to understand, however much you mulled them over. As they emerged onto the Downs and climbed higher along the carpet of lime-green moss, she decided it would be wise to change the subject.

"How was your date with Jean-Pierre?" she asked Hayley.

Hayley went scarlet. "Date? What date? It wasn't a date. Not exactly. We've just been surfing a few times, that's all."

Mick gave an elaborate shudder. "Hmmph, bit cold for that, isn't it?"

"And?" asked Clara, ignoring Mick.

"Um, yeah, he's good fun," said Hayley in a high voice.

"I see." Clara smiled to herself as she charged ahead.

At the top of the hill, Clara paused to enjoy the view she loved the most. Her land lay before her like a sumptuous feast, so beautiful she felt a stab of pain at the back of her eyes. She stood by the little fence and gazed towards the Siri shaft, struggling with now familiar emotions—a bittersweet blend of happiness at what they had achieved, mingled with regret for those they had lost.

"There we are then," she said. "No more Siri shaft. All filled in."

Where the hole had been, only a mound of rocks remained. Apart from the fence and the danger sign, you'd never guess a shaft was ever there. It had gone, and with it their only hope of discovering the fates of Zeno and Jed. Although Clara had known them just for a short while, they'd had a profound effect upon her, and she missed them more with every passing day.

If only she and Rob hadn't gone back to the cavern that night. True, Zeno and Jed would probably still have suffered the same grisly end. But at least she wouldn't have been there to see it.

That was selfish, though, wasn't it? What's more, if they hadn't gone back, Hayley wouldn't have been left on the Downs alone. She wouldn't have found Gail Maunding ... Oh! Rob was right—it really did fry your brain.

A picture of dejection, Mick crossed to the granite

boulder. He heaved himself onto it and sat motionless, hunched in his parka.

"We'll never be sure, then. We'll never know if it worked. That's it."

Clara felt equally dispirited. She didn't know what she'd expected. Why should things be any different today? One puzzle might be solved—thanks to the item in her pocket—but the future would remain a mystery.

Hayley linked arms with her. "It can't be helped."

Rob's voice was unusually soft. "There's no point getting upset. We'll know one day … when the future comes. We'll just have to be patient. We've defeated Maunding. He hasn't got the Luxulyanite."

"You're right," said Clara. "He'll never get that. We've got money now. We'll be able to stop him if he ever tries again. We mustn't be sad. And I do have one more surprise for you."

Hayley whipped her head around. "Tell us, Clara. Don't keep us in suspense."

"Let's sit on the boulder," suggested Clara.

They clambered up beside Mick. Clara rummaged in her pocket and pulled out an envelope. Inside were several hand-written sheets and a photograph. The writing was erratic, the ink smudged in several places.

"This letter came in the post yesterday," said Clara with a grin. "Why don't you read it out, Hayley?"

Hayley snatched it and peered at it in amazement. "But it's …"

Her eyes grew rounder as she began to read.

December 23rd
Somewhere Hot and Sunny

Clara,

Do you like the photograph? Can you recognise me? That's right. I'm dancing on the table at a marvellous restaurant I discovered. I think you'll agree I look considerably better than I did the last time you saw me. That man in the paisley waistcoat is Felipe. He makes a mean Tequila Sunrise, and his souvlaki is to die for.

My dear, I know I could let you wonder about certain things forever. But I'm sitting by a balmy sea, a glass of fine Bordeaux at my elbow. I'm in a generous mood. The temptation to let you know how I found those numbers is hard to resist. Who else is there to tell? Possibly I will think better of my indiscretion in the morning. But if you are reading this, it seems I didn't. You'll know it was an exceptionally good Bordeaux.

I could be making the wrong choice. However, as you said, you already know so much. A bit more can't hurt.

Those last days in the cavern were indescribably awful. For years afterwards, back here, I woke up shivering, dreaming that I had been catapulted forward to that time.

You see, Zeno and Jed were our best hope for any kind of future. I agreed with them then, as I do still, that the only way forward was to go back, to try to change one of the worst mistakes in history.

(I say one of the worst, as daily I am appalled by the foolhardy way people treat our planet. You cannot

323

imagine the frustration I have suffered during my ten years here in your time.)

I told you recently that when you visited us in the cavern, I overheard snatches of your conversation. I heard your plan, listened to what you said about a strange lottery competition. And I wondered.

Of course, we had more important things to worry about. Project Gigi was nearing completion, and daily the Grammets became more powerful.

As I informed you, I was the one chosen for Project Gigi. It was a great honour, but also made me sick with fear. I saw that you and your friends were able to return safely to your own time, but you belonged there. So far, we'd been unable to send one of us back. Would it work this time? Even Zeno didn't know for sure.

The night before they sent me, I was breathless with terror. I considered reneging on the experiment. How I wished I had the nerve! Yet I could not do that to Zeno, and the thought of letting Jed down was more than I could bear, worse than the thought of being vaporised into a million tiny pieces.

To take my mind off my impending departure, I scoured the cavern looking for anything useful I might take with me, which might aid me if my mission were successful.

After hours of futile searching, I scaled the wall of our sleeping cells, and despite my exhaustion I climbed to the very top. I needed to be as far away from my friends as I could be. I did not want them to see my fear.

I crawled into a cell which was seldom used, it was so rough and uneven. Sleep would not come, of course. I was about to embark on a one-way mission. If the experiment went wrong, I faced death. If it succeeded, it meant farewell to everyone I had ever loved.

I was at breaking point. I just wanted it to be over.

I wriggled as far away from the dim light as possible, to where the roof sloped into a crevice. As I lay tossing restlessly, my hand caught on something sharp behind my head. Puzzled, I tugged at it. It was the corner of a briefcase!

By the looks of it, it had been jammed into the crevice a long time before, and by whom, we shall never know. It was slim and battered—and locked. Most interesting of all, there were two gold initials inscribed upon it. I wiped off the dust to read: D. M.

By morning, the Grammets had come. They had breached our defences and slipped through the tunnels when we were least on our guard.

We knew it was all over for us. Zeno and I made it to the Siri shaft just in time.

I brought the briefcase with me.

I will gloss over the terrible times which befell me then. As you know, I did come back—but I arrived ten years early!

I was ecstatic that I was still alive. I was pleased that the project had succeeded. And it was miraculous to breathe pure air, to drink fresh water and feel the sun on my skin.

But I had no money, no identity, just a single briefcase to my name.

As soon as I could, I forced the case open. My suspicion was correct: the case had belonged to Derek Maunding, and hailed from his time running MORE in the cavern.

It contained a strange miscellany of items. There were reports about neutrino research at CERN in Switzerland. There was a small jewellery box containing a lock of auburn hair.

What riveted my attention most of all was a folder at the bottom of the case.

It contained newspaper clippings.

I quickly scanned the dates of these cuttings. Most were from the years before the Disaster, awards won by MORE, features in Sunday supplements, that kind of thing. Then I saw something which made my hair stand on end.

The earliest cuttings were from your time! And two of them referred to Gail Maunding.

The first was a report about her disappearance. The second was the one which changed everything.

It was a clipping from The Bugle, dated the week after Gail vanished.

Perhaps I should explain that, in Temporal Dynamics, there is something called the Mackrami Paradox. It states that although time may indeed be changed, there are certain tendencies which are favoured. In other words, similar things are likely to happen in similar timelines. There is a mysterious link between them, which no one yet understands.

My guess is that, in my timeline, Gail trespassed on Callenick Downs, no doubt secure in the knowledge that the land would soon be her father's. I expect she envisaged all manner of wild parties there, hidden from view of parents and other adults. But she got lost, and fell in the shaft. This time, there was no Hayley on hand to rescue her.

The cutting described another fruitless search. It ended by saying that hopes of finding Gail were slim.

I realise now, of course, that Gail had fallen down our Skeleton Shaft. In my time, Gail died in that shaft. She was the Skeleton! Yet when I lived in the cavern, no one knew who the Skeleton was, or when it had arrived there. I had, I confess, forgotten all about it. It was only when Hayley found Gail that I made the connection.

However, enough of the Maunding sisters.

This report was NOT the important thing on that page.

Being the meticulous man he was, Maunding had cut all the clippings to the same size, so that they slotted neatly into polythene pockets. This meant that other items on the same newspaper page were inadvertently included with the reports he wanted to keep.

I could not believe my eyes. For printed below this final report were the winning numbers of the most recent lottery draw! Saturday's!

So, Clara, I have spent the last ten years of my life convinced that I would give you these numbers, when the time came, if it proved necessary. Although I did not know for sure if they would be the right ones. If I've learnt anything, it's that time is very mysterious, and that travelling within it makes it more mysterious still.

As you will one day learn, thinking is one thing. Doing is quite another.

At the Maundings' party, as I stood on the staircase at Pardeaux Hall, the reality of what we were about to do hit home.

The chances were, as soon as your grandmother's deal was called off, "my" future would be obliterated. Within moments, I might cease to exist. My world would never be. Jed would never be.

My feelings will make no sense to you. You know me as a middle-aged woman, a woman past her prime. But remember that I am, and always will be, a stranger in your times. That cavern was my only home. As dreadful as it was, it contained everything and everyone I ever loved.

Alas, we are but frail, flawed souls, and the will to live is strong. Try not to judge me too harshly. Keep this letter. One day, you may understand.

When you found me on that staircase, I saw hope gleaming in your eyes. I felt the purity of your heart. I saw my Jed again, and his face was shadowed with disappointment.

I knew then where my duty lay. Even if I ceased to be, my final action would be one to make Jed proud.

Do you see? My momentary lapse was about self-preservation. Rest assured, I did not seek to deprive you of your ticket for my own financial gain. You see, my dear, there was no need.

You probably know by now that there were two lottery winners last Saturday night. Clara, have you asked yourself who the second winner might be?

What's life without the odd wheeze? My dear, I had already bought one ticket! The ticket I bought from Polgrehan shop was actually a second one, with the same choice of numbers. That ticket was for you. The first one was mine.

You don't begrudge me my share, do you, Clara? I knew that, if you won, there would still be plenty for your needs.

I had no idea if I would continue to exist, once the past which moulded me was gone. But I hadn't come this far in order to finish my days drumming history into infertile minds.

And I did survive, I am pleased to report! (As luck would have it, one of Zeno's pet theories proved correct: that since I arrived back here before the future was changed, before our timeline was destroyed, I now exist in my own right. Fantastic, isn't it? Time travel really is a right squirly can of conundrums.)

But all that's by the by. I send you my greetings from sunny—ah, but that would be telling.

You will agree it's best if we have no further contact. I suggest you and your friends forget all about Zeno, Jed and me, and what might have happened. What did happen, as far as I am concerned.

Don't drop your guard, though. You can see for

yourselves the daily threats to our planet. Look after it, Clara, it's the only one we have!

With best wishes for your future,

Gina Grundy

CHAPTER 30

HAYLEY read out the letter, her voice trembling with emotion. When she finished, she folded it and replaced it in the envelope. She handed it back to Clara, reserving the photo, which she passed around for Mick and Rob to see.

"Wow," Hayley said. "Just imagine …"

"I must admit," said Rob. "I never thought we'd find out what happened to her."

"She looks so different, doesn't she?" said Clara. "Almost like the woman she used to be. The one we saw in the lab."

"Phew, we didn't kill her. I'm so glad." Hayley gazed into space for a moment, then appealed to Mick. "Kind of weird though, isn't it? I mean, if we've changed the future, Miss Grundy will never be sent back—so how come she ended up in our time? Why didn't she disappear when the future changed? Or, if she was never sent, how can we even know she was here?"

Rob groaned and put his head in his hands. "Oh Hayley, please, please don't start him off again."

Ignoring him, Mick gave a knowing nod. "All very good questions. I'll need to give it some thought. As Miss Grundy rightly said, time travel really is a squirly can of conundrums."

For a moment, they watched two jackdaws squabbling over a worm, stretching it between them like a strand of spaghetti. Then Rob heaved himself from the boulder.

"Shall we go then? I told my dad I wouldn't be too long."

Clara strode across to the little fence and gazed one last time at the destroyed Siri shaft, her mind whirling with an odd mixture of relief and sadness. Rob, Mick and Hayley joined her, and they were all silent for a while.

Rob rested his hand gently on her arm. "We can look at it as many times as we like. It won't change anything."

"Guess you're right."

Clara turned away.

Hayley shrieked, so loudly that the jackdaws took flight, dropping their prize worm. She pointed into the stone-filled centre of the shaft.

"Look!"

Clara's gaze followed Hayley's. "What? I can't see anything."

"Thanks for making my ears bleed," grumbled Rob.

"In there," cried Hayley. "Isn't that the trilloscope?"

Then Clara saw it too. Within the rubble, there was a flash of brilliant white, like a glinting tooth.

Mick jumped over the fence and began pushing aside the stones. With a cry of triumph, he held up the tennis ball-sized sphere.

"Wow! You've got brilliant eyesight, Hayley."

Hayley beamed.

Mick held out the trilloscope, balanced on his palm. They gathered round and peered at it.

Clara felt a glimmer of hope. She picked it up to look at it more closely—then let out a moan.

"Oh no, it's damaged. There's a hairline crack round it." She ran a finger along the tiny dark line.

"What a shame," said Hayley with a sigh.

"Well done for finding it, anyway." Clara gazed into the distance, trying not to let them see her disappointment.

"Let me see." Mick snatched the trilloscope from Clara's hand and turned it against the light, examining every centimetre. "Could be worth a go, don't you think? It might still work."

"We don't have any vinegar with us," said Rob.

Mick frowned for a moment, then rummaged in the large front pocket of his parka. With a little cry, he pulled out a small bottle and waved it in the air.

"Actually, we do. I've been carrying this round for ages, ever since Hayley and I used the trilloscope together. I'd forgotten it was there."

Hayley jumped up and down. "Ooh, try it, Mick. You never know."

Mick perched the trilloscope on a raised, flat stone near the fence. "Okay, here goes. Fingers crossed, everyone."

Clara, Rob and Hayley watched while Mick poured vinegar over the sphere.

"Good job no one can see us," he said. "I feel a perfect idiot."

Clara crossed her fingers. As she expected, nothing happened. No whirring, no pulse of heat, no sparks flying into the sky.

"Try again," she said.

Mick poured a second dose of vinegar over the trilloscope. They all waited. Again, nothing happened.

Rob paced up and down. "How long should we give it? I hate to be a spoilsport, but I think we're wasting our time."

"Shhh!" said Mick. "I'm trying to concentrate."

He glared at the sphere, as if willing it to move.

The trilloscope remained stubbornly inactive.

"Come on, then, let's go." Rob glanced at Clara's face. "Look, maybe it's for the best. Maybe it's better not to know."

Clara nodded. Too upset to speak, she strode off.

"Clara, wait." Hayley chased after her.

"What?" Clara stopped and turned.

Hayley's face bore a strange expression, eager and luminous. "It's just … I've got something that might cheer you up. I've been meaning to give you this for days."

She dropped a small box into Clara's hand. Clara frowned, puzzled. They had already exchanged Christmas presents a few days before.

Clara opened it. Inside she found her silver necklace with the St Christopher pendant. She stared at it for several moments, unable to find her voice.

"Oh, Hayley!"

Hayley glowed. "I didn't give it to you before. I

wanted it to be a surprise. I had it fixed for you. For Christmas."

Clara crouched so that Hayley could fasten it around her neck, then she turned and hugged Hayley tightly.

"You're such a good friend."

She smiled at Rob and Mick, who had caught them up.

"You all are."

Rob and Mick went bright red. Both edged away, as if frightened Clara would hug them too.

The four of them walked on. As they neared a slab of granite, Mick gave a strangled yell.

Rob winced and covered his ears. "What's with all the shrieking today?"

"What's wrong, Mick?" Clara felt sure he must have twisted his ankle, at least. But he was racing back the way they'd come, leaving her in no doubt that he was all in one piece.

"How could we be so stupid," he cried. "It's got to be on granite. Don't you remember? The trilloscope's got to be on a granite base."

"Of course!" Clara gave a whoop, hope surging through her as she turned and bolted after him. "We forgot that bit!"

Mick fetched the sphere and placed it reverentially on the granite boulder. Clara took a deep breath, trying to calm her pounding heart. It didn't necessarily mean anything. The trilloscope was still damaged, and might not work, even on granite.

Mick had only a small amount of vinegar left. He

poured all of it over the sphere. The four of them stood back, hoping and praying.

The sphere emitted a sound. It was barely audible, just a tiny sizzle, like the buzz of a bee.

"Hear that?" Mick peered at it from beneath his glasses, which had steamed up.

Her excitement growing, Clara nudged it with her fingertip. It felt a little warmer than before, didn't it? And was she imagining it, or had its pure white colour begun to darken?

"It's trying," she said in wonder. "It's not the same, but it's doing something."

The sphere went grey. Then it lit again, creamy pink, like a pale eye opening. There was a pulse of heat, enough to warm their cold noses. As they watched in silence, the pink glow faded, the colour leaching out of the sphere, leaving it almost transparent.

"It looks like a lens," said Mick.

There was more sizzling and a smell of citrus. A spark flew out.

Hayley grabbed Clara. "I think it's working!"

Slowly, a bubble slid out of the sphere, as though it were being blown through. It floated upwards and hovered above the sphere, stretching and growing to the size of a football. It was so clear Clara could see the ferns behind it.

The bubble hissed and filled with steam. Now it looked like a round cloud hanging there. Swirling strands of grey mist danced together, mingling and coalescing.

The strands twinkled as they wove themselves into a hazy image, picked out in wisps of blue, turquoise and violet.

"What is it?" breathed Clara.

The image writhed and sparkled, and all at once Clara understood what she was looking at.

An old stone cottage stood window-deep in honeysuckle, foxgloves and hollyhocks. At a wooden table sat an elderly couple, holding hands.

Although he looked much happier, his face less furrowed, it was clear who the man was.

Exhilaration surged through Clara. "Zeno!"

"Dear Zeno," cried Hayley. "But who's that with him?"

The grey-haired woman looked strangely familiar. As Clara watched, she realised why. She had seen her in a picture, a picture drawn with ash.

"That's Siri," she said, softly.

"It can't be," whispered Hayley. "Siri was murdered, don't you remember? By the Grammets … Oh! Of course."

Clara smiled. "That's right. In the new timeline, Siri doesn't get killed."

Siri looked just as Clara imagined her to be: peaceful and serene, her face old and lined, but her eyes still lively and her smile warm.

The image expanded to reveal two more figures within the bubble, a younger man and woman. They stood off to one side, next to a hedge ablaze with roses of every hue.

Clara gasped and pointed. "There's Jed." It was easy to recognise him from his butter-yellow hair, although it was trimmed and neatly styled.

The woman had a plump, pretty face, and looked kind. At her feet, two small children played on the grass.

As they watched, shadows crept through the image. The wisps shimmered and began to darken.

Hayley clasped her cheeks. "It's fading."

In the picture, at the table, Siri lifted a glass. As if to toast them.

The last thing Clara glimpsed was Zeno's face, in profile. He turned a fraction towards her, his eye glimmering. Was that a wink? Clara couldn't be sure.

The colours blended as the image melted away. The four friends stood gazing at the empty space where it had been.

No one spoke for a long time. Then they turned to one another and laughed.

"We did it," said Clara.

Mick's eyes were glossy with pride. Hayley, too, blinked away the tears.

Rob cleared his throat. "We sure did."

Clara had never seen them look so happy. Suddenly, she felt light and airy. It was as if a crushing weight had been lifted from her chest, leaving her free to breathe.

"We changed the future," she said.

Everyone jumped as a crack of gunfire filled the air.

"What the heck was that?" asked Hayley.

Clara grinned. "'Tis only Dad with his cannon. He fires it every Christmas Day. Dads!" She rolled her eyes.

"A real cannon?" asked Rob. "Wow. I wouldn't mind a look at that."

"He'd love to show it to you, I'm sure … Come on, let's go."

They turned and headed for home.

As he passed the granite boulder, Mick slipped the trilloscope into his pocket. You never knew when it might come in handy.

THE END

ABOUT THE AUTHOR

Teresa Bassett writes mysteries and adventure stories for young and older adults, mostly set in her home county of Cornwall, UK. A graduate of the University of Bath, she formerly worked as a foreign language teacher, magazine writer and translator. She also spent eleven years with educational charity *The Eden Project*, where she learned all kinds of wonderful things about plants and people.

In 2013 Teresa was over the moon when the manuscript for her debut mystery adventure *The Time Crystals* reached the final five Young Adult titles in Amazon's Breakthrough Novel Award, going on to win international contest The Next Novelist. More recently, in 2020, she was awarded first prize in Crowvus's Ghost Story competition. Her second novel, *The Mystery of Acorn Academy*, was published by Authors Reach in 2021. *Flight of the Bluebird*, the next book in the Time Crystals series, is scheduled for release in early 2022.

You can find Teresa at:
Facebook
https://treeandleafblog.com.

For the latest author news, including special offers,
please sign up to Teresa's occasional newsletter:

www.teresabassett.co.uk

If you have enjoyed this book, a review or rating
would be much appreciated. Thank you!

THE MYSTERY OF ACORN ACADEMY

A gripping suspense novel with twists and turns and a nail-biting finale.

Can Holly discover the Academy's deadly secret, before she becomes the next victim?

Fourteen-year-old Holly Champion is devastated when, following a traumatic incident, her father sends her away to an exclusive school in Cornwall. Acorn Academy, a magnificent clifftop mansion, looks stunning, but why are the students so docile and obedient? Why does the principal seem to dislike Holly so much? And what happened to the mysterious Lydia, who occupied Holly's room before her?

When Holly's new friend Jess vanishes without trace, Holly's only ally is Jess's aloof brother Adam. Together they must risk their lives in a terrifying struggle, racing against the clock to expose a shocking plot.

What readers are saying:

Exciting Books For All Ages

Fantasy
Adventure
Thrillers
Paranormal
Horror
History
Romance

Visit us at:
www.authorsreach.co.uk
Join us on Facebook:
www.facebook.com/authorsreach

TAKE A LOOK AND LET THE MAGIC BEGIN!

Made in the USA
Las Vegas, NV
09 November 2021